AGAINST THE WIND

AGAINST THE WIND

a novel

&

Jim Tilley

Red Hen Press | *Pasadena, CA*

Library of Congress Cataloging-in-Publication Data

Names: Tilley, Jim, author.
Title: Against the wind : a novel / Jim Tilley.
Description: Pasadena, CA : Red Hen Press, [2019]
Identifiers: LCCN 2019018055 | ISBN 9781597098359
Classification: LCC PS3620.I515 A73 2019 | DDC 813/.6—dc23
LC record available at https://lccn.loc.gov/2019018055

The National Endowment for the Arts, the Los Angeles County Arts Commission, the Ahmanson Foundation, the Dwight Stuart Youth Fund, the Max Factor Family Foundation, the Pasadena Tournament of Roses Foundation, the Pasadena Arts & Culture Commission and the City of Pasadena Cultural Affairs Division, the City of Los Angeles Department of Cultural Affairs, the Audrey & Sydney Irmas Charitable Foundation, the Kinder Morgan Foundation, the Meta & George Rosenberg Foundation, the Allergan Foundation, the Riordan Foundation, Amazon Literary Partnership, and the Mara W. Breech Foundation partially support Red Hen Press.

First Edition
Published by Red Hen Press
www.redhen.org

ACKNOWLEDGMENTS

As I made my foray into fiction from writing poetry, I participated in several fiction workshops at Bread Loaf both in Vermont and in Sicily. I would like to thank the participants in those workshops and the various faculty, too many to name individually, for their combined insights, critique, and guidance on excerpts from early versions of this novel. My wife, Deborah Schneider, has my undying gratitude on many levels—as my literary agent, but more than that as someone who could get through to me her opinions on what was working and what was not in various drafts of the manuscript. Although she does not like to read a manuscript more than twice, she abandoned that rule many times over for me. As always, whether it's a collection of poetry or a long personal essay or a book of fiction, I am indebted to Kate Gale and Mark Cull, the co-founders of Red Hen Press. Kate had me re-imagine the several chapters that conclude *Against the Wind*, not once or twice, but three times. It was a pleasure working with her. I am convinced that Mark is one of the best book designers alive.

for Deborah

AGAINST THE WIND

PART ONE

CHAPTER 1

The details are not unusual. He collapsed during the meeting; the paramedics arrived. They carried him on a stretcher down the freight elevator, gave him some nitroglycerin. Making it to the hospital on time without getting stuck in New York City traffic—that was a bit unusual. It turned out to be a minor heart attack. He stayed in the hospital less than a week recovering from a routine procedure to install stents in two obstructed arteries. It's the longest he's ever spent confined to a room.

It gave him time to think. That part is also unusual. Ralph has led a hard-charging life that has given him little time to think about anything other than work. Little time that he's chosen to take because he knows the answers to his important questions are not what he wants to tell himself. It was easier to focus on the court cases at hand. The notion of a bucket list had never entered Ralph's mind until the episode with his heart. But lying in bed all day with only the occasional stroll down overlit hallways, he imagined the upcoming canoe trip, a reunion of old camp friends. They'd been hard to find after more than forty-five years, and sadly, harder to convince.

The past three months brought another reunion. This one by chance, although, reflecting on it in the hospital, Ralph suspected it was bound to have happened, three onetime grade school friends coming together again, he and Lynn, high school sweethearts, he and

Dieter, high school rivals, Dieter the loser in the battle for Lynn's affections. Thrown together in a fight over wind farms in the county where Lynn now lives.

All in all, the unfinished business of past lives brought forward and played out, offering opportunities to put things right.

Mark, Ralph's second-in-command at the office, visited the hospital only once. When he started to talk business, Ralph told him to carry on running the office without him, much as he has done for the past year. Ralph's sharp-tongued assistant, Mary Ann, came to the hospital every day. On one visit she caught him flirting with a nurse, an attractive woman, a good twenty years younger.

"So you had to have a heart attack to rejuvenate your love life?" Mary Ann said, looking directly at the nurse, not Ralph. The embarrassed nurse excused herself.

"You're such a positive influence. She probably thinks you're my wife."

"I know you too well."

That nurse reminded him of Lynn. The short brown hair, the way she had it pushed back behind her ears, her grayish eyes, and especially her small, thin lips. When Mary Ann left, he lay back and let his head sink into the pillow, closed his eyes, took a deep breath and exhaled slowly. Thought back to a dinner with Lynn three months earlier after not seeing her for more than twenty-five years. Thought back to the twentieth high school reunion. Back to the days in high school. The run-ins with Dieter. The time at summer camp. Canoe trips.

❧

Ralph remembers Lynn's statement word for word. *I'm dying to hear the story of how the boy who couldn't get enough of the outdoors turned into a lawyer representing big energy companies.* She called him out and he had no answer. A week after their dinner at Café Boulud, three months before the heart attack he didn't expect, he still has no compelling answer. Lying back in the recliner watching the trees in the park wrestle with the heavy wind, he muses on the consequences of bad weather on canoe trips and in life.

He eases himself out of the recliner. Standing on a step stool in the guest bedroom, he retrieves a box from the top shelf in the closet and rummages through its contents, setting aside the blue ribbons for winning grade school races, newspaper clippings his mother saved religiously, Boy Scout merit badges, and his Sunday school bible. He digs until he finds the prize-winning essay from his junior year in high school, a piece the judges thought was fiction and mistakenly moved into the story category. He removes the rusted clip from a sheaf of yellowed papers.

TRIUMPH OF THE RIVIÈRE ROUGE
by Ralph Mackenzie
October 18, 1965

All five of us—Jack, Steve, Bill, Maarten, and me—had been camp friends for years, returning to Kiamika summer after summer. We were experienced canoe trippers. Each of us had earned the Voyageur Award. The mission of our last trip as campers was to complete a circuit that hadn't been attempted in ten years, a seven-day route beginning at Lac Rouge, looping north and west, then south and back east to end at the nearby Lac-de-la-Maison-de-Pierre in the Laurentian Mountains of Quebec right outside the boundaries of Parc du Mont-Tremblant. We were led by two counselors, Frank and Geoff, both twenty-two, also experienced canoe trippers. Our prospects were good; though no previous trip had made it around the circuit in years, we expected to. We would find the lost portage and clear it, for ourselves and for others who would follow us. It was a trip with a mission.

Day one it poured. After paddling three miles from the drop-off point up Lac Rouge and Petit Lac Rouge, everyone was drenched right through his rain suit. The canoes were carrying two inches of water. Two short portages and five more miles paddling and we'd all had enough for the day. Instead of pitching camp, Frank and Geoff decided to force the rusted lock on a weatherworn fishing cabin and spend the night under a roof that wasn't made of canvas . . .

Ralph remembers the heat of the fire they were able to get going in the cast-iron stove, so hot they couldn't stand anywhere near it and had to open the door to the cabin to let cooler air in. It was a fire started from and kept alive with the wood that he and Steve had cut, mostly him because Steve managed to let his ax glance off the slippery bark of the maple he was chopping down and plant itself in his leg.

Frank cleaned and disinfected the deep cut and fashioned butterfly stitch-es from several strips of tape. He considered using a sterilized fishhook to sew the cut closed properly, but backed off when Steve refused to go along. Maarten, still chilled from the day, piled logs on the fire in the stove. "Easy," said Frank. "It has to last all night— Hey guys, we have a problem. Steve's going to need real stitches soon and the nearest village is L'Ascension. That's at least thirty-five miles by dirt road. In his condition he can't make that hike. None of us want to carry packs or canoes that far." He unfolded the 1:50,000-scale government-issued topographical map and placed it on the cabin's table. He ran his finger along the meandering curve of the Rouge River, muttering his thoughts as he traced the route to L'Ascension. With the eleva-tion difference between the river's source and the village, there were bound to be several series of rapids around which they'd have to portage. No cleared trails. "I think it's too dangerous to take the river," he said . . .

Pity Frank hadn't gone with that thought. Pity he'd let Geoff sound a countervailing note, encourage Maarten's bravado, build a group consensus. Pity he'd finally caved. Long-forgotten images turn out not to have been forgotten, merely tucked away beneath layers of in-tervening life. Imagine thinking that a night's sleep would somehow change the factors affecting the critical decision. True, by next morn-ing the sky had cleared and the fog was lifting from the lake. As if the improved weather superseded the sum of everything else, Frank turned optimistic and changed his mind. Maarten let out a whoop. "Piece of cake." Ralph felt like asking whether it had chocolate frosting.

And that was that. That's what counselors are for. They lead. They didn't change the lineup in the canoes. Steve continued to ride in Frank's, only three of them.

With no one between Jack in the bow and Steve sitting on a pack in front of the stern thwart ahead of Frank, Steve could extend his injured leg over the portage thwart and keep it slightly elevated. "Best if you don't try to paddle," said Frank. "The current will carry us along fast enough."

Geoff's canoe, with four paddlers to only two in Frank's, took the lead. After an initial meandering stretch, the river straightened out and began to run faster. We negotiated a short section of light chop easily. The river leveled out again. "This isn't bad," said Geoff. "At this rate we'll be there by late afternoon. Or earlier— " he shouted as our canoe rounded a bend and he spotted churning water ahead. "Take the channel on the right." We entered the surge. In the bow, Bill paddled hard to avoid rocks and keep the canoe tracking the route Geoff had chosen. We handled the first set of rapids without getting wet. Then around a mild curve in the river, our canoe plunged into a three-foot drop between a pair of boulders. The bow broke the surface and the canoe took on water. Geoff looked for a place to draw to shore, but the canoe's momentum drove it forward. We hit a barely submerged, jagged rock head on. It ripped through the canvas ahead of the stern thwart and the canoe turned sideways . . .

Only one other time has Ralph found himself lying on his stomach belching water. Coincidentally, that was also on the Rouge River, the Lower Rouge many years later on a rafting trip during his twentieth high school reunion. It was his onetime rival, Dieter, who hauled Ralph from the river and kept reminding him all day long how he'd saved his life. Still, it was good fortune. Then, and years before on the Upper Rouge. On that canoe trip, fate simply would not allow an innocent fifteen-year-old to pay the price for the counselors' atrocious decisions. A beaten-up, rusted-out truck driven by a local who spoke a wholly unintelligible French-Canadian patois was heading along the road toward L'Ascension and stopped to help. Ralph would have liked to think that his French, limited as it was, was adequate to describe their predicament. More likely, it took one look at Steve's wound for the man to understand.

Ralph re-clips the sheaf of papers, sets the essay on the floor, and boots up his laptop. He is back amidst elegant white birches at Kiamika, standing outside the Nature Cabin, waiting to catch a glimpse of Jack's sister, Joan, on her way to pick up her family's lunch at the Dining Hall. He's chopping down small maples for tent poles; he's building a lean-to, making a mattress from boughs of balsam. He's baking a blueberry pie in a reflector oven by a hardwood fire . . .

He is writing a letter.

October 25, 2012

Dear Jack, Steve, Bill, and Maarten:

It's been nearly fifty years since we took our last canoe trip together, the one on which Steve tried to cut down his leg instead of a tree. I'm writing to entice all of you into a repeat performance. Well, not exactly—this time, there will be no axes in legs, no Rouge River debacle. I'm willing to let that river's victory stand, but I don't want to say goodbye to this life without completing the originally intended trip. I need all of you to help me to accomplish that.

I'm about to contact Camp Kiamika's director to ask if they'll sponsor our expedition. Do you remember the camp's founder? He was still taking canoe trips late into his seventies. So I don't expect any excuses from any of you regarding your age.

Please mark your calendars from late June into early July next year. I'm thinking that we'll assemble at Kiamika on Sunday, June 23ʳᵈ and return to camp on Wednesday, July 3ʳᵈ. If you're not like Jack, who's probably already in shape for this, you have almost eight months to prepare. This is a "save the dates" notice and a call for RSVP, no regrets accepted. I'll write you again in the new year after I've had a chance to speak with the camp director and make arrangements. Meanwhile, an early Christmas greeting to you and your families.

Best wishes,
Ralph Mackenzie

CHAPTER 2

As her headlights unfurl the highway in front of her car on the way back from Toronto, Lynn continues replaying parts of the evening's conversation with Ralph at Café Boulud. She congratulates herself for managing to avoid admitting that she took their college breakup hard. Didn't want to let him know that she'd often played the "what if" game. But it always came down to Jules—if she'd married Ralph, there wouldn't be Jules. Not that Jules has been easy. It was hard to adapt to the new reality that he imposed on her and Jean-Pierre. Their Jules started life as Juliette, and now, like their daughter Suzanne, Juliette is gone. Juliette started leaving at a young age, insisting on joining boys' teams, challenging boys on their turf, proving to be every bit as competent—she'd especially loved trampling them in soccer. At age seven, she refused to wear dresses to school, church, anywhere at all. Well before the court approved her name change, she demanded to be called Jules. As he tells it now, it was only ever the illusion of Juliette; Jules was there from the beginning.

The most difficult times with Jules are behind Lynn, but the crisis created a rift with Jean-Pierre. For both Jules and Lynn. Jean-Pierre couldn't adapt. It was hard for her, too, her brain initially unable to reprogram itself to get the proper noun and corresponding pronouns right, but Jean-Pierre made no apparent effort. Jules was dogged about correcting their missteps. In a pocket notebook he carried wherever he went, he recorded the errors with thick black X's, a tally sheet like the one Lynn had taped to the refrigerator when Jules was a young child to track the number of times he misbehaved. A single X for an incorrect pronoun in any form (she, her, hers), three X's for the improper proper noun (Juliette). Never a check mark for getting something right. Only the mistakes recorded. They thought Jules would tire of keeping score. At first he fined them a quarter for each tally mark, but when he saw how little good that did, he upped it to fifty cents and then a dollar. Some days Jules tallied more than a hundred dollars. Jean-Pierre kept telling Juliette it was merely play money, yet asked her what she planned to do with it. Building a fund to pay for top surgery was Jules' answer.

"What's top surgery?"

"Duh—the opposite of bottom surgery. Don't you know anything?"

"You mean a mastectomy?"

"A double mastectomy. That's the easy part."

"I won't allow it."

"You won't have any choice when I'm eighteen."

"What if our health insurance doesn't cover it?"

"It costs less than $10,000."

"You don't have that kind of money."

"At this rate I will soon."

Lynn remembers where that conversation led, how Jean-Pierre's fury built as the tension escalated. When Jules demanded that his father get his name right or he'd never speak to him again, Jean-Pierre spit back, "I *do* call you by your proper name, *Juliette*. That's the name your parents gave you and that's how it's going to stay."

"Not for long, *Dad*. I've been talking to Mum, and she's agreed to file the government form for a legal name change."

"I don't believe it— She'd never do that— Not without talking to me first."

With the road passing beneath her at 120 kph, little traffic to pay attention to, hopefully no cops lurking behind the overpasses, Lynn lets her mind locate the start of that particular episode, the one that essentially ended their marriage. Jules had just returned from school. Walking through the front door, he launched into a tirade about having to carry around the "ugly lumps on his chest," having to wear a tight-fitting spandex top like a corset with a loose-fitting sweatshirt over it to hide what still showed. That day, Jean-Pierre didn't back off. After hearing his bitter exchange with Jules regarding the name change, Lynn came into the living room to defuse the bomb about to detonate. "What's got into you?" she asked Jean-Pierre.

"What's got into *you*?" he snapped back. "You've been playing along with Juliette's charade. Now you've agreed to a name change?"

"Only one parent has to sign the form."

"That may be good enough for the government, but not for me."

"Jules' psychiatrist has written a letter of support. I was hoping it would persuade you to co-sign the form."

Jean-Pierre slammed his fist on the coffee table, knocking the book on the top of the stack to the floor. "The *two of you* are in on this?— You've been scheming behind my back?"

"You and I have discussed it for months," said Lynn, picking up the book and replacing it carefully on the table.

"Not an official name change."

"Sure we have— Where have you been?"

"I feel like I'm not living here anymore. This is my house and nobody tells me anything."

"That's ridiculous. It's our house, too. You've turned a deaf ear to what you don't want to hear."

"Maybe I should live somewhere else," said Jean-Pierre.

"Or maybe Jules and I should."

Jean-Pierre charged out of the house, slammed the door, and went for a long walk in the rain. By the time he returned, soaked to the skin, Jules had already eaten and gone to a nearby friend's to spend the night. Lynn handed Jean-Pierre a towel and bathrobe. While he showered, she set the dining room table and lit candles. After dessert they made love. Angry love. It was the last time she made love of any kind. With anyone.

❧

As he always had, Ralph took charge. He reminded the maître d' that he'd requested a table in a quiet corner. "Better for talking business," he said to Lynn

"Yes, I guess that's what this evening is about. I thought you might be able to help me in my fight against the wind farm projects in my county."

"I've been thinking about your situation. I know you were hoping that my firm could represent your citizens' group— "

" —Not your firm, Ralph— You."

They'd barely sat down. No *Hi, how are you? It's been a long time since our twentieth high school reunion. It's great to see you.* Lynn fiddled with her knife, trying to determine what to say next. Ralph continued as if she hadn't interrupted, explaining that one of his clients had won the right to install turbines on a few of the sites in Prince Edward County and that it would be a conflict of interest for him to represent her group. He referred her to a lawyer working for a non-profit environmental organization.

"I want *you* because I've heard you're the best."

"This lawyer is very good. I've even lost a case to him."

Still arrogant. She asked if he'd toured the sites for the proposed wind turbine installations. He shook his head no and reached across the table, put his hand on hers. "Please give that knife a break. Save it for your steak. It looks as if you're getting ready to use it on me."

"I think I'll have salmon," she said.

"I was hoping we might have chateaubriand for two."

"Not tonight."

"Well, maybe you can cook it for us sometime soon. You know— After you take me on a tour of your county."

She caught his gaze and held it. Odd how it seemed that he was holding hers instead. Intensity in those light blue eyes. Penetrating, but not threatening. They communicated curiosity infused with warmth. Back in college, she'd thought of them as kind. They told you he was interested in what you had to say without telegraphing that he might be interested only because he was trying to figure you out. Deceptively kind eyes that could put you off guard. His appearance hadn't changed much, except the color of his hair, silver now instead of reddish-brown, thick as ever. He was wearing it a little longer, slicked down with gel, a clean part—banker-ish. Only the slightest of wrinkles in his face and neck. Still trim. Well preserved. Amazing for sixty-two. Too damn good.

That's how the evening began. Only hours old, part of it seems as if it occurred a month ago, barely echoes of the conversation left, part of it as if it's happening all over again, right here, as if Ralph is in the passenger seat. She can't say the rest of that evening was uneventful. He refused to answer her question about where the boy who loved the outdoors had gone. He seemed to keep bringing the conversation back to the past. She was sure he'd end up at prom night and what they'd never satisfactorily resolved, but he didn't. She let him reminisce about hiking in the Eastern Townships, willing to let herself tag along in the conversation as she used to tag along with him and his father as they orienteered their way to small mountain ponds for picnics. She let him tell the story about the day the two of them sailed his family's Y-Flyer from the marina to the beach to join their mothers for lunch. After a swim, they headed upriver and upwind toward Lake Champlain, he at the tiller and tending the mainsail, she trimming the jib. A few miles from Fort Lennox, the sky turned dark and the wind picked up. Ralph came about and headed back. The boat made good speed surfing the growing waves, the centerboard whining as the bow planed. Holding onto the jib sheet, she pressed her toes against the gunwale and hiked out over the water. 1967. A few days before she turned seventeen.

"We put into the slip at the first crack of thunder," Ralph said. "Soaked before we could finish furling the mainsail."

"You had something else on your mind."

"Yeah, I can't believe it never happened."

Lynn changed the subject to their days on the debate team. "Do you remember the time Jean-Guy and I beat you and Louise in the provincial championships? You couldn't get over it."

"We had to argue *against* Quebec's secession from Canada. With two French judges and only one English judge, that was the harder side to win."

"Maybe. But you chose a bad strategy. Jean-Guy and I— "

"   —Got lucky," Ralph interrupted.

"Not at all. It was brilliant to have me speak in French and Jean-Guy in English. It blew the judges away."

"Yeah, it was clever." Ralph's expression softened. "A sign of things to come, wasn't it?" He motioned to the waiter to take away their plates.

She frowned. "You've eaten only half your steak."

"That's all I want. Would you like dessert?"

"What do you mean?"

"How about a nice crème brûlée?"

"No— What do you mean about a sign of things to come?"

"Adopting the French point of view as your own— Your love of men named Jean-something-or-other— Your dumping me in college for Jean-Pierre."

Ralph ordered two crèmes brûlées.

"Make that one. I'm going to pass." She got up from the table. "Excuse me— I'm going to the ladies' room."

Her love for Jean-something-or-other? Why had she agreed to this? Maybe for an opportunity—finally—to come clean . . . But maybe now, seeing each other again after such a long time, wasn't the right time. She touched up her lipstick and ran a brush through her hair, still the same length it had been in high school and college. Short. She never let it grow out, her hair the only feature that has resisted the pull of time. But only with regular coloring. She's added more wrinkles than Ralph has. No Botox for her. Let those crow's feet creep toward her gray-green eyes if they must. Ralph always claimed her eyes were gray. She's always seen them as green. Like his, hers can hold a gaze. Does he see hers as kind? Damn him— He's as good looking as ever, still arrogant, still in control. He hasn't changed. She brushed her hair back behind her ears.

"That's not how I remember it— " she said as she approached the table. Their waiter waited for her to sit, then placed a crème brûlée in front of her. "Compliments of the chef, Madame." She nodded to the waiter and tasted a spoonful. "Please give my compliments to the chef." Turning to Ralph, "You took up with your best friend's sister."

"What?"

"It wasn't me with *Jean-Pierre*— It was you with *Joan*."

"That was only *after* you began to see Jean-Pierre."

"No, it was before. I asked if you wanted to discuss our term papers before we turned them in and you said you couldn't because you had dinner plans."

"I hardly remember."

"Convenient. Let me jog your memory— Dinner with Jack and his sister. But Jack couldn't come. You and Joan had dinner alone."

"It was nothing."

"Seriously?— A week later you took her skiing and left me behind."

"That's not how it was— Joan was part of a large group of us who went on the midterm ski trip— You didn't even ski."

"Maybe I would have if you'd asked." She knew it was unfair to dredge this up after so long. But he'd started it. "Face it, you— "

"You face it. The truth is that you fell for him and his separatist cause. Christ, you married Jean-son-of-a-bitch right after graduation and began campaigning for the Parti Québécois!"

The people at the nearby tables stopped their conversations and turned their attention to Lynn and Ralph's escalating argument. The

waiter approached. "Is there something else I can bring you? A digestif, perhaps, compliments of the house, to accompany your dessert?"
With a wave of the hand, Ralph dismissed the waiter's intrusion. Lynn
leaned across the table and spoke softly, "I tried to talk to you, but
you'd have none of it. You said you weren't ready."

"Better late than never."

"Sometimes not."

At the hotel bar after dinner, Ralph ordered a cognac. Lynn nursed a
seltzer-water-with-lime—she had a three-hour drive home. By tacit
consent, they avoided the herd of elephants passing between them.
After the evening's drama, she wasn't about to ask Ralph why he was
still single, knowing that he'd counter by delving into the reasons
why she and Jean-Pierre were living apart.

"You haven't mentioned anything about Suzanne. At our high
school reunion you said she was about to graduate from high school."

Tears welled in her eyes. She could see that Ralph, thinking it safe
territory, felt terrible for having asked. "Suzanne and her husband
died in a plane crash. July 17th, 1996. My birthday. For seventeen years,
I've avoided celebrating it."

Ralph ran his hands through his hair and clasped them behind
his head, his forearms pinched against his ears. "Oh my God, Lynn—
I'm so sorry— That must've been devastating."

"I think about her all the time."

"On the phone you mentioned a grandson."

"Jules. The only part of Suzanne who survived. He was staying with
a nanny. Sixteen months old— "

"You and Jean-Pierre raised him?"

"He doesn't remember his parents. We are the only parents he's
known. He calls us Mum and Dad."

"I'm sure it hasn't been easy."

Ralph was right about that. But maybe harder for Jules than her.
Not because he'd been orphaned before having had a chance to know

his true parents. Because— She decided the complicated story of Jules could wait. She wasn't ready to tell it to Ralph. Another place she didn't want to go. More of those than she'd first thought there would be when she agreed to this dinner. But unavoidable when you see someone again after a long time. A lot to catch up on, the inevitable prying into crannies where the mind has tucked certain events away, not for safekeeping but because the memories simply can't be expunged, merely stowed as far as possible from where they can readily prey upon the mind. "It hasn't."

"Jules is seventeen now?"

"Almost eighteen. He'll graduate in June."

"Is he planning to go to college?"

"University of Toronto. Engineering."

"What type of engineer does he want to be?"

"Mechanical or civil, I guess—he's building model wind turbines for his science fair project this year. Floating windmills. Crazy-looking things."

"Seriously?"

"Yeah— What do you mean?"

"That's Dieter's specialty. When you called me the other day you mentioned you'd seen him recently."

"At a town meeting. He represented International Wind Technologies."

"A German company," said Ralph. "He was recently put in charge of their North American operations." Ralph filled her in on what she didn't know about the Dieter of the present day. Their grade school and high school friend had followed his father's footsteps and become a world-class engineer. "I bet Jules would like to pick his brain."

"Are you suggesting I invite Dieter to my place?" Lynn asked.

"Invite both of us."

"I don't know."

"You've been saying that a lot tonight."

"Have you forgotten your last encounter with Dieter?"

"The rafting trip during our high school reunion?"

"I was thinking of the floor hockey championship in our senior year."

"A horror show," said Ralph.

For sure. Nobody there that night would ever forget the bench-clearing brawl that Ralph and Dieter instigated. To the great embarrassment of parents, teachers, and the principal.

"And don't forget he had a crush on me. He was upset when you and I started going out together."

"I'm sure he got over you," said Ralph.

"Maybe not— Have you?"

That shut him up. Then, barely audibly, he said, *Not really—* As if admitting it to himself more than addressing her. "Make sure you tell Dieter that you've invited me too. Maybe he'll turn you down." Ralph smiled at that.

❦

She sees that the lights are still on. As she enters the house, she calls out to Jules. "You still up?" No answer. She walks down the hallway to the back bedroom she'd had converted into a studio for Jules to work on his science fair project. He's filled the huge fish tank on the wall-length tabletop and is now piecing together mini-LEGOs from his old mechanical engineering set. He's already constructed three stacks of blocks that he's seated on the bottom of the tank. "What are those?"

"Anchoring pylons. I'm going to simulate the effect of waves on the stability of the turbines I'm building."

"Are the others in your group helping you?"

"No. They're researching the environmental effects on fish and birds."

"I wish you'd work with them instead of building your turbines. It would help support my cause."

"That doesn't really interest me."

"You're not interested in helping me?"

"I think Canada should build more wind farms. Especially off-shore— Like Denmark has done."

"Why couldn't you have chosen some other project?"

"Loosen up, Mum. We've talked about this a zillion times."

"Obviously to no good."

"There's no way my project is going to damage your protest."

"What if your team wins and gets some press?"

Jules put down the parts of a pylon he was snapping together. "I hope you'll be happy for us."

"I'd be happier if you won with some other project."

"You're starting to sound like Dad."

That is not what she needs to hear at one o'clock in the morning. But she lets it pass because it's Jules, not Jean-Pierre. "Right— You should go to bed and get some sleep. Goodnight." She leaves the room, walks down the hall to her bathroom, washes the makeup from her face, and rubs in moisturizing cream. After brushing her teeth, she changes into pajamas and slides under the covers. Unable to fall asleep, she lies thinking how much easier it would be for a single mother to raise a daughter instead of a son. A daughter could lie in bed with her and talk. The way Lynn used to with her mother when her father was away on business. Her mother and father—how painlessly they've adjusted to Jules' changed circumstances. They understand that he's the same talented child, merely answering to a different name. Why couldn't Jean-Pierre see that? She'd counted on him to come around rather than lose another child. Okay—lose a daughter, but gain a son. Doesn't every father want a son? *Naturally, but a real son,* Jean-Pierre said, *not a daughter masquerading as one.* He claimed that that was worse than it would have been to discover his daughter was gay. He didn't laugh when Lynn said that Jules might be both transgender and gay.

Lynn hears Jules turn out the light in the studio and go into his bedroom. How does the kid survive on so little sleep? He's like her father, who'd go to bed at eleven and rise at five. Still unable to sleep, she lets her mind run over tomorrow's lesson plan for English class. *Today's* plan—it's already tomorrow. Stephen Leacock's story about the sinking of a small town's steamboat, the Mariposa Belle— Mariposa, a town like Picton, but with a shallow lake, not Lake Ontario with its deeper waters. Deep enough to make erecting wind turbines a challenge, she hopes. She imagines Jules far offshore directing the installation of a farm, she and Ralph sailing close by, their sails whipped about by turbulence from the turbines, the boat changing tacks suddenly, jibing unexpectedly, the boom striking her forehead . . . falling overboard, unable to grasp the whisker pole Ralph extends toward her . . . sinking, sinking . . . her last image a turbine's blades, like a steamboat's paddlewheel . . . more like a giant motorboat's propeller spinning loose from its mount . . . pursuing her to the bottom of the lake.

She awakes from the nightmare, perspiring from her neck and back, pajamas clinging to her skin. She removes her top. Stands in front of the mirror— No, she hasn't aged nearly as well as Ralph. The death of Suzanne and the troubles with Jules have left their marks. But at least she's maintained her slim body. Her breasts haven't yet surrendered fully to gravity. Ralph might still be able to see her as the same young woman he once loved. An older version of her yearbook photos. Not bad.

CHAPTER 3

Ralph used to visit Montreal regularly, but hasn't been there much in recent years, not since he established the base for his Canadian practice in Toronto and not since he handed off most of the responsibility for Canadian clients to his partners in that office. But for Hervé he always makes an exception. Hervé Boudreau, the founder and CEO of Frontier, Quebec's largest independent wind energy company. He and Ralph have been friends for twenty years, from when the wind energy business was in its infancy and Hervé's startup was run from a small warehouse. Unlike most French Canadians, Hervé speaks English with barely a trace of French accent.

A week ago, Ralph called Hervé to say he had an acquisition prospect for Frontier, one that would expand its business considerably outside Quebec. Hervé was reluctant to meet but finally agreed to let Ralph treat him to lunch at his favorite restaurant, Le Montréalais. Ralph joked that it is out of character for his "favorite French Canadian" to suggest eating at the Queen Elizabeth Hotel. Hervé's rejoinder was that he was only trying to please his "favorite English Canadian."

"I've been a U.S. citizen for a long time," said Ralph.

"You're still Canadian at heart," said Hervé.

Knowing that Hervé has punched a hole in his calendar to accommodate him, Ralph dispenses with the standard pleasantries and gets right to the point. He identifies the company Frontier should acquire and explains why he believes it would be a good fit. But Hervé seems distracted, even distraught. Unlike him to avoid eye contact.

"I don't have your full attention— Is everything fine at home? How are your girls?"

"Oui, oui—ça va bien."

The waitress arrives to take their orders, the usual for each of them—salade composée avec poisson frais. Hervé's eyes follow her as she walks away. "Très jolie."

"Your daughters?"

"For sure, but I meant the waitress."

"I guess she's more interesting than my proposal."

"We've already been thinking along similar lines."

"I wish you'd told me that."

"Not similar— Identical— Our bankers showed us the same company a few months ago. We've been in serious discussions for weeks."

"If you were already talking to them, why did you invite me for a last-minute lunch?"

"Ralph— You didn't disclose the name of the company over the phone and you invited yourself. I agreed because I haven't seen you in six months."

"There's something else, isn't there?"

Hervé doesn't say anything for a few seconds. "We've— " He hesitates. "Been considering other acquisitions too. Possibly a merger."

"I'm late to the table," says Ralph.

"Not at all. It's not your job."

"I thought I could help."

"Keep focusing on our environmental litigation. That's what I pay you for— By the way, how's our appeal on the Gaspé case going?"

"We don't have a hearing date yet."

"We shouldn't have had to appeal."

"The judge made a mistake in his decision." Ralph looks into his friend's face for a sign of displeasure or disapproval. As always, Hervé is inscrutable. "It should've been open-and-shut in our favor— I don't know what more anybody else could have done."

"You could have won."

"Our Toronto lawyers proved that Frontier met all regulatory requirements. The personal injury lawyer we brought onto the team argued convincingly that there was no link between the wind turbines in the vicinity of the plaintiff's home and his chronic state of depression."

Hervé raises an eyebrow. "Your man should have been more aggressive in exposing the plaintiff's medical history. He was clinically depressed *before* we installed the farm— Marital problems— Job performance."

"Look— I don't think it's the particular case that's bothering you."

"What makes you think I'm upset?"

Ralph ignores Hervé's attempt to divert the conversation. He points out that the Federal Government has already given clear signs it is on the verge of compelling the industry to fund an independent study of health hazards. The publicity around the Gaspé case put them over the top. "Right," says Hervé, "and now the Wind Energy Association blames my company. Even if we win the appeal, we're stuck with a bad reputation."

"Not *if* we win, but *when* . . ."

"I'm not so sure."

"Set the litigation aside," says Ralph. "Are you convinced there aren't any health hazards from your turbines?"

"I'm not aware of any evidence proving there are."

"Put yourself in the shoes of that poor Gaspé man and his family."

"It's not my job to empathize with plaintiffs."

Ralph scans his friend's face for a hint of compassion. "Would you consider the minimum setbacks adequate if it were your own girls' health at stake?"

Hervé takes a long, slow drink of water and picks at his salad, moving the fish aside. "I don't pay you to be my conscience."

"Really? That's exactly what I think you pay me for."

"That's not how I see it. I'm compensated for profits and share price— You help me avoid taking hits to those."

"I know, but if we suspect something isn't right, we should change it."

"Even if the practice is strictly legal?"

"Even then— Especially then."

Hervé gives a dismissive shrug. "We've had this conversation before— You always fail to factor in the costs of doing more than we're legally required to. Face it— You're an idealist."

"You're missing the point," says Ralph. "It's long run versus short run."

"The point is we should have won the case and you know it."

Ralph pauses to consider his response carefully. No matter how he phrases it his friend will resent the implicit *I told you so* he's about to deliver. "If you'd volunteered to pay for the plaintiff's ongoing psychotherapy and settled out of court, there'd be no adverse publicity at all."

"It's over and done with," says Hervé. "Merely another bump in the road— You've served us well." His friend's tone suggests a finality that Ralph doesn't like.

CHAPTER 4

As he leaves his office in Place Ville Marie and heads to the underground garage, Dieter sees that it's already two thirty. Later than he'd planned on leaving, but still early enough to stick to the speed limit and arrive at Lynn's on time. Germany is different. There he can put his BMW 335i convertible through its paces. The one he keeps in Montreal he has to rein in, all those horses under the hood champing at the bit for a little freedom to gallop away. Sometimes he can't help but yield to the demands of those creatures and the one inside him, an impulse for which he's often paid the price of a big ticket for a speed dangerously close to an automatic license suspension. Not today though. He can take his time and savor the unfolding drama he's directing. An opportunity to write the script for the next act, his old high school rival now clearly in his crosshairs. But tonight he'll disarm Ralph—they'll be on the same team, currying favor with Lynn. Or maybe it'll be good cop, bad cop, Lynn undoubtedly viewing him as the bad cop. His life's story with her. Unlike Ralph, who's always in her good graces.

The weather report is for solid overcast by the time he arrives in Picton, but right now in Montreal it's sunny with high cirrus clouds. If it were still summer, he'd drive with the top down, enjoy the feeling of the wind tossing his hair. It would set his heart racing, yet not as much as when he used to take his car to Circuit Mont-Tremblant.

Courtesy of a friend who knew its owners well, he was often permitted to use the track. Mostly they made him drive his convertible with the top up, but every now and then he'd run the course a little less aggressively with the top down. As a boy he watched a few Canadian Grand Prix races there, one in particular he'll never forget—the high school graduation present from his father, who'd arranged for him to meet Mario Andretti after a Formula One event in 1967, which Mario happened to win. The autographed checkered flag is mounted on the wall of his apartment in Montreal. But he hasn't been to the track in more than four years. His invitations disappeared after his crash in 2008. He totaled the car on the infamous Turn 2 but walked away unscathed. He's also had a few near misses on the highway, but no accidents. So far he's been lucky. Except for speeding tickets.

As he passes into Ontario along a straight stretch of road, clouds striding in from the west to overtake the sun drawing a late-in-the-year shallow arc in the sky, he turns his attention to Ralph and wonders what he's up to. Probably touring Prince Edward County. Will he fall for its natural beauty, be taken in by the bays and inlets and lakeshore, the rolling farms and quaint town of Picton? Will he drive down to the beach and sit on a dune, his former boyhood friend who bounded off to camp every summer to return with tales of sailing and canoe trips? Will he get caught in his reminiscences and let them overcome him or will he see that the proposed siting of the wind farms more than satisfies the legal requirements? Will Ralph support Dieter's views or undermine them with Lynn? Could they ever be on the same team? Ralph cares only about his own agenda. Though he suspects few people have ever seen beyond the veneer, Dieter knows that deeper down Ralph's a fucking prick.

Back in elementary school it was different. As young children they were best friends, playing together almost every day after school. Sometimes with Lynn, at Swiss Village where Lynn and Dieter lived. Lynn's family was granted permission to occupy one of the little brick houses his father's company built so that its expats wouldn't have to find a place for their families to live during their stints in Canada—a Monopoly house, red instead of green. They weren't exclusively for the Swiss; important people working at the company could rent the houses the Swiss didn't need. Dieter lived in the biggest by far—a Monopoly hotel—because his father ran the manufacturing plant. He was Lynn's father's boss. Dieter thought that might have counted for something.

Dieter now sees that what he and Ralph generally played at should have been a sign of things to come. Every time Ralph called him "German," he protested. The Swiss are not the same as the Germans. Maybe to an American, who too often is willing to lump all Europeans together as non-Americans, but not to a Canadian. A Canadian should know better. Why did he have to keep reminding Ralph that Switzerland remained neutral during the War? It was an odd thing to have to say because war was what they played, positioning their toy soldiers in trenches they dug in mounds of earth on construction sites after the workers had left for the day. They blew up each other's troops, Canadians against Germans at the battle of Dieppe. They used ordinary firecrackers unless they'd saved enough allowance to buy cherry bombs. Though the Canadians fought valiantly, the Germans always won.

When Lynn joined them, they put away their soldiers and put on Cowboy-and-Indian outfits instead. Lynn and Ralph let Dieter be the Cowboy. With his six-shooter cap-gun, he'd kill them again and again before they were all called in for dinner. But Lynn and Ralph always refused to die, resurrecting themselves to track down Dieter and fire their suction-cup-tipped arrows at his chest. When they killed him, they told him that he was truly dead, that Cowboys couldn't invoke Indian spirits to bring themselves back to life. Dieter claimed that *Swiss* Cowboys had that power. And Lynn and Ralph had to allow it because their playground was the woods at *Swiss* Village.

That was all play. The true rivalry with Ralph started in high school. The school enabled it, even encouraged it. All students belonged to one of four houses, colorfully named Red, Blue, Green, and Yellow. The houses competed both scholastically, grade averages from quarterly report cards posted student by student on large charts adorning the walls of the school's main hallway, and athletically, results of intramural games displayed on a bulletin board that also charted top athletes' progress toward a coveted Athletic Letter. Ralph was the best student during the first two years of high school, but Dieter took over that spot when the curriculum turned math-and-science heavy in the junior and senior years. In the gymnasium, Ralph and Dieter, each captain of their houses, pitched their teams fiercely against each other in basketball, volleyball, and floor hockey.

One evening, late in senior year, the rivalry spilled out in front of assembled students, parents, teachers, and the principal. It was the final encounter of their high school careers, the championship of the floor hockey season. Spring of 1967. Ralph's Red team was down 4–3 in the third period to Dieter's Yellow team when Ralph stole the puck from Dieter and raced down the left wing. Dieter caught him from behind and cross-checked him off the playing surface into the Red bench. During Dieter's two-minute penalty, Ralph scored to tie the game. And in the final minute, Ralph stood his ground against Dieter's rush through the Red defense and sent him to the linoleum floor with a vicious elbow to the face. Both benches cleared. Teachers had to come out of the stands to help the sole referee separate the players. The principal called the game. Fathers besieged the principal on their way out of the gymnasium, complaining that he should have ejected Ralph and Dieter but let the game continue to a resolution. Mothers collared him near the front entrance, claiming it was a disgrace to run such an undisciplined school.

The principal ordered both Ralph and Dieter to appear at his office at eight the next morning, where he summarily stripped them both of the Athletic Letters they would have been awarded at the upcoming graduation ceremony. Told them they were lucky they'd still receive their Scholastic Letters. But Ralph received both letters anyway, Dieter only the one. It wasn't until their twentieth high school reunion that Dieter found out why. The former principal attended the event and, under pointed questioning from Dieter, admitted that Ralph's father, chairman of the school board, had intervened on his son's behalf, arguing that Dieter had been the instigator and should be the only one punished.

Dieter and Ralph didn't see each other after graduation until that high school reunion. That's when Dieter saved Ralph's life, during a one-day excursion to the Rouge River for a little whitewater rafting. Because of his canoeing experience, Ralph joined the guide at the back of the raft, but didn't make it through the first chute. He fell overboard, was sucked under and bobbed like a cork, choking on the water he'd swallowed. Dieter was the one to pull him out of the river. Ralph was so frightened for his life he must have forgotten who Dieter was and thanked him. Dieter asked him right then, when Ralph was still dazed from the near-drowning, where he stood with Lynn. Ralph didn't say a thing but his look was answer enough. That was the crux of it. By the time Dieter had finished grad school, he realized it wasn't any of their battles in athletics or scholastics that killed the earlier friendship. Since middle school, he'd harbored a crush on Lynn. In high school when everyone started dating, she ended up picking the Canadian over the Swiss. But Dieter thought he'd ruined it for Ralph and was shocked to hear that he and Lynn were still together in college. Not surprised, though, that she found someone else to marry. Ralph not ending up with Lynn was small consolation. She was the prize Dieter had wanted. Still does. Sometime he'll have to apologize for what happened between them. But not tonight. Not with Ralph there.

Dieter checks the rearview mirror and sees a car approaching quickly. *That guy's going to get pulled over. Better him than me— Fuck— It's the OPP.* The illegal radar detector he keeps out of sight on the passenger seat hadn't registered a warning. The cop must have been tailing him at a distance to clock his speed. He's hosed. Quebec plates in Ontario. Doubly hosed. But not as bad as Ontario plates in

Quebec. Dieter pulls over, unplugs the radar detector and slips it under his trench coat on the passenger seat.

"Good afternoon, officer," he says, forcing a smile through clenched teeth. *Bad afternoon.*

"For you I guess. That's a beautiful car you have, but this is not a speedway. Do you know how fast you were traveling?"

"No officer, I'm afraid I don't. I was trying to keep to the limit."

"Really? I clocked you at 150 kilometers per hour. This isn't an autobahn you know."

Why would the officer have said that? How could he know that I reside in Germany? Probably the BMW. "Yes, I know."

"License and registration please."

This guy's like a German. No chit-chat. All business. "I'm sorry sir. I reside in Europe most of the year and I sometimes forget where I am. Here's my international license."

"And your registration please?"

When the officer returns from his patrol car after ten minutes, he looks at Dieter quizzically. "There are no previous infractions listed against your international license, but your vehicle has been stopped twice during the past six months for speeding in Quebec. You were the driver both times. Do you also carry a Quebec driver's license?"

"Yes sir, but I forgot to bring it overseas with me this trip."

"Do you maintain a residence in Quebec?"

"Yes, officer, an apartment in Montreal."

"I would have thought you'd leave your Quebec license there."

"Most of the time I do."

"What is your citizenship?"

"Swiss, sir, but I live in Germany when I'm not here."

"Do you know that I have the right to confiscate your license?"

"Yes sir."

"This infraction carries a huge fine. With your record, the next time you're caught speeding like this, your license will be suspended— Do you understand?"

"Yes sir."

"That means today too. You get stopped again today—here or in Quebec—and you won't make it anywhere."

"Yes officer." Dieter takes the ticket and his documents and tucks them in the glove compartment. For several minutes he sits fuming. *This fucking country. There's no one else on the road. I could have been traveling 200 kph and it wouldn't have mattered. I can't wait to get back to Germany for good.* He looks in the side view mirror and sees the officer approaching again.

"Officer?"

"Why are you still here?"

"I'm trying to catch my breath. My chest hurts."

"Should I call an ambulance? The hospital in Cornwall is not too far."

"No sir— I'll be fine— You can leave— "

"I can't leave until you do. It's dangerous for you to park on the side of the highway."

"Okay. Please give me a few minutes." Dieter raises his window without waiting to hear what the officer has to say. His chest doesn't hurt at all. He is not out of breath. He sprinkles a little water on his handkerchief and wipes his face. Starts to compose himself for the evening ahead.

CHAPTER 5

It was to be a special evening and she had to leave school early to get ready. Lynn told Jules to catch a ride home from school with a friend. When Jules gets home, he finds her primping herself, getting her lashes and eyebrows perfect. In the morning she seldom does more than pull on a clean skirt and blouse and run a brush through her hair before driving to school. She's out of practice, she says—hasn't been out on a real date since they left Montreal. Maybe one, he says. The dinner with Ralph. Jules is happy that tonight won't be a date of any kind, not with him hanging around and Dieter driving in from Montreal.

"Mum, I hardly ever see you in a dress. Trying to impress Ralph again?"

"He and Dieter are coming straight from work. They'll be in suits."

"Just so you know, I'm not dressing up. They're not *my* guests." He leaves her to her finishing touches and heads to his studio.

"Hey wait. How about changing into a nice pair of slacks? I'm not asking you to put on a sports jacket."

Jules turns and crosses his arms over his chest to make it clear he has no intention of complying. "You won't ever catch me in anything like that."

"You'll wear a tux to your prom, won't you?"

"If I go."

"Why wouldn't you?"

"I haven't thought about it."

"Will you go with a boy or a girl?"

"What kind of question is that? I'll probably go alone. If I go— I don't want to talk about it."

He enters the studio, but his mother won't let the matter drop. "In my day, if you went by yourself it meant you couldn't get a date."

"Today's different. And there's a girl I'm interested in. Maybe her. Didn't you hear me— I don't want to talk about it."

"You don't have to get all prickly."

He knows what she's thinking. They talk about it all the time. Too much. Is it his job to help her through this or the other way around? He knows that she feels he's sometimes more than she can handle, the *transgender dimension* of his life magnifying the usual teenage issues, she says. It's at times like this he knows she's most angry with his Dad for forcing her to raise him by herself. Jules has heard her grumble about it, Jean-Pierre leaving all the difficult situations to her then waltzing in from Montreal for his every-other-weekend time with his adolescent child. Jules puts down his backpack and returns to the kitchen. "You didn't answer my question about Ralph."

"We were childhood friends."

"It must have been more than that."

"We went to the senior prom together and then to McGill. It got complicated when I met your dad."

"Is that when you dumped Ralph?"

"It didn't happen that way. We sort of grew apart as I started seeing your father more."

"Do you still have feelings for him?"

His mother hesitates. "I wouldn't have called him unless I needed his help. I think he can advise us on filing a lawsuit against the wind farms."

"That's not all. You had a big smile on your face when you came back from dinner." She smiles. This time he can't tell what she's thinking.

"What did you tell him about me?"

"That you're my grandson and you're building wind turbines for your science fair project and you want to be an engineer."

"That's all?"

"That's all— As you said, I don't want to talk about it."

"Okay, but one more thing. Were you and Dieter ever together?"

"God, you're full of questions tonight— " She hesitates again. " —No. We were merely friends\. He was interested in me, but I wasn't interested in him."

He can see there's way more to it than that. Another of those situations when the truth is too complicated. She tells him that all the time. Especially when he wants to talk about his father and why they can't get back together as a family. "That must have made him jealous of Ralph."

"They didn't get along in high school."

"What about now?"

"I guess we'll find out. Go change your clothes while I finish preparing dinner."

There isn't much left to prepare. She's spent the last two evenings concocting a fine French offering—pistou, a vegetable stew, perfect, she says, in case Dieter is vegetarian, and tourtière, Montreal-style, a meat pie. Jules helped her with the tourtière by grinding the pork and adding cinnamon and cloves. There is Boursin and pepper crackers to start and her famous mille feuilles for dessert. The meal that is his father's favorite. It's not lost on him that she's making a play for Ralph.

❧

In dress slacks and dress shirt, his hair combed and parted as if he's going for a college interview—he decided that his mother was right (though he certainly won't tell her that) and he wants to make a favorable first impression—Jules greets Dieter at the door, takes his bottle of wine and calls out to his mother before realizing he hasn't introduced himself properly. He shakes Dieter's hand.

"Pleased to meet you, Dr. Graber. I'm Jules, Lynn's grandson."

"My pleasure, Jules. I've heard we have a common interest."

"You're working on a science fair project about wind energy, too?" Jules waits for the polite laugh from Dieter that doesn't come.

"Oh yes—offshore turbines, floating platforms."

Lynn appears and takes the bottle of wine from Jules. "Marvelous. Nuits-Saint-Georges, my favorite white."

"As you requested."

"Jules, why don't you show Dieter your project while we wait for Ralph?"

In the studio, Dieter runs his hand along the edge of the thick plywood tabletop screwed into sawhorses placed every meter along the back wall of the room, a work area Jules reinforced solidly to support the weight of the large fish tank filled with water.

"Did you make this yourself?"

"I did."

"Where did you get that tank?"

"From our school. They renovated the biology lab and replaced the aquarium."

"How did you get it here?"

"In my friend's father's pickup truck. It took all three of us to carry it. Empty."

"Is that clay on the bottom?"

"Yes— I couldn't anchor anything in sand and gravel."

"Why didn't you use Plasticine?"

"That would've cost money. Besides, clay is more realistic. A local farmer allowed me to dig on his property." From a pile at the side of the tank, Jules takes a handful of soil. Closing his other hand over it, he massages it into a ball. "See— It clumps easily."

"Clever— It looks as if you've set up the tank for wave tests."

"That's the plan. But the aquarium's narrow. If I'm not careful, I cause reflections from the sides."

"It looks entirely effective for a homemade wave tank. But better for simulating ocean waves than what you'd find on Lake Ontario."

Dieter continues asking questions as if he's a judge at the science fair.

"How many pylons will you need to anchor each turbine?"

"I've been thinking of three. With a level lake bottom, windless surface conditions, and no current, the turbine would essentially float at the center of an equilateral triangle with the pylons at the vertices." Jules, listening to himself, realizing that this is turning into a trial run for the science fair, is pleased with how academic-sounding his answers are.

"Have you considered configurations of more than three?"

"I'm testing a cluster of six turbines arranged in a hexagon within a cluster of six pylons arranged in a larger hexagon rotated sixty degrees, allowing me to replicate the triangular structure after I add a central pylon."

"Economical," said Dieter.

"That's the point," said Jules. "Each of the outer pylons will tether two turbines and the central pylon will tether all six turbines. Seven pylons in all for six turbines. The turbines will be linked to each other to maintain an approximate hexagonal configuration depending on the force of the waves. Let me show you." Jules takes a piece of paper and sketches a diagram that looks like a six-pointed Sheriff's badge.

"I don't think anyone has considered that configuration," said Dieter. "I wonder if the requirement that the turbines be spaced sufficiently far apart to operate efficiently will frustrate the design."

"I hope not. Trouble is, my tank is way too narrow to test it properly."

Lynn joins them in the studio. "Dinner's ready. I wonder what's holding up Ralph."

"Probably traveling around the county scouting out the wind farm sites. That would be like him. Maybe we should go ahead without him."

"What do you think of Jules' project?"

"Amazing. He's studying many of the same types of effect we test in our commercial facility. Do you mind if we spend a little more time together?"

"Not at all. I'll finish up in the kitchen."

Turning back to Jules, Dieter asks, "What kind of topside turbine are you going to exhibit?"

"Eggbeater."

"Vertical or horizontal axis?"

"Both, but I'm leaning toward horizontal— Lower center of gravity, more stable."

"True, but wind speed tends to be higher the higher above the surface of the water you go. And steadier too."

"I hadn't thought of that."

"Vertical-axis turbines can be located closer together. That might render your six-cluster structure feasible."

"I guess I'll have to consider them more seriously."

"Do you have a prototype of the eggbeater?"

"At school. My physics teacher asked to see it."

Both of them standing side by side looking at the tank, Dieter puts his hand on Jules' shoulder. "This is great work. I wonder if you'd like to visit our research center in Germany. Best in the world."

"Are you kidding! Germany? That'd be awesome— But I don't think my mother would go for it."

"Why not?"

"We watch our expenses carefully— And I have school."

"I don't mean right away. How about your summer break? We have an internship program and a few scholarships."

"How would I apply?"

"I can have the forms sent to you. The scholarship would cover your travel and living expenses."

"Do all the interns plan to study engineering?"

"Most will be college students already enrolled in engineering programs. I hear you're thinking of University of Toronto."

"McGill too. I'm going there this weekend."

"I was an undergrad at Toronto and a grad student at McGill. They're both great schools."

"I've read that McGill is better for mechanical engineering."

"It's a toss-up. Have you visited Toronto yet?"

"After the science fair."

"I can help arrange your visit— I still know many of the professors."

"That'd be fantastic."

"Let's ask your mother about a summer stay in Germany before you start college. The monthlong program starts sometime after mid-July. You'd probably want to arrive a week early. Would that fit with your plans?"

"We have no plans yet for the summer."

Lynn is setting out the cheese and crackers in the living room. Through the picture window she sees Ralph pull into the driveway and opens the door to welcome him. Dieter and Jules follow.

"That's special—a welcoming party!" says Ralph as he gets out of the car. "You make a nice family." He hands Lynn a bottle of wine.

Ignoring Ralph's comment, she says, "I was beginning to wonder whether you got lost in the wilds of Prince Edward County."

"Out there enjoying the countryside."

"Dieter thought we should go ahead without you."

"Typical," says Ralph. "I guess nothing's changed."

Lynn gives Ralph a pained look. Jules recognizes it as the one she uses on him when she wants him to shut up. "Jules, this is Mr. Mackenzie, an old school friend."

"You've already told me all about him, Mum."

"Only good things I hope," says Ralph.

"Mostly," Lynn says, laughing. "Jules has been showing Dieter his science fair project. Maybe he can give you a quick tour."

Jules waits until his mother returns from the kitchen, three empty wine glasses in one hand and an opened bottle of wine in the other, before springing the question. "Dr. Graber has invited me to Germany for a one-month summer internship at his company's research center. Can I go?"

Ralph winces. Lynn juggles the wine glasses. "Dieter, do you usually take on high school students?"

"Generally college students. Engineering majors. But every year we admit a few incoming freshmen."

"It's a generous offer, but I don't think we can afford it on my teacher's salary."

"Dr. Graber's company can provide a scholarship."

"Without his having to apply?"

"He'd have to apply, but I can see from what he's accomplished on his project that he's already doing work as advanced as many of our recent interns."

"That's kind, but Jules doesn't speak a word of German."

"Everybody at our company speaks English. It's a requirement for employment. He'll quickly pick up the essential German."

"Jules, we'll talk about it later. Why don't you show Ralph your project and tell him about school while Dieter and I set the table?"

He doesn't want to demonstrate his project again. He's not some talking head with a rewind button. He'd prefer to ask Ralph whether there's something between him and his mother and why he doesn't get along with Dieter. But he's also interested in surviving the night intact. Fortunately, there's little opportunity to pursue his questions, even obliquely. Ralph has hardly begun to survey Jules' project when Dieter calls everyone to the table. Jules excuses himself after the pistou, leaving the adults to discuss the boring politics of wind farms. He's more interested in anchoring his pylons.

CHAPTER 6

It has stopped raining. Wearing her reflective vest, Lynn steps out of the house at six o'clock for her usual walk before school. Light from street lamps reflects off mist still hanging in the air and creates an eerie glow, the kind you see on a movie set to create a sense of impending doom. There is a strong earthen smell, the scent of wet, decaying leaves. Almost no traffic on the road. She loves it here in Picton, such a difference from Montreal. She walks briskly to the marina and makes her way to her favorite boat, a Daysailer about halfway down one edge of the dock.

Last night's dinner unfolded as she had feared. From the moment he entered the house, Ralph had it in for Dieter. Not even someone like Dieter deserved that.

"Nice. I see that Germans are not above wearing fine Italian clothes. Brioni suit and Zegna tie, if I'm not mistaken. Not bad for an engineer."

"Same old," said Dieter. "Trying to keep up with you."

Then the episode over Dieter's offer to Jules. Handing Dieter a stack of plates in the kitchen, out of earshot of Ralph and Jules in the studio, she said, "What the hell are you doing? We're on opposite sides of the wind farm issue and you barely step into my house before offering my son a scholarship for a summer internship?"

Dieter looked crushed. "I know what I'm doing. We'd be lucky to have Jules in the program."

"C'mon. It smells like a bribe— You've put me in an impossible position with Jules."

"How?"

"If the lawsuit I bring against your company succeeds, you'll pull your offer of the internship and he'll resent me forever."

"Giving Jules this opportunity is the right thing. It has nothing to do with wind farms in your county— Or the fact that I still have a soft spot for you— "

He waited for her to react, and when she didn't, he finished placing the plates around the table. "Where's the silverware?"

Lynn opened a drawer of the sideboard. "You're saying that you'd have offered Jules an internship regardless?"

"Certainly— Especially after seeing his work— Ironic, isn't it? I'd never have met Jules without running into you at your town meeting."

"I'd like to believe you." In a perverse way, she was glad that a contentious matter had already sprung up with Dieter, even if Jules had to be at its center.

Dieter turned out not to be a vegetarian. Lynn served them both generous slices of tourtière and took a smaller one for herself. Dieter heaped on ketchup from a small dish that she'd placed on the table beside a cruet of molasses. Ralph waited, watching her pour some molasses onto the side of her plate, then followed her lead. Looking directly into her eyes, with no lead-up to it, he asked whether she believed that wind power is part of a sound energy strategy for the country. It caught her off guard.

"Ah, Mr. Prosecutor, the framing question! No wonder you went into law. By the way, how's the tourtière?"

"Seriously— " said Ralph, "that's the place to start. If you think it's a bad energy policy, it becomes a different discussion."

"Seriously— How's the tourtière?"

"Delicious. Perfect with molasses. I presume that's the Quebec way."

"Yes— I thought this was supposed to be purely a social visit. A chance for Dieter to meet Jules."

"I'm glad I did," said Dieter, "and I love the meal you prepared for us, but while I'm here, I'd like to talk about the proposed wind farms a little more than we were able to at the town meeting."

"I can't tell whether it's the tourtière you like or the ketchup you've slathered all over it," she said, wishing as soon as the words escaped her mouth that she could reel them back before they reached his ears.

Dieter looked crushed again. He'd been caught masking the taste of a favorite food of Quebecers that he couldn't stand, but was forced to eat solely out of politeness—the only thing he found worse was French-Canadian poutine.

"Sorry— I don't like the taste of molasses."

"In principle, I don't think it's a bad policy," she said to soften the blow. "The ketchup I mean." Dieter put on a weak smile. When Ralph stopped laughing, she continued. "Okay, Ralph—*seriously*. I don't think we should place wind farms where there are tourist attractions, recreational parks, or wildlife preserves. We have all three in this county."

"If you take the emotion out of it," said Dieter, "you'll— "

She interrupted him mid-sentence. "We've looked at it the only way residents can. We don't want to see the towers. We don't want to hear the thump-thumping of the blades whipping the air. We care about our wildlife. We thrive on tourist business. Could it be any simpler?"

"That's a self-serving view," said Dieter, apparently unwilling to adopt a lighter touch. Not much of a soft spot for her after all. "Opposition groups tend to agree that the country needs to harness wind energy, but then turn around and say, 'Take your projects somewhere else, thank you. Not in my backyard.'"

Lynn savored a mouthful of meat pie and took her first taste of the wine. "Now that's a good Nuits. Who brought this one?"

"I did," said Ralph.

"You should have opened mine," said Dieter. "It's a better vintage."

Turning to Dieter, she asked, "What's wrong with that view?"

Jules, who'd been standing unnoticed in the doorway to the dining room, answered for Dieter. "If everybody thought that way, the country would never solve its energy problems."

"I don't think I need your help on this," she said. Jules retreated to his studio.

"Smart kid," said Ralph.

"Smart ass— There are plenty of places where wind farms could be located that wouldn't affect people's lives as directly."

Dieter drained his glass and refilled it. "Let's finish this bottle so that I can open the better one."

"You're thinking of places where few people live," said Ralph.

"Exactly."

"Sadly, for reasons of cost, we don't always have that luxury. We tend to site farms in rural areas. From my tour this afternoon, I'd say this is a rural area. Except for the town itself."

"Not rural enough. I meant places where there is virtually no population."

"I guess you don't understand," said Dieter, "how expensive it is to transmit power from remote areas."

"Then build massive farms there and transport a lot of electricity. Make it an economy of scale. Hey guys, there's nothing new here— All you big energy folk are set in your ways and won't listen to reason."

"I think the same could be said of you," said Dieter.

Lynn bristled. Got up and started to clear the dishes from the table. "Anybody want dessert? I've made mille feuilles."

"From scratch?" asked Ralph. "You didn't pick it up at the bakery?"

"All by myself. I can't tell you how many times I helped my mother make it. It is my father's favorite."

"Let me help you clean up," said Ralph. "We need a break."

But Lynn refused to let the matter drop. "What you're both overlooking is that people who live here—or merely visit—consider it God's country. Why ruin it for everybody?"

Ralph, obviously still trying to divert the discussion, or at least keep it on an even keel, said, "Are you saying that if God had wanted us to have windmills here, He'd have built them Himself?"

"You mean *She* and *Herself,* don't you?" By the grimace on Ralph's face, she could tell that her tone had too much edge for his taste. They both let it go and rejoined Dieter who was still sitting at his place, topping off his glass.

"Easy there," said Ralph, "you have a long drive back tonight."

"Maybe we should all get as drunk as we did on prom night," said Dieter. "See where it goes." He glared at Lynn.

Ralph noticed and gave her a puzzled look. She returned his look. "We might as well finish the argument we've started," he said, "and move on to something more pleasant."

If only you knew, she thought. "Okay, go ahead."

"I had a chance to view three of the major sites today on my way here, two on land and the one off Sandbanks."

"What did you conclude?" she asked.

"The proposed onshore farms are located exactly where such farms are typically found. Like Wolfe Island across from Kingston. Essentially farmland. Or Maple Ridge in Upstate New York. Farmland, rolling hills, wooded areas."

"Those developments were highly controversial," she countered. "Many residents were upset with the prospect of turbines near their homes and they're no happier now that the farms are operational."

"Both developments got a clean bill of health from regulatory authorities," said Dieter.

"Despite the protests, those projects eventually got built," said Ralph.

"It ends up being a losing battle to fight them," said Dieter. "You merely forestall the inevitable."

Looking straight at Ralph, Lynn asked, "What about the offshore sites? You're still a sailor, aren't you?"

"I am indeed, and I'm concerned that part of the site off Sandbanks will be seen directly from the beach."

"Wait a minute," said Dieter. "That's my company's project. It's Crown Land—we worked closely with the Federal Government to get that approval."

"I know," said Ralph, "but erecting turbines in plain view of the beach could be devastating to the tourist business."

"Obviously we disagree," said Dieter, "and the government did too when it gave us the nod to proceed."

Lynn noticed the sudden flush in Dieter's face. "Hey boys, it sounds as if this is heading toward a bad place. We're grown-ups now, aren't we?"

"Some of us," said Ralph, "are capable of appreciating the merits of both sides and see good reason to strike a balance."

"What the fuck!" said Dieter.

"Tone it down guys. Jules is down the hall. No floor hockey finals in my home, thank you."

They all laughed. "Got any spare broomsticks?" Dieter asked. "I'd like to show Ralph how to take a proper shot."

"At the net or at me?" said Ralph.

"Let's finish up business before dessert," she said. "Since you've asked, I'll tell you where I stand."

Both Dieter and Ralph, sitting on the same side of the table, moved to the edges of their chairs.

"Here's my little sermon. Listen up—obviously this is what you came for. If the wind companies can demonstrate an openness to other viewpoints, some flexibility on how to protect the wildlife preserve, and a willingness to revisit the location of offshore farms, that may be enough for us to reach an accommodation. We're not unreasonable. But until we see signs that your industry is willing to consider those possibilities, we're going to insist that the entire county be declared off limits, land and lake. We're going to file suit to that effect."

"That's a totally uncompromising position," said Dieter.

"Hardly. I've told you what we'll consider constructive movement on your part."

"Thank you for that," said Dieter. It didn't sound as if he meant it. He managed another weak smile. Both Ralph and Lynn could feel him seething. "And thank you for a lovely dinner. I'm going to pass on dessert— You're right, it's a long drive back. You two can enjoy my bottle of wine."

"That's it? You're leaving?"

"I suspect you and Ralph need to sort something out— Anyway, please consider the summer opportunity for Jules. It would be a great experience for him. And I forgot to say it as I walked in— Lynn— You look absolutely spectacular. You've taken good care of yourself."

After Dieter left, Ralph started to rinse the wine glasses, china, and silverware. At the sink, his back to Lynn, he asked, "What did Dieter mean that we've got something to sort out? And what was that about our prom night?"

"I think Dieter was talking about having to carry you on his back up to your front door and hand you over to your parents. You were too drunk to remember it the next day."

"Is that all?"

No, that wasn't the half of it, but the rest would have to wait—she wasn't going to talk about the post-prom party, not in her own home, not with Jules down the hall. "Yeah, that's all— "

"Well, Dieter's right, you know—you look stunning."

"Thank you. Not so bad yourself, eh?"

"I can stay a while and help you clean up. Maybe another glass of wine? Let's see if Dieter's right about his bottle."

"Thanks, I can handle washing up. You also have a long drive back. Look—it's started to rain."

"I'm in no hurry," said Ralph. "Let's sit down and talk."

"Some other time— I'd love to, but I'm tired and I need to speak with Jules about Dieter's offer."

At the door, Ralph gave her a firm hug, then kissed her lightly on the lips. Holding her by her shoulders, he looked into her eyes. "Sorry this ended up being only about business. We didn't even get to your mille feuilles. I'd like to take a rain check." He looked outside and chuckled at his choice of words.

"Sure, why not?"

"I'll give you a call."

She stood at the door, watched him back out of the driveway, and waved goodbye. Didn't go inside until his taillights passed from view. Didn't wipe the kiss off her lips. Wished that Jules had been staying with a friend that night.

Standing on the dock and looking out at the bay, she realizes that something good had come from the evening: the compliments about how she looked had made her feel good about herself. Good, but not altogether good. She wasn't thrilled that Dieter had been the first to comment. It made Ralph's compliment seem forced instead of freely offered, perhaps a response only to make sure he hadn't been completely one-upped by Dieter. The more she thinks about it, the more troubled she becomes. Dieter is going to continue to pose a problem. He doesn't seem to understand that she will never forgive him. And Ralph—would he still be interested if she hadn't kept herself trim? What if she'd put on another thirty pounds over the years? Had let her hair grow long, making her look more like an old witch than an older version of her graduation photo? Would he fall for her today if they hadn't been sweethearts in high school and college? Even more troubling than those questions is why she keeps rejecting his overtures. How long can that continue before he'll walk away? For good this time. She wonders if he is thinking the same thing.

CHAPTER 7

Right on time. Nine o'clock as Lynn enters the lobby of the Marriott on the lakefront in Kingston. Ralph hands her a key card on which he's marked the room number. "Top floor—great water view. You'll love it. Right next to mine."

"Hi Ralph— Nice to see you, too," Lynn says.

He can't tell whether she's irritated or kidding. He takes the card from her, moves back a little, then steps forward and gives her a hug. "Lynn. I'm glad you decided to come. I appreciate it."

"Me too. That's much better."

He hands her back the key card. "Have you eaten breakfast? They have a buffet here every morning. It's edible."

He's relieved that she turns it down. On the way to his parents' place, he tells her that they moved last year from their scenic water-front home in the Thousand Islands to an assisted-living facility with a view of commercial buildings and open fields that will soon be built up into more commercial buildings. His mother finally decided she could no longer cope with the housework and cooking and caring for his father, whose dementia has now progressed beyond the early stages. His father can still carry a conversation and tell a joke, but keeps asking the same questions over and over. It exasperates his mother. He tries to visit often to offer some relief.

After registering in the guestbook at the front desk of the facility, they take the elevator to the top floor. Lynn notes the wide, well-lit hallways.

"Wheelchairs and walkers. It's a two-lane highway. The faster folk need to be able to pass the slower ones."

"I bet it's a highly controlled environment."

"You have no idea. No stoves, hot plates, candles, matches. No smoking. Nothing that might start a fire. Microwave ovens. Emergency cords in the bathrooms. No tubs or sinks that hold water for very long. Mind you, no plastic caps on the wall outlets, but otherwise childproofed."

They knock on the door of Room 400 and are met by his parents. "Mom and Dad, I'd like you to meet an old friend—Lynn Adams. Lynn, please meet Claire and Gordon. I guess it's more like *meet again*." After hugs all around, they sit in the living room, Gordon in his recliner, Claire on the small sofa, Lynn and Ralph in adjacent armchairs, everything oriented to face the television.

"Would anyone like tea?" his mother asks. "Ralph, you can boil water in the microwave and make what you want: Chamomile, English Breakfast, Earl Grey. You know where the tea bags are."

"Mom, do you remember Lynn? She and I were in the same homeroom from first grade through high school."

"I remember her," says his father. "She's the one you wanted to marry."

Lynn laughs. She's glad Ralph has warned her. "That's right. Forty years ago he did, but a French Canadian snatched me out of his arms. He's never got over it."

Ralph makes a point of pouting, but his father is not easily put off. "Why are you here now?"

"We met up again a few weeks ago. I asked Ralph to help me find a lawyer."

"Are you in some kind of trouble?"

"Not really. They're trying to put wind turbines in my backyard."

"Where's your backyard?"

"In Picton."

"Has Ralph been able to help you?"

"He's recommended a good lawyer."

"But he's a good lawyer himself. Why not him?"

"That's what I asked him."

Ralph doesn't comment. He sinks back in the armchair and allows the conversation to take its natural course. With his father, it's like a river seeking the gradient of the land. He's curious to see where it will end up today. Lynn seems game, but Ralph knows her patience will run out when she gets trapped in one of his father's oxbows, the questions and answers eddying round and round.

"It didn't work out for the residents of Wolfe Island," says Claire.

"It probably won't for us either," says Lynn.

"What day is it?" Gordon asks.

Here we go. "Saturday, Dad."

"Who's your friend?"

"Lynn. From high school and college. Back in St-Jean and Montreal."

"What's she doing here?"

"She lives nearby in Picton. I thought you and Mom might be glad to see her again."

"I am. She's very pretty. How did you find her?"

"In St-Jean, back in grade school. Do you remember?"

"I don't remember much these days." Gordon shifts his body, trying to find a more comfortable position in his recliner.

Claire glances at Ralph and sighs. "We'll be able to have an easier conversation after lunch when he takes a nap," she whispers to Lynn. "I hope you brought a book—Ralph and I like to work on Sudoku while Gordon dozes."

"I like puzzles too," says Lynn.

"Great— Here's one I did yesterday. They called it 'devilish'— I'll copy it onto a blank template for each of you."

While Claire works on today's puzzle, Lynn and Ralph start on yes-terday's. After a few minutes, he says, "Mom, there's no low-hanging fruit."

"That's why I set it aside for you."

"What's low-hanging fruit?" Lynn asks.

Ralph tells her that he coined the term to refer to the squares that are easy to fill in, the ones that can be solved for quickly, merely by scanning horizontally or vertically. "Picking the low-hanging fruit first makes the rest of the puzzle easier."

"Tarzan's queer younger brother," says Gordon chuckling, obvious-ly pleased with himself.

"What?"

"Low-hanging fruit."

Lynn laughs so hard she almost falls off the ottoman to which she's moved. "Gordon, are you always this funny?"

"I try— Especially when there's a pretty girl in the room."

A half hour later, Gordon snoring lightly, Claire engrossed in her puzzle, Ralph struggling with his, Lynn exclaims, "Ta da!" and puts down her pencil.

"Ralph, she beat you," says Claire.

"That's why I don't do them," says Gordon, stirred from his snooze. "They're not a true test of intelligence."

"Now, Dad. You know they are— You hate to lose."

"No more than you," says Claire.

"True enough— " Ralph replies. "Except to a pretty woman."

With his father napping in the bedroom after lunch, Ralph comman-deers the recliner, lies back and closes his eyes, shutting out the con-versation between Lynn and his mother. It's always like this when he visits, his parents sitting around all 'day talking, snoozing, reading, more and more of the same in the retirement home, the residents more like inmates in a low-security compound, all surrounded by the walls of themselves and others more or less the same, less and less they can remember each passing month, the same conversations, a wonder any of them can recall what day it is, his father checking the date in the newspaper on the table beside the recliner, and if his mother hasn't yet picked up the paper from the mailroom, his father digests the same news, the world stuck in its wars, murders and scandals, the same sports teams winning by the same margins, the same people getting married and dying, the comic strip characters up to the same antics. Does his mother ever regret trading their waterfront home for this? Every day at that house brought different patterns of wind and waves on the river, different reflections of sun and clouds. In the summer, boats motoring by, cormorants diving for perch. In winter, fresh trails of footprints in the snow covering the ice, sometimes the neighborhood fox presenting herself. It was exhilarating to watch a storm race across the river and slam against the picture window. Man against the elements. Man finally harnessing those same elements. From their old property he could see the turbines at the far eastern end of the Wolfe Island wind farm. He found the lazy spinning of the blades soothing. That had not been his battle to win. His father, who'd sit for hours on the screened porch watching the activity out on the water, organized the locals into a group to protest the project across the river, but dementia dulled his fire and, one by one, homeowners sold out to younger families with different sensibilities. Out on the island, the citizens lost heart. The wind farm was erected largely as originally planned.

Ralph opens his eyes and finds Lynn gazing at him. "Where were you?" she asks.

"Back at their waterfront home. Windmills. Growing old. The need to set things right before the end."

"I could tell it wasn't anything light. Look— Your mother fell asleep reading her book."

"It's another Harlequin romance. She never seems to get enough of them. Same old, same old."

"Can one ever have enough romance?" Lynn asks.

He senses a wistfulness in her tone. "I suppose not." She doesn't reply. "When Mom and Dad wake up, let's say goodbye for the day. We'll take them to tea and leave them with their friends. Tonight there's live music— They won't miss us."

❦

Lynn parks her car in the underground garage at the hotel, and walks with Ralph along the waterfront in the park. They sit down on an unoccupied bench.

"Few sailboats out there this time of year," he says.

"Yeah, most are in for the winter. Are you still sailing?"

"My boat at the Cape is up on land now and shrink-wrapped for winter. Too bad, it would be fun to get out with you."

"It's been a long time, hasn't it?"

They sit silently for a quarter hour watching the surface of the lake sparkle in the sun's late-afternoon glancing rays. Then he touches her cheek and suggests they head over for an early dinner at Curry Original, his parents' favorite Indian restaurant before they moved, tucked away at the end of an alley, near the waterfront but without a view of it. Though Ralph hasn't dined there in a few years, the owner remembers him and asks after his parents. They order Naan, Chicken Saag, and Chicken Tikka Masala, all of which they agree to share. She selects a Napa Valley Cabernet that she says will cut the spiciness of the food. A better start to dinner than at Café Boulud.

"In Toronto you asked how the outdoorsman could have turned into a lawyer arguing cases against environmental activists— I have an answer."

"Is it one you believe in?"

"Yes, but it's hardly self-flattering. Funny thing— I know why I went to work for a big law firm and I know why I broke away to start my own practice, but I can't tell you why I'm still doing it."

"I'm confused," she says.

"Money— There's no money in working for a nonprofit. But when you've already earned a lot, there's no need to continue what you're doing if you don't fully believe in it."

"You mean quit and work for the other side?"

"Possibly. Or plain quit. Instead you keep doing what you've always been doing because it's comfortable to do that. You turn off your conscience—you don't let any concerns creep into your thinking."

"The devil you know," she says.

"Right."

"That's not a satisfying answer."

"No. It's not." He takes her hand, "But it's the only answer I have right now."

"Sounds as if you're in a rut."

"Yeah— Do you mind if I ask you something personal?" He pauses to gauge her reaction. She looks concerned.

"Try me."

"I feel there's something you haven't told me— "

She looks even more troubled. "I don't have to ask if it's going to upset you— "

"No, go ahead."

"It's about Jules. He's a good-looking boy. You might even say pretty. Not what I'd expected."

The worry leaves her face. She swirls the wine in her glass and holds it up to the light, looks into the semi-opaque red, sees the legs crawling down the insides of the glass. She breathes it in and takes a mouthful, swishes it across her palate, lets it bathe her tongue. "A taste consistent with the bouquet and a finish that's not much different from the first impression," she says. "Are you sure you want to venture into this territory?"

"For American reds, I've always preferred the Willamette Valley," he says. "But my true favorites are the Italian reds." Why is she stalling?

"It's deeply personal. I'm willing to discuss it, but I'm not sure you're prepared to hear it."

Ralph picks up his glass and clinks it against hers. "Here's to a wonderful evening— I'm a lawyer— I'm used to handling the unusual."

"Okay then— Jules was born Juliette."

"You mean a girl?"

"Yes, he's transgender."

Lynn tells the story of Jules, beginning with Jean-Pierre's temporary estrangement from their daughter Suzanne after she abandoned Montreal to live in New York City with an American she'd met at McGill and married right after graduation. Jean-Pierre's hard stance softened when Juliette was born. It helped that Suzanne chose a French name for her. Suzanne and Jean-Pierre were back on friendly terms by the time the TWA flight crashed. He took her death as punishment for the prior estrangement and wouldn't forgive himself until he came to view Juliette as his second chance. As if he still had a daughter with the same flesh and blood. Everything was fine until Juliette renounced her birth gender and announced she was a he. That he was actually Jules. Lynn recounted the years of escalating conflict between Jean-Pierre and Jules that finally led to the rupture and the separation. Lynn called it her evacuation from the war zone of their city home in Outremont to the tranquility of rural Picton. It was a week before her birthday two years ago, almost fifteen years from the day that Suzanne died, that Lynn and Jules left Quebec behind.

She pauses while Ralph digests the story. He takes a mouthful of wine, squeezes it between his tongue and teeth, inhales and swallows. "When did Juliette decide she wanted to be Jules?"

"Juliette didn't decide she *wanted to be* Jules. He *realized he was* Jules, not Juliette. There was no transformation."

"Of course there was."

"That's how we first thought of it too, and how Jean-Pierre was still thinking of it when Jules and I left."

"That makes sense to me."

"Sort of— But as soon as you truly embrace that Jules was always a he, you see it differently."

"You mean Jules believes that Juliette never existed?"

"Exactly."

Ralph knows he's no poker player. He's sure his face registers incredulity as he lets out a long sigh and pushes his chair back from the table a little. "Do *you* really believe that?"

"Now— But not at first. Not for a long time. I thought it might be an extreme case of poor self-image, you know, that all teenagers struggle with."

"Instead of?"

" —Gender dysphoria."

"That sounds like psychiatrist-speak."

"It is— A lot of therapy."

He wants to let her continue talking about the therapy, but senses there's a more pressing issue behind what she's told him. "Did Jean-Pierre see a therapist too?"

"He would have none of it. Thought it was a phase and Juliette would grow out of it— "

" —But she didn't, and you left when you realized that Jean-Pierre wasn't going to change. Why did you choose Picton?"

"A friend told me of an open position for an English teacher at the high school— We came without even visiting it first. We were that desperate. Luckily, it's worked out well."

"And Jean-Pierre?"

"We haven't had a serious discussion since I left. I see him once a month when he picks up and drops off Jules."

"When are you going to resolve the marriage one way or another?"

"Soon— Tomorrow, after Jules gets back from his weekend trip to Montreal."

Ralph can't help but interpret her response in terms of his own selfish desires. It's good news or bad depending on how it'll work out between her and Jean-Pierre. Either way, a no-lose outcome for her. She'll get back together with Jean-Pierre or move on. He doesn't want to think about it; he'd prefer to hear more about Jules. "How did you convince yourself that Jules' situation was gender dysphoria?"

"How can you ever know something like that?" She pulls her chair closer to the table and leans forward as if she's finally on the verge of divulging a long-held secret. "Please— Let's not go there. I've already had enough therapy."

He shuffles his chair back up to the table and takes her hand again. "What did it do for you?"

"It helped me realize that Jules is a survivor— That I'd worry less if I trusted him to take charge of his life."

"But he was too young for that."

Lynn wells up. "The alternative was unacceptable."

"Would it have come to that?"

"Who knows?— Jules is tough— He's put up with a lot— "

"Like what?"

"I found blood on his sheets one morning when he was sixteen. He'd used a paper clip to scratch 'I am not me' into the underside of his forearm. Can you imagine doing that to yourself?"

She says that Jules had himself committed to a mental institution. Jean-Pierre drove to Picton to sign the papers because she couldn't bring herself to do it. Jules missed Christmas at home that year. "When he was discharged— " She dabs her eyes with her napkin. "When he was discharged, I had a stack of presents for him. He refused to open any. Said he didn't deserve gifts— Had six weeks of schoolwork to make up for midyear exams. I'll never forget— I didn't think it was possible— I know I couldn't have done it."

He takes both her hands in his. "Done what?"

"Learned the course material in two weeks. Two A's and two B's, the only B's he's ever had."

"Seriously?"

"He's the best student in the school. I think getting those B's scared him more than anything else."

Ralph squeezes her hands gently and releases them. "I could tell when I met him how smart he is."

"You have no idea."

No, he doesn't. Doesn't have any idea at all about what Lynn has been through. With Jules. With Jean-Pierre. The conversation has been difficult for her. Ralph suspects she hasn't been able to speak about it with anyone other than her therapist. He draws back a little from the table again, unsure of what to say next. She breaks the awkward silence.

"I've learned that Jules knows what he needs to do to keep going. He changed his name— Made a corset to hide his breasts— Insisted on top surgery— Began hormone therapy."

"Testosterone injections?"

"Yes."

"How did you get comfortable with that? Don't they cause a woman to become sterile?"

"They do. I didn't get comfortable— I had no choice."

"If you could do it over, would you do anything differently?"

"That's a question I try never to ask myself. I don't know— I'd probably have tried to persuade him to have some of his eggs harvested and frozen— Too late now."

"That wouldn't have been consistent with the view that Juliette never existed."

"You can't expect everything to make sense— " she says as she fidgets, using the nail of her right index finger to scratch away the polish from the nails on her left fingers. "Life for us was a state of constant triage."

"And now?"

"We're doing much better. We take it a day at a time."

Ralph notices her use of *we*. He takes her hand again. "It's not as bad anymore," she says. "These days I worry about the future, not the present."

"Life's going to be tough for Jules," he says.

"Until he has bottom surgery. Afterwards too probably— Whenever that is— Can you imagine not having a normal sex life?"

"Yes—unfortunately," he says. They both laugh and let the conversation end there. He pays the bill.

They leave the restaurant and amble back to the hotel. When they reach the entrance, Ralph suggests walking along the waterfront. There's something he wants to show her. He keeps hold of her hand until they come to a large inlaid stone compass on the promenade. He leads her to the western compass point, leaves her there and walks to the southeastern point. "Face outward," he says. "I'll do the same— These are the directions to our homes. As we travel along these lines, we move farther apart." He walks back to her. "Isn't this better?" He puts his arms around her and kisses her on the lips, more firmly this time than he had at her home. He clasps her hand again. They walk back to the hotel entrance and through the lobby to the elevator.

Outside his room, Ralph says, "Come in for a drink. It's too early to call it a night." He expects her to hesitate but she doesn't.

❦

Ralph and Lynn arrive at the retirement home as his mother is returning from church. They wait in the lobby as Claire goes up to the apartment to bring Gordon down to go out to lunch.

Aunt Lucy's, his father's favorite restaurant. They are greeted warmly and shown to a booth in an alcove. Claire recaps the minister's sermon for Gordon. He asks several times why he hadn't attended the service. Lynn learns firsthand why a meal off the premises with Gordon is an ordeal. At first he can't remember whether he's ordered and then, after he's been reminded that he has, can't recall what he's asked for. Answering the same question for the third time, Ralph says, too curtly, gauging by Lynn's expression, "Dad, the food will be here shortly. They're going to poach the salmon the way you like it—pink in the middle." He looks to Lynn and shrugs, partly in frustration, partly in apology for his tone. To her, he says, "All salmon is pink in the middle." She squeezes his hand.

After lunch, Ralph and Lynn drop off Claire and Gordon at the retirement home and excuse themselves. Ralph announces that he'll be back in the evening to say goodbye before returning to Toronto. They drive downtown to the lakefront and stroll through the park talking about one hundred thirty-five degrees of separation.

"We're walking west along the lake," Ralph says. "Toward your home. I'd like to spend time with you there."

"I've thought about it since our dinner in Toronto," she says. "I'd like to have you visit, but I don't think the timing is right."

"Why not?"

"It's taken nearly two years for Jules and Jean-Pierre to come to a peaceful understanding. Another father figure in Jules' life right now might be confusing. It'll be different when he's at college."

"Not until then? What about the weekends Jules is in Montreal? I don't have to see my parents every time I come to Toronto for business— Or you could visit me in New York."

"I'm not sure."

"How can I ease your mind?" He brings her close and kisses her. "Do you know I still love you?"

She blushes. "A part of me loves you too."

"When were you last in New York City?"

"Nearly twenty years ago."

"It's time to fix that. Why don't you come to my place in two weeks? We can visit a few museums and cook a meal together."

She kisses him.

"I'll take that as a yes," he says.

CHAPTER 8

Lynn parks the car and waits with Jules on the platform at the Belleville station, as she does every month and, as is always the case, the VIA Rail train from Toronto is almost on time. All Jules has with him are his clothes and laptop stuffed into a backpack. It's only a weekend with his Dad and, unlike that evening with Ralph and Dieter, he doesn't need dress-up clothes, not even for the visit to McGill.

"Have fun," Lynn says. "Say hi to your Dad for me. Remember to get off at Kingston on Sunday—your train won't stop here."

Jules can tell something's different with his mother, but there's no time to ask. She's been upbeat the past few days, as if she's looking forward to something and can't wait to get rid of him for the weekend.

At the other end of his trip, the Dorval station in Montreal, his father is waiting at the gate right where Jules expects him to be. Nearly every month for two years Jean-Pierre has been there as Jules steps off the train. They have the routine down. During the twenty-minute drive to Outremont, Jean-Pierre explains that he's scheduled a morning's worth of meetings at McGill, three different engineering professors followed by the Dean. Afterwards, they'll catch lunch nearby and return for the campus tour in the afternoon.

"I've asked for a French language tour," Jean-Pierre says. "I want to see how far the university has come since my days."

That's his father, still at it decades later, still deploring how slow the English have been to adapt to the language reality of Quebec. The old-timers. The English who didn't leave the province when the separatists came into power in 1976 under René Lévesque. Jules knows he'll have to hear about Université de Montréal versus McGill all weekend. "No problem."

"The only other thing I've planned is dinner at Enfants Terribles. We haven't been there since you and your mother left Montreal."

"I remember it—avenue Bernard."

"A friend of mine might stop by for dessert. She's the one who helped schedule your college visit. I thought you might want to thank her."

Same old Dad. Revealing only what he wants to. When it's convenient for him. *Slipped that in as if I wouldn't notice.* He should have been a politician in the National Assembly instead of a political science professor. "Are you dating her?"

"No, no— She's a friend. A politician. Quebec's new Minister of Natural Resources."

"How do you know her?"

"Through my consulting."

"Did she go to McGill?"

"Twenty years ago. Mechanical engineering."

It seems his parents happen to know engineers who can arrange college visits. "She's a lot younger than you— Is she pretty?"

"I suppose."

"She *might* stop by for dessert? Dad, you can do better than that— "

"You sound like your mother— "

"Don't go there— "

For once, Jean-Pierre heeds the warning. "Anyhow, no plans after McGill. We can hang around the house or go out to a movie— I'd hoped we could take in a Canadiens game, but that damn lockout is still on."

"Dad, you and your hockey." They pull to a stop at a red light and wait an eternity for the left-turn arrow.

"I was the fastest skater on the varsity team. Your mother loved dating a hockey player."

Jules has heard this story a hundred times. It's annoying how old people have to recycle information, as if by telling the stories over and over they can convince themselves that the true accounts are the embellishments they've become. Part of the ritual is playing along. "She's never mentioned that to me."

"She watched every home game."

"I still can't see you as a hockey player. You're too small to push your weight around."

"Ever hear of Yvan Cournoyer? They called him The Roadrunner."

"He played with Le Gros Bill and the Pocket Rocket," Jules says.

"I'm surprised you know."

"You can't live in Montreal and not know the Canadiens' history. Dad, why didn't you teach me to skate?" They've had this conversation before too.

"You were small for your age. I didn't want you to get banged up."

Much better. This time his father doesn't say that girls shouldn't play hockey. "I'm stronger than you now." Jules doesn't know if that's true but he's bulked up since taking testosterone injections. Every day after school he works out in the gym. But he wishes he were taller, a deficit he blames his grandparents for, not for the genes they passed down to him through his birth mother whom he never knew, but for ignoring his demands to have his pediatrician prescribe growth hormone. Too late now, one of the things for which Jules will never forgive Jean-Pierre, who never gave Lynn a say in the matter.

"I doubt that. But you're right—that's why I never played professional hockey."

"You became interested in other things."

"Yes, I know— Another story I've told you a thousand times."

"That's right. Quebec politics and more Quebec politics."

There is no pause or stop button Jules can press. His father runs through the list: the famous McGill français march, the birth of

the separatist movement and the Parti Québécois, Premier René
Lévesque as a greater hero than the country's first Prime Minister, Sir
John A. Macdonald. His father's map of Canada has Quebec at the
hub, the other nine provinces as mere spokes on the wheel. The part
of the joke he conveniently omits is that each of the other provinces is
Canada's national animal, a beaver, and they're all pissing on the frog
at the center. "Don't forget meeting Mum."

"How is she?— Does she talk about me?"

"Sometimes."

"Favorably?"

"Sometimes."

"Is she still angry with me?"

"She's pleased that you set up the visit to McGill— Said you're
becoming an 'involved parent' again."

"Awfully serious conversation for a child."

"It's how we talk all the time."

"A heavy responsibility," Jean-Pierre says with a smile. He turns
into the driveway of their stone house on avenue Davaar and pulls
into the garage. "It would be easier for you if we were together as a
family again."

"Yeah," Jules says and heads straight into the house.

Jean-Pierre shouts after him, "Are you hungry? I can make you a
sandwich."

"I had one on the train."

"Then get some sleep. Your first meeting is at eight."

Jules stops in the doorway to his father's study and walks into the
room to get a closer look at a photograph on the bookshelf. "Dad, this
picture wasn't here the last time I was home."

"What Jules?" Jean-Pierre calls out from the kitchen.

"This picture of me when I was eight— With long hair."

"It was in the album your mother left." Sandwich in hand, Jean-
Pierre joins Jules in the study. "I had it framed."

"You know that's against the rules. No pictures of me in a dress. No pictures of me with long hair— I thought I'd destroyed them all."

His father stands between him and the photograph. "Why would you do that? They mean the world to us."

"Because that person never existed. You only thought she did."

"The pictures prove it. You can't change facts by shredding photos."

"You don't get it. Why does Mum understand but not you?"

Taking the picture from the shelf and holding it face toward Jules, Jean-Pierre says, "Our hearts are attached to these memories. You can't erase them."

"Look at my face— Do you see happiness?"

"Hey— Are you asking me to believe that Juliette was never born?"

"You got it right. As soon as it becomes legal to change my birth certificate, I'll set the record straight."

"What about your passport and social insurance card? Your birth announcement in our scrapbook— There's a record of Juliette every where."

"I'll hunt them down." Jules glares at him. "Give me that picture. I'll start with it."

Jean-Pierre clutches the photograph. "No way— It's my property, not yours. I have every right to display this picture in my home."

"I want it destroyed. Have you forgotten?— This is *our* home."

"I'm shocked. By now I thought you'd be able to accept reality."

"Dad, *you* need to accept reality. Call me by my proper name— Treat me as your son."

"I have finally accepted that. You know I have."

"Not if you keep that picture. Every time you look at it you're thinking of someone else, not me."

"Okay, okay— I get your point— I'll throw it away." He retrieves a hammer from the garage and wraps the picture in newspaper. With a few blows, he smashes the glass. He opens the paper gingerly and inspects the photo a last time, shards symbolically cutting into Juliette's head. "Satisfied? I'd say that person's been brutally murdered." In the newspaper he wraps the frame with its broken glass and marred pho-to and tosses the bundle into the trash. "Now please settle down. Get some sleep. It's going to be a long day tomorrow."

Jules doesn't move. He stares at the empty spot on the bookshelf and grins.

☙

They find an Italian restaurant on rue de la montagne. Jean-Pierre says it was formerly known as Mountain, but not after Lévesque's Bill 101. He tells Jules again how life changed after the Language Act. For some it was the name of the street they lived on, for others the name of the town they lived in. For everyone it was the signs inside and outside places of business that had to be marked only in French or more prominently in French than English. Macdonald's had to be-come Macdonald. No possessive apostrophes in French.

"And you were okay with all of that?" Jules asks.

"They should have had French names to begin with," Jean-Pierre answers.

"As if their English character never existed, you mean. Because with English names they were forced to appear as something they were not."

Jean-Pierre can finally see the bind he's worked himself into and moves on as gracefully as he can. "Well, Montreal mostly stayed Mon-treal," he says. "Mountain or montagne—it was the same old street. Always a few good eating spots. I hope this is one of those."

They sit at a table against a wall, look quickly through the menu and order. "How did your morning go?"

"I met with two professors, a fourth-year student, and a graduate student. The professors were cool, especially the hot-looking Italian. He designs underwater robotic vehicles. The kind you could use to install offshore turbines."

"I thought you had three professors on your schedule."

"They felt that speaking with a couple of students would be better." Jules describes his conversations with the two foreign students and said how much they enjoy the experience of living with other students in the residences. "Would I have to live at home?"

"We'd probably have to pull some strings to get you admitted into a residence— They're usually reserved for students whose families live outside the city."

"Picton is outside the city. It's outside the province."

"Sorry— I keep hoping you and Mum will move back to Montreal."

Following the standard one-hour campus tour, conducted by a third-year French-Canadian student whom Jean-Pierre kept badgering with questions about French content at the university, they head toward the Arts Building.

"When we've seen the spots Mum suggested, can you show me the residences where the guys live?"

"I think they're all co-ed now. Will that be a problem?"

"I'm sort of co-ed all by myself."

"That's the first time I've heard you make a joke about it. Does that mean you like both guys and girls? You called the Italian professor hot."

"It doesn't mean anything— "

"Whatever."

"Dad, you're way too old to say that."

The classroom where his mother and father met is still there. Not truly his mother and father, he reminds himself. His real mother and father also met at McGill, but he's never heard that story. Someday. Jean-Pierre says the spot has hardly changed. Jules asks why each desk has a hole in the top of it. His father tells him about India ink and fountain pens. The room looks ancient. Jean-Pierre says the Faculty of Arts must not be getting its share of government funds. Jules asks where in the room they were sitting when they met. As if more than forty years ago were only yesterday, Jean-Pierre points to two desks side by side. Jules sits in his mother's spot. "Where was the professor when he caught you flirting with Mum?"

Jean-Pierre moves the large desk at the front of the classroom closer to the corner. "He was sitting on the edge of the desk when he asked the students to introduce themselves one by one to the class. Mum gave her name, said she'd grown up in St-Jean and though she'd lived in an English-speaking household, she'd been speaking French all her life, often mixing up the languages. She told the class that one day when she was only three, she came in thirsty from playing out in the yard and said, *Mummy, I'm soif.*"

"What did the professor say?"

"He asked if she was also *faim*, but before he could add to that, I spoke up and told her that she wouldn't get confused in this class—it would be clear which language is more beautiful."

"Were you in love?"

"At first sight of her green eyes."

Jules begins to tear up and his father asks him what's wrong. "I wish it could still be that way."

"Me too— C'mon, let's get out of here and head over to Molson Stadium. I want to show you the section the engineers owned."

They climb rue University to its intersection with avenue des Pins— Pine back in the day, Jean-Pierre points out—to the entrance to the football field. The gates are unlocked because the Redmen are taking their final practice of the season. In the south stands, they cross a row to the section that was commandeered by the engineering students for every home game.

"A rowdy bunch," says Jean-Pierre. "Somehow they always managed to smuggle their giant cooler into the stadium. They cared more about their beer than the game."

"I won't be like that."

"As the game progressed, they passed the most shit-faced students down."

"Passed them down?"

"Students in one row would lift a drunken student, turn him on his side, and hand him off to students in the next lower row, and then another until he arrived at the first row where they'd slump him over the railing and let him puke onto the track."

"I definitely won't be one of those."

"Don't be sure—everyone wants to be a member of the tribe. But it's probably not like that these days. Everybody's parents have a lawyer."

They leave the stadium and walk further up University to the residences at the edge of Parc du Mont-Royal. Jules asks about the large cylindrical building nestled among the dormitories.

"Bishop Mountain Hall. The residence cafeteria. I heard the food was good. No food fights, but there was a running contest to see which dorm could get the most pats of butter to stick to the ceiling. I doubt that happens anymore."

"Dad, you make it sound as if the old days were way better."

"Not really, I guess, but maybe in their own way. It's nostalgic being here."

"I'm surprised to hear you say that. You spend your life on a campus."

"It's different in your student days."

They climb the stairs to Gardner Hall, the farthest up the mountain of the three undergraduate dorms. At the front desk, they seek permission to look around. After checking out the lounge and the recreation area, they ask to see a dorm room. Not possible, they're told, while school is still in session.

"It doesn't matter," Jean-Pierre says. "Every room is a single. Perfect for you."

Jules imagines living apart from his parents, no adults controlling his life. McGill is a much bigger place than his high school in Picton. Much bigger even than the school he left in Outremont. He could get lost in this population. That wouldn't be a bad thing.

That evening they see the last showing of *Argo* at the Cineplex Odeon. On the way home, they comment how ironic it was that the six Americans who'd escaped the storming of the U.S. embassy in Tehran had to hole up in the Canadian embassy for more than two months before masquerading as a Canadian film crew to escape the country.

"One of the few good things that happened on President Carter's watch," Jean-Pierre says. "And Canadians made it happen as much as the CIA did."

Jules mutters something about the movie being a good example of what it's like to feel hostage in a situation not of one's own making. His father rolls his eyes.

At one o'clock the next afternoon, having finished a draft of a history essay due when he gets back to Picton, Jules begs to go to Parc du Mont-Royal and visit the cross at the top.

"Why? You've been there before."

"Never with you. I want you to tell me how you pulled off the Halloween stunt." Jean-Pierre has told the story many times, but has never been completely forthright about some of the key details. Neither to Jules nor to Lynn, who has told Jules that it's sometimes better not to know too much.

"It was one of the greatest trick-or-treats ever," says Jean-Pierre.

The day is warm, a late Indian summer's last gasp, leaves still hanging on, not all turned, patches in peak color interspersed among trees almost bare. The park is crowded, its paths clogged, whole families out for picnics, children tossing Frisbees, police here and there on their mounts.

"See how happy everyone is," Jean-Pierre says. "It wasn't like this in the fall of our senior year."

"Why not?"

"The FLQ bombings and kidnappings. Prime Minister Trudeau invoked the War Measures Act— Ordinary citizens couldn't enter the park. There were machine gun nests everywhere."

"Dad, you're still a separatist."

"But never a terrorist."

They arrive at the cross. Jean-Pierre explains that their infamous feat can no longer be accomplished the way they had done it, not only because the protective fence around the cross is now higher and more secure, but also because the city long ago replaced the old-style bulbs with LEDs. "We'd have to hack into the computer system instead of climbing the cross. Probably easier, but nowhere nearly as thrilling."

"Why LEDs?"

"To change the cross's color easily."

"Red and green at Christmas?"

"And purple before a new pope is elected."

"That's useful," Jules says with not a little sarcasm. He peers up at the steel latticework as tall as a giant tree. "How did you finish before the police arrived?"

Careful planning, Jean-Pierre says. A team of five sophomores. One on the ground, who served as the sentry, and four on the cross— one guy scaling the uppermost part to turn out those lights while three on the crossarm's platform selectively turned out and added lights to form the word *T-I-L-T*. After they finished, one of the guys replaced an ordinary bulb with a special blinker to make the letters flash on and off in unison. On the way down, everyone loosened bulbs on the lower part of the cross, leaving only the world's largest pinball machine for Montrealers to see.

"Didn't someone get hurt?"

"The last guy down— But not on the cross."

"Was that you?"

"Thank goodness no. The police almost caught the last guy before he reached the steep path down the McGill side of the mountain. They refused to hitch up their horses and pursue him. But in his hurry to escape he slipped and ended up sliding down the path on his rear end. A rock gashed open his butt. The other three climbed back up to help him the rest of the way to the residence, then called a cab to take him to the emergency room at Montreal General. He took more than fifty stitches. For weeks he had to sleep on his stomach and eat standing up."

"Did you go to confession for defacing the cross?"

"Absolutely not. That's not the kind of information you want to put in the wrong hands."

"Did you tell your father?"

"No, Jules— I didn't tell Mum either— Not until she discovered a photograph of the transfigured cross."

"Who took the photo?"

"Our sentry."

"Dad, which of the five were you?"

"Who do you think?"

"The photographer."

Jean-Pierre puts his arm around Jules' shoulder. "It's getting late. Let's go home and change for dinner."

As they walk along avenue Bernard toward Mile End, Jules notices that a few of his favorite restaurants are gone. "I can't believe you're taking me to Enfants Terribles."

"Do you know what the name refers to?" his father asks.

"Children like me— Holy terrors to their parents."

"They're a pair of children, brother and sister, characters in a Cocteau novel your mother and I studied in the classroom I showed you yesterday."

"It must have made you want children."

"That's why we stopped at one."

This is one of the few times he's reminded that Jean-Pierre is not his real father and Lynn not his real mother. He never knew his parents. The plane crash is forbidden territory. Too hard for his grandparents, his surrogate parents, to deal with. Jules has seen them break down. But he doesn't cry about it. His real parents don't exist in his memory. The best he can muster is empathy for his grandparents. To him they're Mum and Dad and always will be. He stopped leafing through the old family photo albums long ago. He hates photographs. They capture how other people see you, not how you see yourself. A mirror is even hard for him. At least that image disappears when you walk away.

His father, tearing up, tries to rescue the mistake. "And then you came along."

"Dad, don't get sentimental."

"Jules, you alone have been like a pair of children. But now I see it more like a child and his twin ghost."

"Do we have to talk about this?"

"No we don't— I thought you might be willing to admit that the child who's gone can still have a positive influence on the child who stayed."

"There were never two of us," Jules says, almost in a whisper.

They arrive at the restaurant. On the corner across the street, the first story of the building is boarded up with plywood, in stark contrast to the quaint red-brick buildings along the avenue and the modern glass façade of Les Enfants Terribles.

"Didn't that used to be a restaurant?"

"La Moulerie—one of my favorites. Hey, let's go in and wait for the Minister."

The maître d' directs them to a table for four and removes a place setting. Jules sits beside his father. "Please, Jules, your best behavior tonight." The Minister arrives a few minutes late. Jean-Pierre makes the introductions.

"What shall I call you? Madame Beaumont? Madame Ministre?"

"Monique will be fine."

Monique takes the seat opposite Jean-Pierre. She's taller than his mother, younger, darker hair, almost black, a more prominent nose, much more makeup, and large gold hoop earrings—his mother seldom wears jewelry, certainly not gaudy earrings. Monique and Jules each wait for the other to talk. Finally he speaks up and thanks her for having arranged the college visit. She asks how it went. He describes his conversations with the professors and the Dean. During the meal, he asks Monique about her years in the engineering program and what had made her decide to become an engineer. Then about her time working at Hydro-Québec and her decision to enter politics. His father has briefed him well. He even asks about why she chose to represent the Parti Québécois rather than the Liberals.

"You ask a lot of questions."

"It's because I'm an 'enfant terrible.'" Jean-Pierre groans.

"Is that an inside joke?"

"No, not at all," says Jean-Pierre. "It's an unfinished conversation from our walk over here tonight."

"It was finished." Jules says. "I have another question if you don't mind."

"Fire away, enfant terrible," says Monique.

"Are you married?"

"Jules!" Jean-Pierre thumps the table, making the silverware jump and drawing the attention of patrons at neighboring tables. "That's rude— It's none of your business."

"It's okay, Jean-Pierre." Monique reaches across and touches his arm. "It's a perfectly fair question." Turning to Jules, she says, "I've been divorced for almost a year. I know what you're really asking— Whether your father and I are nothing more than good friends— We are— He's a wise man when it comes to politics. He's helped me in my career. And still is."

"What are you working on now?"

"We've been discussing the Ministry's proposal to build a huge wind farm to make Quebec completely energy independent forever. It's a project that grew out of our collaboration years ago when I was working at Hydro-Québec. I expect we'll be working together closely— But how do you say it?— *No worries.*"

"Good to hear," Jules says, too obviously trying to sound like the adult he's not, "because I want you to know that my father is not available. He and my mother are getting back together."

"Good to hear," says Monique, trying to keep from laughing at her obvious sarcasm while giving Jean-Pierre a puzzled look.

"When I attend McGill, I'll be living at home with my parents." At that comment, Jean-Pierre chokes on his food.

"Wonderful," says Monique. "Please let me know what I can do to help you get into McGill."

"Thank you, but I'm sure I can do that on my own."

Jean-Pierre elbows Jules. It's not a friendly nudge. "I apologize for my son's directness. Sometimes he surprises even me."

"Every child should surprise his parents. You're lucky— Now, if you'd kindly excuse me, my girls are home from boarding school this weekend and I promised I'd get back early."

Jean-Pierre stands. "You're not staying for dessert? Did Jules scare you away?"

"I don't scare that easily." She winks at Jules.

Jean-Pierre gives her a hug and Jules rises to shake her hand. "Thank you for telling me about McGill. Maybe my mother will get a chance to meet you at Christmas."

"I look forward to it."

After Monique leaves, Jules sits in her place, directly across from his father, who seems barely able to contain himself.

"What the hell was that? What are you up to?"

"Getting you and Mum back together. Christmas would be the perfect time to start living as a family again."

"You have to graduate from your high school in Picton— Don't tell me you're thinking of leaving Ontario to come back to Quebec? Changing schools with only one semester left?"

"I am indeed."

"I won't hear of it— Have you discussed this with your mother?"

"I will on the drive home tomorrow."

CHAPTER 9

The bed has been turned down, but the curtains aren't drawn. As Ralph rummages through the minibar, Lynn turns off the lights and stands at the window, gazing down at the lit tree, most of its leaves yellow, some green, all about to become the past, but still holding on. Beyond the tree, out on the promenade, the inlaid stone compass on which they stood not more than five minutes before. Southeast to where he lives, west to her house. One hundred thirty-five degrees of separation. She looks south across the lake. Red lights blinking in unison along the horizon—wind turbines on Wolfe Island warning aircraft to stay clear. *If you must fly low, don't do it here.*

Ralph is flying high. He joins her at the window, a glass of wine in each hand. "To us," he says. "Better the second time around." Not the second time, she thinks. Though they'd come close, they'd never made love as teenagers. She takes a sip of wine and puts her glass on the nightstand, then draws the curtains closed. Ralph puts his glass beside hers. He unbuttons her blouse and unhooks her bra. "My God, you're beautiful." He takes off his shirt, undoes his belt and lets his pants fall around his ankles. She eases herself out of her skirt.

"This is as far as we got on prom night," she says as he sweeps away the covers with one hand and pushes her onto the bed with the other.

"Almost," she says.

She awakes at eight thirty, Ralph still asleep, rolls out of bed, goes straight to the window, and opens the curtains, only to be blinded by the sun scintillating off a shimmering Lake Ontario. Shielding her eyes, she peers out to Fort Henry on the hill. Sees the Martello tower on the spit of land at the tip of the Royal Military College campus. Stares across the lake to the wind turbines strung out like beads on a giant string along the expanse of the island, their blades turning slowly, the red beacons no longer discernible. Once around every three to four seconds, a slow spin in seeming defiance of the stiff breeze. Petals on giant white stalks, reacting to the impulse of nature, snatching a fraction of the wind passing through. Mesmerizing, those blades rotating gently on the horizon, reflecting the morning sun. Adjacent pairs sometimes in unison, strange harmony, as if they are bound to each other, dancing to the same music.

She puts her hand on Ralph's chest and runs it slowly up and down. "Good morning. Is this what you wanted me to see? Windmills glinting in the sun."

"Yes, works of art. Sculptures on a grand scale. Giant sequoias. Majestic."

"Isn't that a bit over the top?"

"Probably," Ralph says.

"Have you ever seen them up close?" she asks.

"Yes, have you?"

"No."

"Then maybe we should take the ferry to Wolfe Island this morning. You can see for yourself that they're not situated close enough to people's homes to do any harm."

"No thanks."

Not put off easily, Ralph presses on. "There's a great bakery where we can have lunch. I've been there with my parents. You'll love it."

"Then we can go there some other time when you're not trying to sell me on the virtues of wind turbines. Besides, we promised your parents we'd take them out to lunch."

"Then we've got time before we have to leave. Come back to bed."

She sits on the bed next to him cross-legged. "Ralph, there's something I have to tell you. No good time for it, but better now than later."

"You're going to say that this was a one-night stand?"

"Ralph. This is important. Remember what Dieter said at my house?"

"About the prom?"

"Yes."

"You were evasive. Why?"

"Because Dieter raped me that night."

Ralph sits up. "Raped you?"

"After he deposited you in a lump at your parents' feet, he was supposed to take me home, but he didn't. He raped me on the back seat of his parents' car."

"How? Didn't you resist?"

"Shockingly, no. I was drunk enough that I thought we were back at the party and that you and I were finally going to make love. I must have imagined he was you."

Ralph starts to shake, opens his mouth, but no words come out. Instead, a howling sound, as if he's been the one raped, silly thought, as if he can possibly know what that would be like. A primitive cry, hurt growing into rage.

"Perhaps I shouldn't have told you."

"You should have told me years ago. The next day."

"I was ashamed. I couldn't tell anybody. Especially not you."

"Your parents then."

"They would have called the police. I expected Dieter to come clean and when he didn't, I couldn't rat him out—we'd all been close for such a long time."

"You let him get away with it— Have you carried it all these years without telling anyone?"

"No one."

"I'm sorry, Lynn. Very, very sorry. No wonder you never allowed us to make love."

"I couldn't."

"You've never told Jean-Pierre?"

"No one."

"Are you ever going to confront Dieter?"

"I can't stand the thought of it."

"But he's come back into your life— Especially with that offer to Jules for a summer internship."

"I can't."

"Well then, I'm going to see that he pays."

"You can't tell him that you know. I'll never forgive you."

"I won't. But I'll make him pay. I'll find a way to take away what he cherishes most. Like he took you away from me."

"I don't want this to come between us."

"It won't. It wasn't your fault. I'm sorry it happened to you. I fucking hate him."

"It was long ago."

"Not long enough."

❧

The weekend has been a whirlwind of emotions. Making love to Ralph. Coming clean about the prom night rape. But, sadly, having to deceive Jules about what has put her in such a good mood, what she did while he was visiting his father in Montreal. On the way home from the Kingston train station, he tells her about his weekend. The picture smashing, McGill professors and students, the old classroom in the Arts Building, drunken engineers in the football stadium, Gardner Hall, watching *Argo*, visiting the cross.

"Did you go out to dinner?" she asks, thinking it an innocuous question.

"At Enfants Terribles. With the woman who set up the meetings for me at McGill."

"Who's that?"

"Monique."

"Does she have a last name?"

"Beaumont."

"And how does your Dad know this Monique Beaumont?"

"She's the Minister of Natural Resources. They've been working together on a project involving Hydro-Québec."

"I haven't heard any of this before."

"You should talk to Dad. He misses you—   He told me we're all getting together for Christmas in Montreal."

"He told you what?"

"You need to talk to him."

"Not tonight. I'm tired. There's school tomorrow."

～

It shouldn't have required Jules' blatant manipulation of the family situation for Lynn and Jean-Pierre to realize it was time to resolve their separation. Jean-Pierre called her the day after Jules returned from Montreal. Hard as it was for her, especially now that Ralph had become a complicating factor—she'd agreed to visit him in New York—she invited Jean-Pierre to spend the coming weekend in Picton. It was finally time for them to end their separation or turn it into divorce and move on. Maybe it would be easier than she feared—with Ralph back in her life, she was heading for the exit and, for his own reasons, she suspected Jean-Pierre was too. But she'd need his help in handling Jules. Early on Friday evening, Jean-Pierre arrives in Picton with a dozen long stem red roses and a college textbook on mechanical engineering. He gives the roses to Jules and the text to Lynn.

"Jules—   You deserve these for all I've put you through. Lynn— Jules tells me that if you learn how to build wind turbines, you might appreciate them more." Jules hands his mother the roses and takes the textbook from her. The gifts serve as a satisfactory icebreaker and the evening quickly assumes the air of a date, not a first date, but a later one when the woman asks the man to stay over at her place and he says yes. Not even that in their case, because they have had a long history. After dinner they dispatch Jules and finish the bottle of wine. Afterwards they sit at opposite ends of the living room couch facing each other, their legs intertwined. Jean-Pierre asks if she remembers the day they met at McGill.

"How could I forget? You were showing off in class."

"I was surprised to find someone so pretty in my French literature class. An English-Canadian girl."

"You complimented me on my accent. That annoyed the professor. Do you recall what he said?"

"C'est une classe pour étudier la culture française, pas pour l'amour."

"Yes. And then you shot him down—*Mais l'amour, c'est la culture française!*—I'm surprised he gave you an A in the course."

They relive their cat-and-mouse game. He kept asking her out for a date and she kept refusing, saying she already had a boyfriend. After months of never seeing this supposed *petit ami,* he insisted she come home with him after class one day to study together for an exam. Either that or agree to a dinner where he could meet this other fellow. She chose the study date. After she'd climbed the eight steps to the massive wooden door of his Outremont *château,* he told her there'd be no turning back. On their third date they made love in his tiny, dark bedroom.

"It seemed perfect that first time," she says.

"Except that you weren't a virgin."

"I was— "

She doesn't finish the sentence. He's puzzled, but her expression telegraphs nothing. She leaves the half-truth hanging on her tongue. It had been easier to tell Ralph the whole truth. That should tell her something. She can't find the words to finesse it with Jean-Pierre. He can see she isn't about to explain and lets it go. "Yeah, that's what you told me, but that's when I knew you really did have a boyfriend."

"You thought I was cheating on him. You never believed me— "

"I didn't care. I told you to ditch him. That's when you finally told me about Ralph. And still you didn't ditch him. It took a different French-English war for that."

They reminisce about the McGill français rally. Jean-Pierre had persuaded her to join him in the protest march from Carré St-Louis to Roddick Gates, the main entrance to the McGill campus, each blowing a whistle and chanting the slogan printed on the flags they waved, *McGill au peuple.* The marchers surged toward a three-deep line of riot police at the gates. Then stopped abruptly, each side staring the other down across a few feet of pavement. They stood arm in arm, shouting McGill français over and over in unison with the rest of the demonstrators. After the rally, they walked to Ben's Delicatessen. Sitting across from her and holding both her hands, he asked whether she'd spoken to Ralph yet.

"I haven't figured out how."

"Okay then— After our coffee, we'll march on his residence hall and tell him the French have finally taken over— He's out and I'm in."

"Non, Jean-Pierre. Laisse-moi le faire. Je te promets."

She made good on that promise and another when she married him right after college, then worked side by side with him kick-starting his political career, campaigning vigorously for René Lévesque in three elections until the journalist-turned-politician finally succeeded in becoming Quebec's first separatist Premier.

"I stood by you as you became René's chief of staff," she says. "Why couldn't you stand by me when I needed your help? If you could deal that easily with the politics in Quebec, why couldn't you handle the pushback from Jules?"

She expects him to say that pushback is an understatement, but after her generous efforts at peace on this first night back together, he settles for: *I don't have a good answer.* He takes her hand and leads her to the bedroom where he undresses her, stands taking all of her in for a moment, as if drinking in slowly all he has missed, and then undresses himself. He edges over to her side of the bed right away, but she turns her back to him. It is too fast and she senses she's being too easy. This soon after being with Ralph, why is she eager for this? Why so comfortable? Because she and Jean-Pierre have found themselves in a place they've been countless times. A good place. It has always felt right in the past and it does now. Why shouldn't it? It's what she's wanted and needed for a long time. When he snuggles up to her, she doesn't move away. He slides one hand across her breasts and runs the fingertips of his other hand lightly up and down her spine. Then massages her shoulders and kisses her neck, raising goose bumps on her thighs. She recalls the first time they made love, fumbling beneath the covers of the single bed in his tiny dark room at the château.

❧

They awake to Jules knocking on the bedroom door. "Get up you guys. It's late."

"Hey Jules, give us another half hour."

"No, Mum. We have to be at school by ten."

"Okay, okay— I'll be right out to cook breakfast." She puts on her robe and slippers, passes a brush through her hair, and jostles Jean-Pierre. "Come on. Jules will need help emptying the tank." She leaves the bedroom and heads for the kitchen to make scrambled eggs, bacon, and toast, and press some French roast coffee. No time for anything fancier this morning. Crêpes with berries and whipped cream will have to wait until tomorrow. She asks Jules to bring in the newspaper.

She hears Jean-Pierre splashing cold water on his face in her bathroom. He appears in jeans and a sweatshirt and joins Jules. Having not seen them together for a few years, she's curious to observe how they'll get along, father and son. She abandons the cooking and moves down the hall, stands barely out of sight at the doorway to the studio.

"How are you going to empty the tank without spilling water all over the place?" Jean-Pierre asks.

"With a garden hose. I'll empty it out the window into the backyard."

"That won't work."

"Ever hear of a siphon? You don't have a clue about science."

"I've been reading an interesting book on philosophy and quantum mechanics. Its author claims that quantum mechanics can explain almost everything. Even consciousness and thought."

"So it explains why you don't understand who I am?"

"That might be difficult even for the author." Jean-Pierre smiles, but Jules ignores his father's weak attempt at humor. "I suppose it does. We need to think of you as having been born in one state and then later we find you in a superposition of two states. After a phase transition, you're in the other state. Sort of like the twin and his ghost we talked about in Montreal. And now the ghost is gone. How about that?"

"That's absolute crap, Dad. Your book, however informative it might be in someone else's hands, is dangerous in yours. Whatever *science* you might think there is in political science is pretty soft. But it's all you know about science and it doesn't explain how a siphon works." After this put-down, Jules opens the window and climbs through it. He hands the end of the hose to his father and asks him to put enough of it in the tank to lie on the bottom. He turns on the water.

"You're going to fill the tank or empty it?"

"Empty it. But first I need to fill the hose. Tell me when the water level starts to rise."

"Now," says Jean-Pierre.

Jules turns off the spigot and unscrews the hose. Water begins to flow immediately from his end of the hose onto the ground, more than a trickle but far short of a gush. He climbs back through the window and stands beside Jean-Pierre.

"How does that work?"

"Gravity. The ground is lower than the tank. Gravity pulls the column of water down— It'll take a while. Let's go eat."

Lynn scrambles back down the hall. She asks Jules to set the dining room table while she finishes the bacon and starts the eggs.

"Mum, are you coming to school with us?"

"Are all the exhibits being set up today?"

"Yes."

"Sure, I'll join you. I can walk around the floor while you and Dad set up your project."

"Why don't you help us first? You can mount the poster boards and then we can check out the other projects together."

"Is Amy going to help?"

"She has a dentist appointment this morning. She could have come in the afternoon, but I said I'd take care of everything."

"Who's Amy?" asks Jean-Pierre.

"A friend," says Jules.

"Jules' date for the prom," Lynn says.

"Mum, you promised we wouldn't talk about that. I don't even know if I'm going. Amy's a friend."

"Are you going out with her for lunch today?" Jean-Pierre asks.

"No— This is our family weekend. I thought we could have a picnic at Sandbanks. It's supposed to be sunny and warm. Let's stop at a farm stand for apples. Mum, you could make a pie tonight."

"It sounds as if you have everything planned," says Jean-Pierre.

"Mum has made your favorite dinner. You know—tourtière."

"And the pistou?"

"Indeed," Lynn says. "Some part of the meal has to be authentic French cuisine. Every now and then you Québécois need to be reminded of your roots."

It takes all three of them to load the fish tank into the van that Jean-Pierre has rented. Jules wraps it carefully with blankets and uses cushions from the living room sofa to buffer it along the sides. Lynn places the poster boards in her car. At the school, it takes an hour to set up the exhibit to Jules' satisfaction, most of that lugging pails of water from the men's room to fill the tank, no garden hose available to make it easy. Jean-Pierre asks what Jules will do without a siphon when he has to dismantle the exhibit. He says he'll get his friends to form a bucket brigade. They spend an hour looking over the other exhibits.

On the way home, they stop at the deli for a loaf of French bread, some sliced ham and imported Swiss cheese, and a container of potato salad. Lynn makes sandwiches and packs the picnic basket. "The park shuts down in the off-season," she says. "We'll take my car in case it hasn't yet. It has our permit on the windshield."

Jules struts into the kitchen in a wetsuit with a bundle of clothes under his arm.

"What's that for?" asks Jean-Pierre.

"Windsurfing. It'll probably be the last good day of the year."

"I didn't know you windsurfed."

"You haven't been around."

Jean-Pierre helps Jules strap his gear to the roof rack—surfboard, boom, mast, sail, harness and lines. On the way to Sandbanks, they drive past picture-book farms set in a late autumn landscape, foliage mostly gone, oaks a shiny leathery brown, any other leaves still on trees a dull rust. At a farm stand near the park entrance, they purchase a jug of cider and a carton of apples.

"Too bad we'll have to drink the cider cold," Lynn says. "It's much better hot with a stick of cinnamon and a splash of rum."

"What, no wine?" Jean-Pierre asks.

"Not today. Look what happened last night."

"Last night?" says Jules.

"He fell asleep while I was talking to him— Typical."

There are few cars at the park. Jean-Pierre grabs the blankets and helps Jules lug some of his gear. Lynn carries the picnic basket. They walk past the spot where the only other family on the beach has set up for lunch and continue toward the dunes. Facing into the wind, Lynn peers out at the lake. "That's a big surf. Jules, please stay close to shore today. There's no one around to help if you get into trouble."

"Mum, you worry too much."

They devour the sandwiches and cider. Jules rigs his board and zips up his life vest. "See you guys later." He pushes out through the waves, climbs aboard and sails off obliquely to the shore.

"That's got to be hard work on a day like this," says Jean-Pierre.

"He'll be okay. The weight training at school has made him strong."

Jules goes down in a gust, struggles to right himself and goes down again. Pointing a little more into the wind, he climbs onto the board easily and is surfing again. For several minutes Lynn and Jean-Pierre watch him crisscross his way farther from shore.

"Jules is right, you know," she says. "We need to talk. Let's walk to the other end of the beach."

She strides off. Jean-Pierre hurries to catch up. "Slow down. We'll get there soon enough."

"Can we have a real conversation this time?"

"Didn't we communicate well last night?"

She gives him the compliment he's fishing for. "The sex was great— It always has been— But we can't seem to talk about the important things."

"You mean Jules? I've made a lot of progress   Last weekend came off perfectly."

"Except for the picture smashing."

"I couldn't believe his reaction to the photograph. You know the one."

"I know you— But it's not your temper I want to talk about." She stops and pinches both his arms, shakes him to make sure she has his full attention. "We're no longer the same people we were. At least I'm not. What's important to you may no longer be important to me."

He pulls away from her and looks out to where Jules is still tacking, moving farther and farther from shore. Standing at the edge of the water, he lets the breakers surge over his feet up to his ankles. He shivers. The water is cold. "Did you feel that way when you left Montreal?"

"I was worried more about Jules' welfare than about us. Since then I've had time to think."

"It's dangerous to overthink," he says and puts his arm around her. "You've got to listen to your heart too."

Her turn to pull away. "What matters most to you, Jean-Pierre?"

"Being with you and Jules."

"I don't believe that."

"What do *you* think matters most to me?"

"Living in Montreal, teaching at the university, winning the next referendum on separation— Jules and I are secondary in your life."

"How can you say that?"

"If you had put us first, you wouldn't have waited two years to resolve this."

"Why is it so important all of a sudden?"

"Because I'm sixty-two. I can't afford to waste time with someone who thinks that what he wants is more important than what I want."

"After all this thinking, have you figured out what's important to you?"

Lynn sighs. She knows he's mocking her—mildly, with no ill intent—but still mocking. "You've managed to duck my question again— Okay, I'll go first. But please listen for a change— Jules is most important to me. His life is going to be difficult. We need to be there for him."

"We don't disagree," says Jean-Pierre.

"I'm sure we don't."

"But what about you? Other than Jules."

"I love living out here in the country. I'm tired of a big city."

"You could live in Montreal and spend summers in the Laurentians."

"It's not the same. Jules can windsurf nearby whenever he wants." She points to where Jules' yellow sail is barely a speck.

"Didn't you ask him to stay near shore?" Jean-Pierre asks.

"I wonder if he's having trouble handling this wind. He must be freezing out there."

"He's wearing a wetsuit. I bet he's having a great time."

"You know he can't do this in Montreal."

"Why does it matter? He'll be in college for four years."

Jean-Pierre has a point. This isn't only about Jules. It's about taking control of her life, setting her own agenda, not blindly following his. "You're right. I grew up in a small town, spent my childhood playing in the woods. That's what I have here in Picton. I take a walk every morning before school. I ski cross-country in winter."

"Don't you miss city life? Art galleries, museums, fine restaurants, guest lectures at the university— You can't get those in Picton."

"Unlike you, I don't need a heavy dose of that stuff. And it's more than that—I'm tired of fighting political battles. I need a simpler life."

"Tired of politics? Then why are you leading a protest against wind farms?"

"To preserve the beauty of this place."

"It's your new cause. Admit it— You need a cause to fight for. You used to be happy joining me in mine."

"In its time the McGill français movement made sense."

"You went way beyond that. We worked together in René's campaigns and for the referendum."

"I was madly in love with you."

"You're not still?"

"Not enough to put your dream of Quebec's secession ahead of my interests."

"What happened? Did Ontario get into your blood?"

Ralph happened is what she's thinking, but she says, "You say that as if Ontario is some kind of disease. I don't hate Quebec. But there's more to life than we had before."

"What we had was good. You didn't give it a second thought until I screwed up with Jules. If that hadn't happened, we wouldn't be here."

"But you *did* screw up and we *are* here. Things are different now." Indeed they are—she has the prospect of a fresh, new love, an old love really, but one that seems fresh and new. More fulfilling than resurrecting a marriage that is all but dead. "Jules and I have moved ahead with our lives— Have you?"

"I'm happy with life as it is— Except for not having you and Jules with me— I don't like what you're implying."

"What's that?"

"That my life is narrow and self-serving."

"Then tell me what you're up to these days that's different."

They stop walking. They stop talking and sit side by side, their backs to the wind to keep the flying sand from getting into their eyes. She holds her hair behind her head with both hands. It feels as if the wind will pull it out by the roots. She lets Jean-Pierre collect his thoughts. After several minutes, with the howling wind the only thing breaking the silence between them, she speaks up. "Jules mentioned a Hudson Bay project."

"James Bay. A wind farm with a few thousand turbines, all linked to Hydro-Québec and its grid. It would complete René's legacy."

"And provide you a little personal glory, n'est-ce pas? Isn't it ironic? Here I am in Ontario fighting against energy companies and you're in Quebec fighting for them. Don't you see that as a metaphor for our lives?"

"Not at all. I understand your position— Erecting wind towers here is a different proposition from situating them at James Bay." Jean-Pierre stands and scans the lake. "Hey, where is Jules?"

Lynn gets up too. "When was the last time you saw him?"

"When you did. About twenty minutes ago. I'm sorry— I was distracted by our conversation."

"Maybe he's gone down again."

"Has he ever been out in winds this strong?"

"Not like this."

"Has he ever got into trouble?"

"He got tangled up in his gear one day this summer. But it wasn't a problem. He's a strong swimmer and wears a life vest. He doesn't panic."

The wind is now almost gale force. White caps roll far up onto shore. They both find it difficult to keep their balance as they hurry back along the beach toward their picnic spot, struggle to keep from getting blown sideways. The blankets are where they left them only because the loaded picnic basket has pinned them down, but it's shaking in the wind and appears ready to lift off. Lynn digs her feet into the sand and braces herself, surveys the lake again. Nothing. No sails. No boats of any kind— Nobody else on the beach— She feels herself starting to crumble. *This can't be happening. Jules is all I have left of Suzanne, the part of me that didn't die in the crash. He is both grandson and son. A tough child who's had the strength to withstand Jean-Pierre's censure, a brilliant boy who wants to become a renowned engineer. Too young to drown. I've taken my eye off the most important thing in my life to have a nearly fruitless conversation with a man I no longer know.* Somewhere beyond her reach, way out there on the lake, Jules is lost to the ravages of this raging wind. She grabs Jean-Pierre's arm and shouts, "We need to call the police."

"My cell phone's in the car," he says.

"Mine's here." She retrieves it from the bottom of the picnic basket and starts to dial. "Not enough signal. Let's get back to the car."

They scan the lake again, shield their eyes from the flying grains of sand stinging their faces. Still nothing. No one crazy enough to be out there. They sprint back toward the cottages on the private road where they've parked and stop breathless as her car comes into view. Jules' gear is lashed to the roof.

They wait at the car. After a few minutes, Jules, wearing his street clothes, walks out of the woods from behind one of the cottages. "Hi Mum. Hi Dad. I've already changed. I was taking a leak before coming to get you."

"Oh Jules! We couldn't see you out on the lake," Lynn says, holding him tight and sobbing.

"I'm okay, Mum. I came in because it's freezing out there."

"You should have let us know."

"I wanted to surprise you by packing up the car— I was going back to pick up our picnic stuff."

She holds him tighter. He allows his father to make it a group hug.

Over dinner they agree to convene in Montreal in early December to plan Christmas. Jules and Jean-Pierre are upbeat; Lynn remains subdued. What matters most to Jean-Pierre hasn't changed. That night they do not make love.

CHAPTER 10

When you look back over your life, some days stand out more than others. Days for which your memory needs little assistance. Over time the details remain sharp, the cascade of ensuing events particularly auspicious or ominous. One such day in mid-November that year will continue to come to Ralph's mind unsummoned, a vortex in which he got caught with Lynn and Dieter, a whirlwind that drew in Mary Ann and Mark as well, and his longtime business friends, Hervé and Peter. A day he should have started by paying more attention to the framed prints on the wall behind the desk in his New York office. His three favorite Miró reproductions arranged side by side. Staring at them, Ralph can concoct a scenario of the future. Often they've offered portents, but sometimes they yield nothing but a means to make sense of the present. His fascination with these objets d'art started out as mere amusement, a way to engage the artist's work and bring it to life, but he's fallen into the habit of paying them too much heed; the act has assumed an importance that would embarrass him if he confided in anyone about it. It's better than foretelling by astrological signs only because he gets to appreciate fine art in the process. That day he would focus most on the central print. Its title gives away nothing: *Plate 15*, an etching from the *23 Gravures* collection. The print contains a group of figures childlike in their representation—crude, roundish heads, some miniscule, others normal-sized, a few with elongated torsos, everything blob-like. A group portrait in the manner a kindergartener might depict her family. Was it Miró's gift *for* a child or his rendition of a gift *from* a child? Depictions of particular people or purely random souls? In the middle of the etching, a figure whose head is all but hidden lurks behind another figure, like somebody about to burst into your life, or perhaps someone retreating from it but not yet completely gone.

Ralph arrived at work that day after ambling through the park like a young boy, scuffing his feet along the path and kicking at the last leaves of autumn. Piles of them on the ground beginning to swirl into the air as the wind picked up after a lull. This is the part of the city in which he is most at home, the closest to wilderness the city has to offer, especially early in the morning when it isn't crowded. He wondered what it would be like to take a canoe trip in autumn; the foliage might be doubly splendid with its early morning reflection in a calm lake, but portages would be even harder to find and follow under a layer of leaves.

Ralph stood at the windows of his 37th floor corner office and looked down to the intersection at 53rd Street and Fifth Avenue. On that blustery morning, everyone was wearing a heavy coat and rushing to get in out of the cold. The clouds were a nondescript gray, unlike the colorful balloon shapes in *The Song of the Vowels*, the Miró print to left of center behind his desk. Like the people down on the street, the clouds above seemed purposefully in a great hurry to get where they were going. He was not. It was delightful when he had a slow day and could stand at the window and muse for a while, scan for portents outside before consulting his Miró prints inside. Savoring such moments still didn't occur often enough even though he'd reached a point in his career when he was finally able to work less than he used to. He had let Mark take over most of the daily operations. Ralph recognized Mark's talent early and brought him along in the group defection from Bourke Donovan Fraser almost twenty years ago after having become dissatisfied with putting all that money in the pockets of the senior partners at the large law firm and not enough in his own. Ralph evacuated with the core of the environmental practice he'd built there and started his own firm. Then carefully cultivated Mark to be his successor as managing partner.

By noon, Ralph has accomplished the few tasks on his list for the day and has girded himself for the call to Lynn that he's been putting off all morning. He hopes to catch her on her lunch break. They haven't spoken in a week. Her visit to New York is still a week away. There's no particular reason they've needed to talk, but it feels as if they should have and that it's his fault they haven't. That feeling turns to certainty when she answers.

"You seem distant. Is something wrong?"

"I've been waiting for your call— I've had second thoughts about our getting together in New York."

"Why?"

"Jules and Jean-Pierre."

"I thought we talked about that— This isn't about them— It's about taking care of yourself."

She doesn't respond right away. "I know. But you're used to considering only your own needs. My situation is more complicated. I owe it to both Jules and Jean-Pierre."

"Have you contacted Jean-Pierre?"

"This past weekend he came to Picton and we talked."

"How did it go?"

"I can't say it was easy or that it all went well, but we decided to get back together and give the marriage another shot."

"Was this Jules' doing or yours?"

"As I said, it's complicated."

Ralph swivels his desk chair around to look at the Miró print to the right of center, a photograph he shot with the curator's permission following his private tour at the Fundació Joan Miró in Barcelona, a picture of the artist's near-end-of-life mural consisting of a long

sweeping brushstroke along three walls. Ralph imagines that brushstroke coming full circle along the nonexistent fourth wall. He's feeling closed in again. Back to his days at McGill when Lynn dumped
him for Jean-Pierre. End of his romantic life. "Are you going back to
Montreal?"

"For Christmas and New Year's. We won't move before summer."

He can't find words. She's knocked the wind out of him. Out of
his sails. The metaphors are starting to mix in his head. That happens
when he feels himself losing control of his emotions. He fixes his gaze
on the wall where all three prints are screaming at him.

"Ralph?"

"You caught me by surprise. I was planning a great weekend for
us— "

"I'm sorry."

"I don't know what to say. Why can't we see each other?"

He hears her sigh. "I don't know how to say this other than straight
out. Jean-Pierre and I slept together last weekend. I'm not the kind of
person who can be in a relationship with two people at the same time."

"But you are. You slept with me hardly a week ago. You're clearly the kind of person who can do that." It didn't come out right. It
sounded like an accusation.

"That's not fair. Are you angry about what I told you?"

"About Dieter raping you? Yes, I'm angry about that, but with Dieter, not you. I'm disappointed in you."

"That's not fair either. You don't understand my circumstances."

"I can imagine us having a great life together. You can too. You're
not nearly selfish enough to grant yourself that after all these years of
unhappiness."

"It's not been all bad. There have been some good times."

"They're in the past. There will be few in the future unless you start
over. With me. With us."

"You're probably right, but I can't right now. If it doesn't work out
with Jean-Pierre— "

"I'm second choice again."

"You're not second choice. In many ways, I'd prefer to be with you. But I can't simply throw my marriage away. Jean-Pierre says he's committed to making it work."

"I hope that's true."

"Is that all you have to say?"

"What else can I say? What I want doesn't seem to matter."

"I'm sorry— "

She does sound sorry. Sounds as if she regrets having to turn him away. She's been separated for more than two years and was doing fine without Jean-Pierre in her life. Why can't she walk away? It's not Jean-Pierre. It's Jules. Nothing Ralph can do to fix that.

"I do have something more to say. I'm not going to accept your answer. I did that once and I was wrong. You and I are going to be together. I will fight for you. I will help you with Jules. You know he'll succeed at whatever he does—the science fair, summer internship, college, career   Everything. We'll make sure his life turns out less difficult than you fear. I will help you keep wind farms out of your county." He pauses to calm himself down. His heart is beating fast, fluttering in his chest like a bird flapping to free itself from its cage. This may be his last chance to keep the door from closing completely. The metaphors are swirling again. "If you must say goodbye, it's only goodbye for now. Until next time and the next. Until we're together again."

"Okay. Goodbye— For now."

He doesn't know how he's going to prevent it, but he's not going to let one of Miró's stick figures be suddenly erased from *Plate 15*.

"Ralph?" Mary Ann has returned from lunch and is standing in the doorway to his office. "I have Dr. Graber holding for you. He called while you were finishing up your other call."

He hadn't noticed line 2's blinking light. Too distracted in his conversation with Lynn. "Hello, Dieter. What brings you my way?"

"I have news."

"Good I hope."

"I believe you know Hervé Boudreau."

"Yes. The CEO of Frontier. One of my clients and a long-time friend. I had lunch with him about a month ago. How do you know him?"

"I met him about the same time you had lunch with him. I heard all about it—about a possible acquisition."

"Why would he discuss it with you? That was confidential information."

"It was. But now I'm able to tell you that Frontier's board has approved the deal."

"The deal I suggested to him? What does it have to do with you?"

Dieter doesn't answer straightaway. Then, "It's all in the family now."

Ralph has no idea what Dieter means. Hervé, whom he's known for twenty years, whose business he's defended successfully in many lawsuits over those years, Hervé in Dieter's circle? That makes no sense. Where is Dieter going with this? He seems to want to spill out something else. Ralph tries to slow him down by saying nothing, but Dieter presses on.

"After voting on the deal you suggested to Hervé, his board unanimously approved International Wind Technologies' acquisition of Frontier."

"Are you kidding? You were talking with Frontier and Hervé didn't tell me about it?"

"He couldn't— It was confidential."

Ralph couldn't help but prickle when he heard Dieter's tone. "Sounds like a double standard— "

"Call it what you like."

"Typical— Let me guess. Since you're in charge now, you're calling to fire me from the Frontier account?"

"It's hard for me to tell you."

What a lie. Dieter is still the prick he was in high school. People don't change. "Was it Hervé's decision or yours?"

"Mine. I'm bringing Frontier into the fold under our current law firm."

"May I ask who that is?"

"Bourke, Donovan, and Fraser."

"You're fucking kidding! BDF?— That's my old firm— I built their environmental practice."

"I didn't know— Sorry."

"I bet you are. You've been playing me." He can picture Dieter. Not the seething, frustrated suitor he witnessed at Lynn's, the unapologetic rapist, but a face breaking out into an insidious victory grin. Maybe even high fiving the air. Retribution for high school days. The adolescent boy satisfied at last. But still adolescent. "I'm going to call Hervé and give him the full scoop on you. He has no idea what's in store."

"Too late now, but do what you need to do."

"You fancy yourself a dealmaker now more than an engineer? Let me tell you something—you're in way over your head. Someday one of your deals is going to jump up and bite you. You'll be finished. You won't even see it coming."

"Spoken like a loser, Ralph. You're jealous because you can see that I'm going to make a bigger impact on this industry in the next few years than you've made over your whole career."

"Are you pleased? After all these years— "

"Don't flatter yourself."

"Remember this, Dieter— In the end, the Germans always lose." Ralph knows it's an uncalled-for comment, hearkening back to the teasing in childhood. But this time it has a deeply bitter edge. He immediately wishes he hadn't said it.

"I'm Swiss, not German. You keep forgetting that."

"Whatever— "

"You've always been too dismissive of me."

"Because you've never learned how to deal with people properly."

"Ralph— You've always judged me too harshly— It's your fail-
ing, not mine. And since you insist on being such a prick, let me give
you something else to think about. Lynn isn't who you think she is.
There's something— ”

"What?"

"Never mind. I forgot— It's confidential."

"Ah, you mean there's something you know that I don't know. Don't
be too sure. Remember, there's no statute of limitations . . ."

Ralph hears Dieter hang up. Dieter's figure in the center print
Ralph doesn't mind scratching from *Plate 15*. But it's not yet fully
erased. The pleasure of that will have to wait. He buzzes Mary Ann
on the intercom and asks her to have Mark come to his office.

"What's up, Ralph?"

"Dieter Graber called me a moment ago. International Wind Technologies has acquired Frontier and fired us—fired *me*—from the
Frontier account."

"Did he say who's getting his business?"

"Our former firm. Can you believe it?"

"I guess what goes around comes around."

Ralph turns his desk chair toward the wall again and imagines
Miró smiling at him while continuing to brush the meandering line
in the right-hand mural back on itself, life ending where it began or
perhaps offering a second chance instead of reminding you that an
opportunity has been taken away forever. "Unfortunately, it's worse.
Frontier has acquired one of our Ontario clients. Two gone with one
swing of Dieter's ax." *My God, now I'm chopping down trees!*

"What's Dieter got against you?"

"Personal stuff. Left over from high school."

"You're kidding?"

"He's been looking to get back at me for a long time."

"What can I do?"

"Dieter's crowing. He'll make sure the news gets out. We need to contact our clients and tell them that it was purely personal, nothing at all to do with our performance— "

"I gather there's more?"

"I have a hunch that something big is brewing in Quebec that involves Dieter. I want to find out what it is."

"What makes you think so?"

"In my lunch with Hervé Boudreau several weeks ago, he didn't answer when I asked him about Frontier's expansion plans. All he'd say was that he'd been spending more time in Quebec City than Montreal."

"Is this personal too?"

"You bet it is, deeply personal— But if I'm right, there's a huge business opportunity. We need to be on the right side of it."

"The opposite side from Graber."

"Exactly— Please call Peter Devlin. Ask him to have his people at their Quebec subsidiary dig around."

"Yeah, they're well connected with both Hydro-Québec and the Ministry. Why do you want me to work this through Peter?"

"I need to keep it on the QT. Peter will be able to control that. Tell him I'll call later today. One more thing— After you speak with Peter, we'll hold a meeting of the partners. Please let Toronto know."

Hervé Boudreau and Peter Devlin. Hervé, his "favorite French Canadian." Peter, an even better friend, shares Ralph's passion for sailing. Once a summer, they spend a day on Peter's yacht on Long Island Sound and Ralph returns the favor with a day on his much more modest boat on Nantucket Sound. Peter has been at Global Energy for nearly ten years. Ralph has watched him rise from president of the energy sector to become CEO of one of the biggest conglomerates in the world. After the partners' meeting, Ralph asks Mary Ann to set up phone calls with Hervé and Peter as soon as she can.

"I need to leave early. Dinner and a play tonight."

"Are you okay?"

"We were fired from Frontier. Mark is handling the damage control."

"That's why you want to speak to Hervé?"

"Yeah— Personal damage control."

While he waits at her desk, she dials Frontier and speaks with Hervé's assistant. "He'll call you back in five." Ralph closes his office door to shut out the world for a few minutes. He stands at the window again. For the first time in days the sun is out. A day filled with irony of all kinds.

Line 1 lights up. "Hello, Hervé."

"I knew you'd want to talk."

"Yeah, I can hardly believe what I've heard from Dieter."

"What did he say?"

"Basically that he was happy to fire me from Frontier. I could almost hear him laughing on the other end of the line."

"I was afraid of that. I wanted to be the one to call you."

"Why didn't you? We're friends."

"Dieter insisted on telling you the news."

A weak excuse. He thought his favorite French Canadian was stronger than that. "But you're no pussy. Why did you let him push you around?"

"He's my new boss."

"Is that why you acted strange at our lunch? Except for making eyes at the waitress, it's like you were somebody else."

"I knew about these deals and it killed me that I couldn't tell you."

"You must have huge plans in the works you haven't told me about."

"No— Nothing special."

Ralph doesn't believe him, but there's no point continuing to pursue it. That he's fishing must be obvious to Hervé. "I'm sorry I won't be there to see them through with you."

"You won't be missing much. Anyhow, I can't imagine you haven't been thinking about your retirement. You've been at this a long time."

"Do you think I'm getting too old?"

"I've always admired your ability to see the other side. You've helped us understand our exposure to litigation. But— "

"Yes, always a but— "

"But— I wonder whether you still have the industry's interests at heart."

"Are you saying you'd have considered dropping us even if Dieter hadn't come on the scene?"

"Like it or not, the business has been getting more bruising. Going forward, we're going to need a hard-nosed litigator with blinders on."

Ralph should have picked up the hints at their recent lunch in Montreal. Hervé was uncharacteristically upset about the lawsuit they'd recently lost. He said that Ralph had let him down, hadn't been willing to rip the plaintive to shreds in a case they should have won easily. The judge made a mistake, Ralph protested, but Hervé wouldn't listen, didn't want to hear that they'd win it on appeal. Hervé must have known then what was coming. Their long friendship should have counted for more. "You mean you're going to build lots of wind farms where people don't want them."

"It's inevitable— You know, like Prince Edward County."

"I see. Dieter told you my views about the offshore turbines there."

"He thinks you were playing up to your old girlfriend."

"Trust Dieter to distort things. I hope you realize what you're in for with your new boss— He's utterly self-serving."

"I don't know your history."

"It exploded in my face today. You need someone to cover your back and now it can't be me."

"So far I've enjoyed working with him. We're a lot alike. We both started our companies."

"Is that what he told you?— I found out years ago that his father's Swiss company put up the seed money yet wouldn't install Dieter as CEO."

"He was honest about that."

"Well, good luck. I hope it works out for you."

"Thanks, Ralph. I'm sorry it didn't work out for you."

Ralph wishes his old friend no harm, but can't imagine how it can be avoided. It goes beyond Dieter's personality. The history between the Germans and the French will play out again. Hell, even the French disdain French Canadians. It's hard to figure out why Dieter chose Montreal over Toronto, especially with the separatists in power in Quebec. Probably his German boss insisted. Another chance to bash the frogs.

Three unexpectedly difficult calls in one day. Ralph leans all the way back in his chair and puts his feet on the desk, not even bothering to take off his shoes. A quarter to four. No time left to line up a last-minute date for the evening. He buzzes Mary Ann.

"I've never done this," he says as she enters his office, "but I've got great tickets for tonight's performance of *Book of Mormon* that shouldn't go wasted."

"Are you offering them to me?"

"I was thinking you might like to accompany me. I know you don't get out much. We could have dinner first."

"Did your date cancel?"

"I never got around to inviting anyone."

"I'm your last resort?"

"Only if you want to be— It wouldn't be a date." They've often teased each other about their status as singles, always careful to stay away from any intimation that there's an easy solution.

"Sure— I'll call my son and let him know. He should be home from school by now."

"Great— Someone's on line 1. I'll pick up— Ralph Mackenzie."

"Mr. Mackenzie, this is Mr. Devlin's assistant. He's holding for you— " Ralph motions for Mary Ann to close the door as she leaves.

"Hi Ralph. Good to hear from you."

"Same here. I asked Mark to call you earlier."

"Thanks for sending him our way. We've already done the digging he asked us to do on your behalf."

Ralph hopes Peter has gone about it quietly. "Any paydirt?"

"Easier than we thought. The new Minister of Natural Resources will be going public in January with plans for an enormous expansion of the province's strategic energy plan."

"More hydroelectric?"

"No, a giant wind farm on the shores of James Bay. The Ministry will invite proposals from energy companies to work with Hydro-Québec."

"How many turbines?"

"It's a two-phase project, one thousand each phase."

"What capacity?"

"Five-megawatt turbines, ten thousand megawatts in total when the project's completed."

"Can you handle something that size?"

"Not from our Quebec subsidiary as it stands. We'd have to expand it."

"What about your U.S. facilities?"

"We could ramp up production there more quickly."

"Your major competitor will be the Germans."

"International Wind Technologies?"

"Dieter Graber. He acquired Frontier and fired me."

"So you want to kick his ass?"

"All the way back across the Atlantic to where it belongs."

Peter laughs. "Happy to oblige you."

Ralph asks whether Peter's contacts had mentioned Professor Jean-Pierre Giroux. Peter says he's never heard of him. Ralph fills in the background about Jean-Pierre's involvement with René Lévesque and Hydro-Québec and the drafting of the original ten-year strategic energy plan for the province, the one that pressed for development of wind energy that was not taken up but now seems to have been revived.

"Do you want me to ask around?"

"Please, but as quietly as you did today. I don't want to tip off Graber. He offered Giroux's grandson a summer internship at their research facility in Germany. The kid's a bright high school senior who wants to become an engineer."

"I won't ask how you know this."

"Don't— It's a long story with an unhappy end in the offing. Some other time over drinks— Good luck in the beauty contest— Happy Holidays."

"You too. Thanks for the heads-up. We'll be in touch."

CHAPTER 11

The Faculty Club at McGill is generally a safe place to meet when you don't want to be seen in public. Sometimes, though, Monique feels as though her political enemies, even her colleagues, have planted spies, if not sitting right at tables in the dining room, then peeping from the pictures hanging on the walls, having disguised themselves as distinguished Englishmen drawn from the history of this venerable institution to which her father saw fit to send her for a quality education. Over and over he told her he understood the politics in Quebec. As if somehow she didn't or couldn't. She's glad he's still alive to see that she does. Her father was wrong—the Parti Québécois is remaking Quebec, and Canada had better come to grips with that. Yet he was right too—she sends her girls to an English private school. But there's nothing wrong about meeting a like-minded separatist in enemy territory. More ironic than traitorous. Scheming right here under their watchful eyes. And nothing morally wrong either. Not now that she's divorced and he's separated from his wife. Still, it's unnerving to hear nothing but English being spoken. A place still beyond the reach of the Language Law.

The air is not poison here, but the Faculty Club wouldn't be the place of her choosing. It is Jean-Pierre's choice because it's the habitual dining spot of his best friend Georges, a political science professor at McGill. Imagine. McGill and Université de Montréal collaborating on a book about the future of Quebec. That's why she lets Jean-Pierre get away with insisting that they meet here most of the time. Georges and Jean-Pierre stand to greet her as she sweeps into the room. So much for hiding herself. Spies, get ready to take notes. This promises to be a momentous evening.

"Great to see you, Monique. I'm sorry I can't stay." With that, and kissing her on both cheeks, Georges ushers himself out.

"I'm glad you could make it," says Jean-Pierre as he pushes in her chair. "It's been a month."

He gives her the once-over as if meeting her for the first time. *Yes, you silly cock, I'm wearing the large hoop earrings you gave me and a silk dress as black as my hair. I see you've thrown on a jacket but couldn't bother with a tie. You never dress as well as I do.* "That's because you've been with your wife instead of me." She's sure that's not the romantic start to dinner he'd hoped for.

"Only on weekends. Your calendar and mine haven't meshed well. It seems as if you've dedicated your soul to the James Bay project. You're in Quebec City all the time."

"We've almost finished putting together the RFP."

"I want to hear the details."

"Later— I want to know where you stand with Lynn."

"We're trying— I don't know whether it's going to work out."

"You mean you're hedging your bets."

"Please don't put it like that."

"How else to put it? It seems you want the best of both worlds."

"French and English, you mean?" Jean-Pierre forces a chuckle at his feeble joke. As if it could possibly ratchet down the tension. "Please remember that you were in the same situation until you chose to go through with your divorce."

"I didn't *choose* to go through with it. I never tried to put my marriage back together."

"Yours was a lost cause. You found Henri with another woman."

"Maybe I should invite Lynn to watch us?"

"That's not even funny."

"Don't forget that she abandoned you. Who knows what she's been up to?"

"Nothing. She hasn't been seeing anyone."

"Well, *you* have— I don't like sharing you while you figure it out."

Jean-Pierre summons the waiter, likely hoping that a few minutes not arguing might put the evening back on course. Without looking at the menu, Monique orders a garden salad with oil & vinegar.

"That's all you're going to have?"

"The way this is going it won't be a long evening."

Jean-Pierre shrugs. "I'll have the same. Russian dressing. And bring us two extra-dry martinis with olives."

"Only one," Monique says. "I'll stick with water tonight."

"What's got you this riled? Bad day?"

"It was a great day."

"So it must be me— "

"You know it is."

"What is it you want?"

"I want you for myself."

"I can't give you that. Not yet— But nothing's changed— "

"Yes it has. Put yourself in my position— If you can."

"You're changing the rules."

"It's not a game. And what about Jules?"

"What about him?"

"I'm sure he suspects. "

"Why?"

"He saw me reach across the table at Enfants Terribles and touch your arm. That dinner was a stupid idea. I should never have gone along with it."

"You're imagining the worst— No one knows."

"Except Georges. I hope you reimburse him for these dinners."

"We have an understanding."

Monique removes the vibrating cell phone from her purse, puts on a frown and slips it back into the purse. "That was my office. Tell me, before I have to leave— Do you still love Lynn?" A straightforward question, even a fair one. But he must not have been prepared for it. The waiter approaches with his martini. He takes a sip and swallows quickly, coughing as it burns its way down his throat. *Come on, Jean-Pierre. No is the wrong answer. No will paint you as callous and you don't want that. You can't say you're not sure—that will appear indecisive. Or waffling. Come on.*

"Yes."

"And me?"

"Yes. Of course."

"How can you be in love with both of us?"

"Because I can shut off thinking about her when I'm with you."

"How can you do that?"

"I compartmentalize my life. She's in one part and you're in another. I don't let the two get mixed up."

"But Jules is now in both parts. How do you manage what Jules #1 can know and what Jules #2 can know?"

"That will complicate things."

"What you're telling me is that you shut off thinking about me when you're with her?"

"Not as well."

"Maybe that should tell you something."

"That's why I'm here."

"It was different before," says Monique. "Neither of us was with anyone else— Before your weekend in Picton— " She's probing and can see that he knows it.

"I know— I have to see if it's going to work out with Lynn. I owe it to her and Jules."

"And what do you owe me?"

"When we first started this, we agreed we'd owe each other nothing. No matter what happened."

"But that's not how it's worked out."

"For you it's changed. For me too, but unlike you I'm conflicted."

"That's not good enough."

"I know— You're talking marriage, aren't you?"

"Do I have to spell it out?"

"I'm not there yet."

"Then why don't you set me aside until you see what happens with Lynn? Why do you want to keep seeing me?"

"You challenge me in ways Lynn doesn't. We have a great time together. Why do you want to cut that off?"

"Don't you understand how alone I am when you're not around? Especially when my girls are away at school."

"Monique— I'm not trying to hurt you— What do you want me to do?— "

"I've already told you."

"I mean whether you want to continue seeing each other."

"We get together only when *you* want to, not when *I*— "

That was the crux of it. He'd fit her in when he wasn't with Lynn or Jules or lecturing or writing his book with Georges. Monique knows she's his last option. When he's lonely. When he can no longer stand the abstinence.

"Lynn and Jules are going to stay in Picton until the end of the school year. You and I will have plenty of time together."

"Until summer. Then what?"

"Maybe things with Lynn will have collapsed by then."

"And if not?"

"Then you and I will probably break it off."

"That's no good. You win either way— I don't."

"Okay. Then it's totally up to you— But I hope you're still planning to spend the night."

"Is that all you can think about?"

"Of course not, but that's why you came, isn't it?"

"I was truly looking forward to getting your views on how to streamline the selection process for James Bay. The Premier is putting pressure on me to get the project going. And I thought I was aggressive—she's been in office a little more than a year and she's already thinking of legacy. Finishing the job that Lévesque started."

"You know I care deeply about that," Jean-Pierre says. He puts his napkin on the table, stands, and holds Monique's chair for her. "But let's get out of here."

And this is where she's weak. Where she caves every time. He smiles and looks into her eyes. He puts his hand on her shoulder. In the open, in this supposedly private place that's way too public. Damn him. She'd like to think she's merely humoring him when she says, "That's the best idea you've had all evening," but she's not. Despite all her resolve, she withers. "We'll take our cognac at your place to celebrate another successful meeting with the Minister." There's an ironic edge to her utterance, but she can't hear it. Once again she's put the evening on autopilot when she's supposed to be in control. Next time she'll be stronger. Next time. À la prochaine fois.

❧

Monique spent the first week of her girls' Christmas break at home in Longueil and then drove north to their place at Mont-Tremblant. Jeannine and Christine have turned into excellent skiers. Now they can all ski together on any trail on the mountain, north or south side, including the double black diamonds and mogul fields. Off-trail skiing has become the girls' passion, and though their mother prefers a slope with "bumps," she can't leave either a fourteen- or a sixteen-year-old alone in the woods. She's been their instructor from the beginning, as her father was for her. He'd preferred the smaller hills at Ste-Agathe and under his tutelage she honed her slalom skills to the point she could compete in high school meets. But her girls prefer the natural slalom through trees on ungroomed slopes. When back on trail, they seek speed, racing each other to the bottom of the mountain where they wait in line for her to catch up. They all ride the chairlift together, but the girls talk between themselves, teenage stuff, leaving their mother alone with her thoughts. Today, their last day before returning home for New Year's, Monique wrestles with how a man can genuinely feel romantic love for two women at the same time. Can it be as simple for Jean-Pierre as he claims? Out of sight, out of mind? She doubts it. Yet what is romance but a state of mind? The little acts—giving flowers, writing notes, holding hands—linger in the mind long after they occur. They are the source of joy in coming home to a spouse after an absence, of inner warmth while sitting alone thinking of someone you want to be with, and of the gnawing ache of lost love. How can a man shift those feelings back and forth between his lovers? As always when her mind wanders into the domain of the heart, there is nothing in her engineering background she can reach for to extract a satisfactory explanation. And then—invariably—she arrives at the top of the mountain without any answers. But she smiles as they ski off in search of a little powder.

Today they've pushed themselves hard. Only one rest break, for ty-five minutes for lunch. Seven runs from the top of the north face of the mountain. But the girls aren't tired. They want a last run before the long drive home. Monique surrenders to her fatigue. She's the one who has to do the driving. The girls can take the last run by themselves, but they have to promise to ski the trail. It's no longer light enough to see obstacles clearly in the woods. They give their mother their word. She removes her skis and enters the lodge. Though it violates a rule she's established with Jean-Pierre—that when she suspects he's tied up with family she won't call—she takes out her cell and calls him. She expects him to have silenced his phone to let it ring into voicemail, but he picks up and speaks before she can even say hi.

"This is a bad time."

"Nice to speak with you, too. I guess you've been thinking about me and missing me. Sorry you haven't had a chance to call."

"I said it's a bad time."

"Why? Did I catch you in bed? When you're with her, you're not thinking of me— "

"What's wrong?"

"You know what's wrong. I don't get to be with you enough."

"I have to go— Sorry— I'll call you tomorrow."

"That's it?"

"Sorry."

It would have been better if she hadn't called. She buys a cup of hot chocolate and sits at the fireplace trying to look through the flames. Carbon. Carbon monoxide. Incomplete combustion. Soot lining the chimney. How many trees had to be felled to keep a few skiers warm? To fill their nostrils with that exhilarating charcoal scent. Incense without its cloying sweetness. She looks at her watch. It's time to start back home. She gulps down the last of the hot chocolate, goes outside, retrieves her skis, and waits at the base of the lift. Ten minutes. The lift line has been roped off and members of the ski patrol are gathering to perform their final sweep of the mountain before dark. She approaches one of them and says that she's worried about her girls.

"Are you sure they aren't in the lodge?"

"I didn't see them and we always meet out here at the end of the day. They should be here by now."

"Okay, we'll keep an eye out for them."

"We often ski off-trail. I told them not to without me, but I can't be sure they didn't."

"I'll inform the rest of the patrol. Please check the lodge again and let us know as soon as you find them— What are their names?"

"Jeannine and Christine. Thank you— I'll be waiting here."

She returns to the lodge and checks the ladies' room and cafeteria. She walks slowly throughout the entire space. The end-of-day crowd is thinning. She'll spot them if they're here. After a second pass, she's certain they're not, and goes back to where she spoke with the ski patrol. Why didn't she choose to ski the south face today where the light lasts longer? It will begin to cool off rapidly now that the sun has set behind the mountains. She should have taken the last run with them. What on earth does Jean-Pierre matter against the well-being of her children? Calling him was a selfish act. In a way, though, she feels that he'll be responsible for anything bad that has happened. Silly thought—he doesn't even know them. He's met them only once, when he dropped her off at home after dinner in the city. He came in for coffee before driving back across the river and spent a few minutes asking them whether they liked private school and whether they were planning to follow their mother's path into the world of engineering and politics. The kind of casual conversation when you know enough to ask an ostensibly sensible question, but ask only because it's proper etiquette, and you're thinking about something else as your questions are being answered. She remembers the look in Jean-Pierre's eyes that night: *You should have found a sitter so that we could make love at my place.* She catches herself. *Here I am again, absorbed with my own well-being.*

A few ski patrol have already returned from their runs. No one has come up to her. They take off their skis and head to their station in the lodge. A few more return. Same thing. This time she follows one, stops him, and asks after her daughters.

"No, Madame, nothing to report yet. The rest of the patrol should be back within fifteen minutes."

"Thank you." *Thank you for nothing but being polite.* Two more ski patrol arrive. No, only one. The other is Christine. "Where's Jeannine?"

"Oh Maman, she had a bad fall."

"I told you girls to stay on trail."

"We did, but Jeannine took a straight shot at some big bumps."

"What?"

"You know, tracking the fall line— Absorbing the shocks with the knees like you taught us."

"What happened?"

"She caught a tip—   Somersaulted head-over-heels—   She didn't get up."

"Was she unconscious?"

"Not when I got to her, but she couldn't move her leg."

"What did the ski patrol say?"

"They think she broke it. She can move the other one."

"Madame, it was a bad fall. We're bringing your daughter down in a sled. She'll need to be transported to a hospital for scans to make sure she doesn't have a concussion."

"Or worse," Monique mumbles, half to herself, half out loud.

"Fortunately it doesn't look that way. But after the celebrity accident here a few years ago, we insist on an immediate trip to a hospital."

"Where is the nearest one?"

"We've radioed for a helicopter to medevac her to Montreal General."

"Can we go with her?"

"It would be better if there were only one of you. An adult. Is your husband here?"

"No, my ex-husband is in Montreal."

"Maybe he could meet the helicopter at the hospital. You could drive back to Montreal with your other daughter and meet him there."

"I can call and find out."

"Maman, I don't want *her* there."

"Who?"

"Papa's new wife."

"Christine, this is an emergency. We'll have to deal— Okay?— "
Monique would have preferred to have Jean-Pierre at Jeannine's side, but there'd be too much to explain to too many people. She can't avoid asking Henri. She hopes he won't refuse.

During the drive back from Tremblant with Christine, Monique received a call from Henri that Jeannine had been delivered safely to Montreal General. The hospital had performed an MRI of her head that showed no serious injury, but the X-rays and subsequent MRI of her leg revealed a torn ACL, a multiple fracture of the tibia, and a rupture of the plantaris muscle in her calf. They were about to perform surgery to set the tibia properly, repair the ACL, and examine the plantaris more closely to determine how well it would heal on its own. In digesting that report, she'd forgotten to ask Henri to make sure, for Christine's sake, that his wife, Celine, was not present when they arrived. Thankfully she is not. Neither is Jeannine, still in surgery.

"I guess it'll only be Christine you take back to school on Wednesday," Monique says to Henri.

"It looks that way. Jeannine will have to stay in the hospital overnight and then at home for a few days. I can drive her to school Thursday or Friday after she's got used to her crutches. What's another ninety-minute drive each way?"

That last bit is exactly the kind of sarcastic comment she hates from Henri. She fought hard to make sure the bastard wasn't awarded joint custody in the divorce, merely visiting rights every other weekend and one holiday a year. In a rare act of generosity, he offered to drive the girls to and from their school in the Cantons de l'est to let her travel to and from the Assemblée nationale without having to make a long detour. She doesn't feel the least bit guilty about the extra driving he'll have to do this week—he should be happy for some additional time with his older child. But always more considerate than he is, she suggests, "Why not wait a day or two and take both girls at the same time?"

"Christine should be back for the start of the semester."

"Fine. Suit yourself." As it had been toward the end of their marriage, and still is, Monique finds it easier to mollify Henri than to argue. Since the divorce, her interaction with him has become purely transactional, free of the hurt and anger that had taken her a few years to work through. Though Henri is the father of her children, she's now assigned him a minor role in her life. She doesn't ask after him or mention him in conversations with the children. She greets him at the door of her house—a different house than they lived in before the divorce, back to her roots in Longueil, happy to escape the ugly memory of Notre-Dame-de-Grâce—when he picks up the girls. She never inquires what they talk about with their father, and whenever they start to talk about him or his new wife, Monique leaves the room or changes the subject. That is how she deals with the residue of Henri's affair.

That's how any woman would cope with it after coming home unexpectedly one day to find her husband with another woman, the two of them so absorbed in their ministrations that they notice her standing in the doorway of the master bedroom only after they're finished and have collapsed in each other's arms, exhausted and sweaty. When you don't need the walls to tell you what happened at the scene of the crime because you witnessed the deed first hand. The picture of them entangled enraged Monique. She took a belt to Celine before Henri could wrestle her to the floor. She kneed him in the balls and spit in his face. She would have whipped Celine into oblivion if he hadn't interceded. Monique has flashed back too many times to the image of the two of them naked, dripping with perspiration and their other bodily fluids—you don't forget something like that and you don't ever learn to forgive it.

Henri waits with Monique and Christine a few hours before the surgeon appears to tell them that the operation has been a success. "It will be a long recovery," he says. "She will need extensive physical therapy to rehabilitate the knee. The fractures will heal well. Her calf muscle should heal within a few months but the injury will leave permanent scar tissue. Whenever it's stressed she will experience pain. But for normal activities everything should be fine."

"Will she be able to ski again?" Monique asks.

"Yes, but I don't think she should ski competitively. She should avoid moguls. Recreational skiing with a knee brace should be fine."

"That's not Jeannine," says Christine.

"It is now, I'm afraid," says the surgeon.

They thank him, and Monique tells Henri he can go. "Please stop by the house at noon on Wednesday. I'll write a note to the headmaster explaining the situation." She tells Christine that the two of them will wait to say goodnight to Jeannine. Then Monique collapses as her thoughts collapse in on her. Being in Henri's presence is an ordeal. He represents all that can be bad in a marriage. Is she on the verge of putting herself in the same position with Jean-Pierre? Or will it be the reverse, Lynn walking in on the two of them one night at his place? Different ugly images invade her head, make her suddenly feel small. Not from the guilt that she's carrying on an affair and might hurt Lynn and Jules, but remorse for letting her obsession with a man who isn't smitten with her deflect her attention from her girls when they needed it. She could have skied with them on their last run—she hadn't been too tired.

⌒

Monique will never cease to be amazed at how a night's sleep can refresh the body and the mind. Despite her feelings the evening before, she finds herself waiting for Jean-Pierre's call. She's certainly not going to call him this time. When her cell phone sounds the ring tone she's assigned to him, she goes into the study and closes the door.

"Happy New Year's Eve Day," says Jean-Pierre.

"The same to you. Thanks for calling— We need to talk."

"That sounds ominous."

"It depends on you. Are you available this week?"

"I'm driving Lynn and Jules to Picton on Wednesday and staying through the weekend. How about next week?"

"That's bad for me. I'll be in Quebec with my senior staff finalizing the RFP before we announce it officially. How about the following Wednesday?"

"Sure— I've been thinking about our last dinner. I have things to tell you."

"They'll have to wait." She's tempted to ask, but quells her curiosity about what he can possibly mean. His news can't be good. Would he drive his wife and grandson home if things hadn't gone well over the holiday? Christine knocks on the door. Monique speaks softly into the phone. "I have to go."

CHAPTER 12

Lynn hasn't seen the inside of the Outremont bedroom in almost two and a half years, or stood in the front yard, such as it is, minuscule compared with the acres of open land near her home in Picton, all of which seems to belong to her when she takes a walk. Nor has she been on avenue Bernard for a family meal at one of their favorite restaurants. She hadn't expected it to be like returning to visit her childhood home, shocked at the emotional distance that time creates, but it has been. Shocking because two-and-a-half years is not fifty and the mind hasn't had enough time to file down the sharp edges of memory, barely enough to dull recollection a little. And there have been plenty of good memories here. But it's now Jean-Pierre's place. It has already assumed the new label—his, no longer hers or theirs. What she sees isn't different—the house hasn't been altered in any material way; Jean-Pierre hasn't redecorated or moved furniture around or assigned rooms different functions. Everything is virtually identical to what it was before she and Jules moved out, as if time froze and Jean-Pierre's life hasn't advanced a single frame. It looks the same, but doesn't feel the same.

As if Jean-Pierre has been reading her thoughts, he says, "It will start to seem like home again— Soon— By the end of the Christmas break— You'll see."

"How did it feel for you to stay at my place?" she asks.

"A bit odd, except that you were there and we were together. That made it comfortable."

"Did it feel like your home?"

"No— But it never was— I'm sure if I lived there a while, it would start to."

"Who else has been here since I left?"

"Almost no one. Jules. And Georges. We often work together here on our book instead of at one of our offices at the university."

"No women? No dates?"

"Why do you ask?"

"Why don't you answer?"

"Because there's nothing to tell."

"Are you saying you haven't been on any dates?"

"I've gone out for dinner a few times, but always business."

"That's hard to believe— You've always needed a steady diet of sex."

"I was waiting for us to get back together."

"What about *Monique*?"

"She's a friend."

"Did you campaign for her?"

"I made a few speeches, organized a rally in East Montreal for the party."

"I know how it is when you get into the heat of a campaign."

"You're thinking of when you and I knocked on doors drumming up votes for René. I'm older now."

"Why her, Jean-Pierre?"

"I'm surprised you don't remember. We met years ago when she worked at Hydro-Québec."

He recalls for Lynn how he and Monique met when the Liberal party was in power. They collaborated on the ten-year energy plan for the province, a landmark document charting the path to economic self-sufficiency. Without realizing how caught up he is in his recollection, Jean-Pierre continues as if Lynn is not present. He describes how Monique pushed the task force toward a more rapid expansion into alternative energy sources, especially wind. But the consensus view at the time turned out more modest. To lighten Monique's disappointment, he used the words he'd whispered years before to René Lévesque after the defeat of Quebec's first referendum on separation, now-famous words that René adopted as his slogan. À la prochaine fois. Next time. He convinced her to enter politics and use her position as a springboard to accelerate the energy plan. *Now* is that next time he tells Lynn. Monique is the new Minister of Natural Resources. Quebec can adopt the aggressive plan it had been afraid to espouse earlier.

She can see that Jean-Pierre has entered his own world and closed the door behind him, unaware that he's shut her out. "It sounds as if you're committed to Monique."

"I'm committed to all my clients— Please— Let's stop talking business. That's not why you and Jules are here."

It turns out that Jean-Pierre was right. As each day passes, Lynn feels more at home. She takes walks on Mont-Royal, stands against the stone balustrade at the top of the mountain and gazes out over the city toward McGill and beyond to the St. Lawrence, the panorama more part of her history than the harbor view of Picton. Some days she goes alone, up and about before coffee has stirred Jean-Pierre's brain sufficiently for him to be coherent. Some days she consents to walking later in the morning with him. On those days, they talk about many things, Jean-Pierre always tying the conversation back to the investment they've made in a shared life. Until one morning, tired of talking, though she'd originally been the one to insist, she says, "Please— No more propaganda— I don't need convincing that we've had good times. I need to feel good going forward. Let's see what happens."

Some days Jules joins them for an afternoon walk after spending the morning on his science fair project, working out equations to express the stresses in underwater cables for different configurations of anchoring pylons. He tells them about the different possible designs for floating turbines. He says he still favors eggbeaters with low centers of gravity despite what Dr. Graber cautioned. All of it is over Lynn's head, but she listens because his enthusiasm is infectious. His team has won the regional science fair and is now entered in the provincial finals in Toronto, where the competition will be much tougher and there will be a premium placed on original work. He claims that finding an optimal, cost-effective combination of anchoring configuration and turbine architecture will be necessary to advance to the nationals in Ottawa. There will be only a month to construct more sophisticated models once he gets back home to Picton. On and on he goes. He talks about his project to them as if they are the judges at the upcoming fair. Lynn feels she could almost stand in for him, but realizes she'd only be parroting his words. Any probing question would expose her lack of understanding. She knows he wants a new laptop for Christmas, but he's asked them for a gift of money instead to buy building materials to enhance his exhibit. Jean-Pierre and Lynn pool their meager resources to meet his wish but also want to put something under the tree for him, something wrapped in fancy paper and ribbons, not merely an envelope containing two checks. They buy him an iPod Nano.

On Christmas Day, the family voted Jules' gift to his father the most thoughtful of all the Christmas presents. At the school's workshop, he'd fashioned a wooden container that when wrapped appeared to be a leather-bound tome with a rounded, ridged spine. Some classic book on history or philosophy or political science Jean-Pierre guessed as he unwrapped it carefully. Inside the box, also wrapped with perfect corners, was a picture frame holding a recent photo of Jules decked out in sports jacket and tie, his hair combed and parted. Jean-Pierre laughed when he saw it. "I know exactly where to put this," he said, and strode to the bookshelf in his study, right to the spot that had stood bare since the November assassination.

Lynn was overwhelmed by Jean-Pierre's gift to her—a single large freshwater pearl pendant on a gold chain, a gift she'd once asked him for. When she opened it and started to cry, Jean-Pierre said, "I bought it a month before you and Jules left. I hoped I'd have another chance." Because of that gift, she had thought momentarily about dissenting in the family vote, but hadn't wanted to upset Jules, who was clearly thrilled with Jean-Pierre's reaction to receiving the photo. Now, with all the presents unwrapped, Lynn stands before the bookshelf and asks Jules, "Who took the photo?"

"Amy. When she was at our place a few weeks ago."

Lynn is stunned at how handsome Jules looks in a jacket and tie. She knows that he'll be a knockout in a tux. She wonders if Amy will be the one he asks to the prom. Assuming he's finally decided to go. Not wanting to start anything and spoil Christmas, she keeps these thoughts to herself.

Christmas afternoon, by unanimous agreement, they decide to embark on a movie fest for the rest of their time together in Montreal. They make a list of all the films they think are destined to capture Oscar nominations and a few that won't, like *Skyfall*, the latest Bond thriller. Lynn insists that *Argo* be included on the list. Jules and Jean-Pierre put up only token protest about having to see it a second time. Jules arranges the schedule on a spreadsheet—six straight days of two movies a day, late afternoon and late evening, with a restaurant dinner between. He concocts a contest in which they all indicate their picks for nominees in the four major Oscar categories. He devises a schedule of rewards and penalties, preliminary points up to the date the nominations are announced and then bonus points if they end up having selected the ultimate winners. He starts to describe the scoring in detail. Lynn and Jean-Pierre raise their arms in surrender. It smacks of his scheme for recording their errors with pronouns and proper nouns. They don't want to know.

"We'll get together on Oscar night," Jules announces.

"It will have to be in Picton because you'll have school the next day," Lynn says.

"What's the prize?" Jean-Pierre asks.

"It has to be something we can all appreciate," says Jules, "because we don't know who will win."

"But then it doesn't matter who wins," says Jean-Pierre.

"I guess that's the whole point," says Lynn. "We'll all be winners."

"I've got it," says Jules. "It's obvious. Something we can all enjoy is being together."

"And?" Lynn and Jean-Pierre say simultaneously.

"And that would be a weeklong holiday."

"A road trip somewhere?" asks Jean-Pierre.

"Exactly. We don't have to figure out where right now— *Zero Dark Thirty* starts in an hour."

❧

Jean-Pierre's cell phone starts vibrating right before the first movie on the last day of their cinematic orgy. He's just come out of the restroom and joined Lynn who is holding a large bag of popcorn and two bottles of water.

"I've got to take this call," he says. "It's business. You join Jules in the theater— I'll be right in."

She hands him the popcorn and takes the bottles of water with her. She turns the corner into the corridor to Theater 10 but pauses within earshot of Jean-Pierre.

"This is a bad time— "

"I said it's a bad time— "

"What's wrong?— "

"I have to go— Sorry— I'll call you tomorrow— "

She hurries down the hall and ducks into the theater. Jules waves— he's been holding the seats. "Dad will be here in a moment. He's bringing the popcorn."

As Jean-Pierre takes his seat on the end of the row, his favorite spot because he can lean into the aisle to get an unimpeded view of the screen if someone tall happens to sit in front of him, Lynn asks, "Who called you on a Sunday afternoon?"

"It was the Minister. Bad timing— Sorry."

"What did she want?"

"We were supposed to meet tomorrow about the James Bay project. She has to cancel, but needs to tell me about something that has come up. I said we'd talk by phone instead."

"You're right," she says. "It *is* a bad time."

Jean-Pierre glares at her. "I said it was bad timing."

"C'mon guys," says Jules. "The trailers are starting."

As the main feature begins, Jean-Pierre clasps her hand. She doesn't withdraw, but doesn't squeeze back. Her mind is stuck on his words. *What's wrong?* You can make mistakes interpreting only part of a conversation, the half you hear. She's given that as a writing exercise to her high school seniors, asks them to fill in the missing speaker's words, then has the students read in pairs to the rest of the class. It's a vivid lesson in how false assumptions can be. Yet she can't wrest her mind from the place it wants to go. Jean-Pierre grips her hand more firmly, leans toward her and whispers, "What's wrong?"

CHAPTER 13

Mary Ann has provided Ralph interim progress reports. She located Jack and Steve quickly because they'd attended McGill and could easily be tracked through the alumni office after the clerk there was persuaded to overlook the matter of the university's policy on privacy. Finding Bill took a few more days. He'd married, divorced and remarried, and moved from Montreal to Edmonton where he's currently a senior executive for an oil and gas company. Maarten was the most difficult. Ralph had forgotten to supply a key detail. Maarten's roots were Dutch—he was born in Holland and emigrated to Canada when he was young. With that information, it only took a week for the private investigator hired by the Toronto office to discover that Maarten had died of cancer in a Rotterdam hospital. The obituary indicated that a wife and two children had survived him and that he'd repatriated from Canada in 1995 to start his own sporting goods company. Ralph smiled when Mary Ann told him.

"I thought you'd be saddened to hear of his death," she said.

"I am. But I never thought that crazy Dutchman would find someone to marry him. He was always full of bravado and off-color jokes. Our canoe trip won't be as fun without him." Mary Ann presented him a list of addresses and telephone numbers. "Only four of us, then."

"Maybe not. When I talked to Jack, I got the impression that he'll be a tough sell."

"I can't imagine why. We were best friends at camp."

"He said you should give him a call."

Ralph sees from Mary Ann's notes that Jack is a professor in the physical education department at the University of Victoria. He dials the number.

"Williamson here."

"Hi Jack. It's Ralph Mackenzie. Been a long time." Silence on Jack's end of the line. "I understand you've spoken with my assistant."

"Yes. About some wild idea for a canoe trip with Steve, Bill, and Maarten."

"Not too wild I hope. I think we can make it all the way around the Maison-de-Pierre circuit this time."

"Why do you think that all of a sudden I'd want to spend time with you after such a long time?"

"What do you mean? You and I were best friends."

"The last I heard from you was in our second year at McGill. After the ski trip to Mont-Tremblant."

Jack's tone conveys hostility more than hurt. "Jack, we simply lost touch. I bet you haven't heard from Steve either and he was at McGill when we were."

"No, but he's not the one who mistreated my sister."

"Joan?"

"Yeah, Joan. Don't you remember?"

"Not exactly."

"You and she finally got something going and you said you'd call her after the midterm break. She never heard from you again."

"Jack, that was more than forty years ago. What's the big deal?"

"I thought you were better than that. Taking her sailing, writing her letters, visiting us. What was that all about?"

"What does it have to with the canoe trip?"

"It's a question of trust. You weren't honest with Joan. You let her down and she took it badly. It made me change my mind about you."

"I'm sorry to hear that. I wish you'd told me then. We could have cleared the air— You know we can't do this trip without you."

"Why not? Without me, there will still be four of you. That's two per canoe."

"No, Jack. I found out that Maarten died a few years ago. We need you. I know we've all changed, but we'll have a great time."

"I don't think so, Ralph. But let me know if the others are in. It might be good to see *them* again."

Everything he has planned might fall apart. But he can't drop it and move on. Like ultimately getting back together with Lynn, the reunion canoe trip is too important to him not to resurrect. He asks Mary Ann to send out his letter by FedEx from the Toronto office to everyone, including Jack. He makes a few changes to the original draft, principally to inform the others of Maarten's passing—he detests that word, but realizes that most people prefer it to the explicit mention of death. Pass away, as if a person slips quietly from existence without being noticed, like an image on a computer screen fading out, dissolving and leaving no noticeable hole, a piece of the background suddenly visible where previously it had been obscured by the recently deceased. He had wondered about putting anything in the letter regarding Maarten, a downbeat bit of news in an otherwise upbeat note. Debated about whether to place it up front or near the end and decided to put it first, get the sadness out of the way by suggesting that the trip will honor Maarten's memory, a tribute to the boy who had buoyed their spirits on the ill-fated trip. Perhaps that would soften Jack's attitude and prevent the canoe trip from passing away.

Several days after the letters were sent, Ralph asks Mary Ann to try Steve at his office at McGill. Steve, the fifteen-year-old camper who'd ruined their trip by swinging an ax into his calf out in the wilderness a long way from the nearest village, had become a distinguished professor of history at Ralph's alma mater. Who would have guessed? Summer camp was an escape from the school year, especially for the boys who attended high-powered private schools, Lower Canada College in Steve's case. As a camper, you felt comfortable asking where another camper lived and went to school, but that was all. You didn't talk about school—sports maybe, but nothing scholastic. Now and then you might hear that so-and-so was a star student, but you never inquired as to the details. Now Ralph knows that Steve had been a star student and had decided to pursue an academic career. After earning a doctorate in the humanities he joined the faculty at University of Toronto but several years later returned to McGill to occupy a prestigious chair. Maybe Ralph would have known if he'd ever bothered to read the notes in the alumni magazine. Maybe not, because who takes the time to send in such news? Line 1 lights up.

"Hello Steve. It's Ralph. I hope you received my letter."

"Hi Ralph. I'm still digesting it."

"That's why I called. I haven't heard back from anyone yet. I thought I'd get a thumbs-up from you to pass on to Jack and Bill."

"The trip's a great idea, something I'd never have thought of— But— "

"Please, no *buts*— "

"I'm scheduled to begin a sabbatical at Oxford on July 1ˢᵗ."

"Couldn't you push it off a week? What better way to clear your mind and start fresh overseas."

"If I were single, but— "

"Your wife is accompanying you."

"And my son."

"How old is he?"

"Still a teenager— I married late."

"notff they'd wait a week for you to take this trip. How could they deny you a once-in-a-lifetime second shot at success?"

"They might not want me to hack off the other leg."

They both laugh. "Say yes. Make my day."

"I'll check with Oxford."

"I'm going to assume that's a yes."

"Okay— Yes."

"Steve, there's something else."

"What?"

"I spoke with Jack before I sent out the letters. He's a bit cool on joining us, not because he doesn't like the idea of the trip, but because of me."

"Why? You guys were best friends."

"That's what I thought, but apparently he's never forgiven me for making a pass at his sister and not following up."

"You're joking."

"Sort of silly, eh? That's what he told me. It seems that she mistook my intentions."

"Did she? Or did you leave her hanging?"

"Maybe left her hanging. I was trying to get over breaking up with my high school girlfriend. I told Joan I'd get back to her to arrange a date and never did. That must happen all the time— "

"Not to your best friend's sister."

"Hey Steve. This is petty. It was long ago— I need you to sell him on the trip."

Steve did call both Jack and Bill on Ralph's behalf. Both wanted to say no initially, inclined to find an easy excuse for declining, especially Jack, but Steve told Ralph he was able to persuade them not to deny the fumbling ax-man an opportunity to redeem himself. He promised to avoid careless injuries this time. They warmed to the idea that the group of four would shatter the record for the highest combined age for participants of any canoe trip Kiamika has ever sponsored, far exceeding the two-person three-day trip that the camp founder at seventy-two and his lifelong friend at ninety-one had taken. Four sixty-somethings attempting to pull it off, one hundred ninety-two combined years older than when they'd failed. Ralph was ecstatic at the news from Steve. They arranged to have dinner in Montreal after the holidays to start planning the trip. Jack and Bill had said they'd leave that task to Ralph and Steve. Steve offered to treat.

❧

The holidays burst upon Ralph with a vengeance. Although Steve had resurrected the reunion canoe trip, a huge gift, Ralph felt wrung out from the triple massacre wrought by Lynn, Dieter, and Hervé. He couldn't shake the disappointment. Lynn was the worst. It wasn't as much the feeling of being set aside, more not being permitted a chance to get started, but it felt the same. From the moment he began to plan their weekend together in New York City, he'd counted on becoming involved with her again. He'd thought ahead as far as the holidays, imagined spending a part of Jules' school break with him and his mother. Ralph's profound disappointment forced him to reflect on its source, not only the mere fact of it, but also the deeper reason behind it. He's never been able to say goodbye to Lynn, a real, honest, final goodbye. He wouldn't let her do that when they parted in college, hoping there'd be a reprieve, that her attachment to Jean-Pierre didn't represent a clean break. Even after her marriage, Ralph held on to hope. His romantic fantasies in the intervening years have been about getting back together with Lynn and only Lynn. Now, unless he comes up with a plan, even those will slip away, the hopes and the fantasies. The goodbyes at the end of their last call were not farewells in his mind. As long as he can cling to that.

As he's done for many years, Ralph celebrated Christmas in Kingston with his parents. This time, he kept finding his thoughts creeping their way westward up the lake against the prevailing wind—the "what might have been" game that eats away the insides while leaving the rest of you looking normal to the outside world. When he'd shopped in New York City, he'd found many things he'd happily have bought for Lynn and Jules. Browsing the stores along Fifth Avenue, he picked out dresses in Saks and a diamond and sapphire necklace in

Tiffany. In the Apple Store on Broadway near his condominium, the latest iPad with retina display and an iPod Nano. He picked them out but didn't buy. Except for the iPad, which he purchased for himself to put under his parents' stubby artificial tree—a gift from them to him, a thoughtful gift for a man who likes the latest gadgets. How could he expect them to know what to get him? For them he bought the usual from L.L. Bean, what they'd wanted every year for as long as he can remember: a plaid flannel shirt for his father and a light blue woolen hat for his mother, what he used to call a *toque,* a word no American seems to know. And a scarf for each of them. You'd think by now they'd have enough shirts and hats and scarves. The winters in Kingston aren't that cold.

When his mind gets stuck in the present trying to imagine how he can make the future turn out to his liking, Ralph turns to the past, the parts of it that have brought him the greatest joys. Summers. Sailing and canoeing. On New Year's Day, home from Canada, he resolves not to let anything get in the way of the upcoming canoe trip. Whether or not he succeeds at bringing Lynn back into his life, he'll relive his camp days one more time. On the first business day of the new year, he arrives at the office before Mary Ann and drafts a short note to his old friends, informing them of the camp's requirement that they all pass a physical. She arrives as he finishes.

"Happy New Year, Ralph. How was Christmas?"

"The usual—only my parents and me in Kingston. And yours?"

"Only my son and me— What's up? Why are you here this early?"

"My New Year's resolution is to make sure this canoe trip comes off without a hitch. I've written another note to my friends."

"You sound tired— Didn't you get any rest over the break?"

"I'm starting to feel old. I hadn't thought about it much before seeing my parents over the holidays. Now I'm worried I might end up like my father."

Putting on a smile to signal that she isn't serious, Mary Ann says, "Maybe you should make a bucket list instead of writing letters."

"That's morbid— Anyhow, apart from this trip, there wouldn't be much to put on it."

"How about settling down with a woman?"

"That too, I guess."

She has obviously been buoyed by the holidays and is trying to joust with him, poking fun at his long bachelorhood. But today he doesn't feel like playing. "Hey— Would you mind taking care of this letter?" He tears off the top sheet from the legal pad. It's not like him not to use his laptop or his new toy, the iPad. More and more these days he doesn't feel like himself.

❧

Steve is a few minutes late for their dinner at the Faculty Club. It takes only a glimpse for Ralph to see that Steve hasn't changed much since their camp days—a little taller, still thin, the same Alfred E. Neuman face, but the boyhood freckles gone. The ugly braces gone too. Ralph gathers the maps spread out in front of him on the table.

"Hey Steve, thank you for persuading Oxford to indulge us on this trip, and thanks to your wife and son. I haven't been as excited about anything in a long time."

"I see you brought the maps."

"Yeah. Someone other than me should have a careful look at our itinerary. I tend to think we can do anything."

"Then I guess you'll do fine as Maarten's replacement. I can hard-ly believe you're so serious about this. Is there something you're not telling me?"

"Like what?"

"Like maybe this is a bucket list item for you."

"That's what my assistant said. Why do you ask?"

"You mentioned in the first letter that you wanted to succeed at this trip before you die— Also the way you worded the news about Maarten."

Ralph hadn't realized the letter might convey that impression. "There's nothing wrong with me. I'm getting closer to retirement— Merely pondering the future, which I'm sure there'll be less of than the past."

With a clear view of the entrance to the dining room, Ralph sees Jean-Pierre walk in with an attractive woman who isn't Lynn. Jean-Pierre pulls out her chair and puts his hand on her shoulder as she pulls it up to the table set for four. He sits to her left rather than across from her, closer, more intimate. "Steve, please excuse me for a moment. Someone's arrived whom I haven't seen in a long time. I'd like to say hi. Be right back." He walks over to Jean-Pierre's table and stands across from him.

"Hello, Jean-Pierre. Good to see you. It's been twenty-five years. You look as if life has treated you well. I hope you and your family had happy holidays. Happy New Year."

Jean-Pierre rises from his chair, as does his companion from hers. He shakes Ralph's hand. "Good to see you, Ralph. Thank you—the holidays were good. Happy New Year to you too."

Jean-Pierre's expression, shock turning to puzzlement then dismay, seems to belie his words, but Ralph can't tell whether the holidays have been good for him or not. "Please introduce me to your lovely companion."

"Sorry— Yes— Ralph, I'd like you to meet Monique Beaumont. Monique, this is Ralph Mackenzie."

Ralph shakes her hand, soft, a bit clammy, as if she, too, is flustered by his arrival. In her eyes he finds a look as puzzled as Jean-Pierre's was a few moments before. "Monique, I recognize you but I can't seem to remember from where."

"Ralph, clearly you don't spend enough time in Quebec. Monique is the new Minister of Natural Resources for the Provincial Government."

"What do you do?" the Minister asks Ralph.

"I run an environmental law practice. My clients are primarily energy companies, all of which I'm sure you're familiar with."

She quickly regains her composure. "I'm sure I am— If we meet again, I hope we find ourselves on the same side."

"Me too. It's a pleasure to make your acquaintance. And a pleasure to see you, Jean-Pierre. Please give my best to Lynn." Ralph turns away, then turns back. Knowing of Jean-Pierre's history with René Lévesque, he says, "À la prochaine fois." But directs it more toward Monique than Jean-Pierre. It seems to unnerve her further.

"Who are they?" asks Steve when he returns to the table.

"Jean-Pierre Giroux was at McGill the same time we were. He stole my girl and married her. The woman he's with is Quebec's Minister of Natural Resources."

"I wonder what they're discussing."

"A business project I suspect, but it looks as if there might be something personal as well."

"Is he still married?"

"He's been separated going on three years. I've heard he recently got back together with his wife."

"Or maybe not," says Steve.

Over dinner Ralph recounts his discussions with the camp director and walks Steve through the maps, indicating where they'd camped overnight in the fishing cabin their counselors broke into and where things went wrong on the Rouge River. He points out Carp Lake, which goes by a French name on the government map, and the probable location of the overgrown portage to reach it. The difficult part of the trip will be the middle stretch where the low-lying terrain is likely swampy. "Few lakes, almost no paddling, a lot of portaging. Much of it through alder thickets, I'm guessing. There might be some slogging through bogs. I'd like to set aside three days for that part of the trip."

"I'm not sure we'll be able to handle the overgrown portages with the camp's heavy wood and canvas canoes," says Steve. "Have you considered taking Kevlar canoes instead?"

"The director advises against lighter canoes because the winds are generally strong on the Baskatong. They'll be harder to handle."

"But they'll be weighed down with packs," says Steve.

"Not as much at the end of the trip with the food almost gone by then— The director's pressing us to take the camp canoes. I believe he's thinking of exposing his brand more broadly, you know, the camp crest on the bow of each canoe."

Steve selects two of the maps and spends a few minutes studying them. "How about an alternative route a little farther north or south with more water, less land? The Baskatong is huge— Does it matter where we enter it?"

"There aren't any good alternatives," Ralph says. He picks at his meal while Steve has another look at the maps. Jean-Pierre and Monique get up from their table and leave. A quick dinner. Ralph wonders if he's been the cause. Jean-Pierre appears distressed.

"You're right," says Steve. "But I'm concerned. The middle portion can break the whole trip. It will defeat the purpose of our reunion."

"That's why I plan to cheat a little. I'm going to commission a pilot to fly us—only you and me—in a seaplane over the entire route. From the air, we'll pick out the most difficult portages in the middle section."

"Then we'll know where they are," says Steve, "but that won't make them any easier."

"I'm thinking that you and I can blaze the most difficult trails before the trip— Not clear them, merely mark them."

"That could take several days, maybe a week or more."

"Consider it a little extra for us. Two consecutive weekends in May should do it."

Steve frowns. "The beginning of May is the end of my semester. I'll be grading papers and exams. How about the end of the month?"

"Fine with me."

"Are you going to tell Jack and Bill?"

"You bet— Jack's already told me he doesn't consider me trustworthy after that episode with his sister. I plan to let him know everything you and I talk about."

CHAPTER 14

The government papers arrive on Dieter's desk in mid-January as promised by the Ministry. This year he has a single New Year's resolution—by whatever means win the James Bay bakeoff. It will be his ticket for a triumphant return to Munich as the next Managing Director of International Wind Technologies. Airlift him out of this godforsaken province and back to the old country. Not Switzerland, but second best. Wearing the brass ring has always been his goal, especially since his father passed him over when the company was formed. It will prove that he can be more than an engineer.

Despite his optimistic outlook, Dieter is worried about the outcome of the contest for the right to build the wind farms on James Bay. It will be the largest single installation in the world and International Wind Technologies does not have a longstanding track record of goodwill with the province of Quebec. His major competitor does. Dieter thumbs through the Ministry's RFP. Everything appears routine—indeed, everything is startlingly close to the plan he had hatched and his company would have presented privately to the Minister if there hadn't been a general call for proposals—he considers the entire project his brainchild. Pity it has to be competitive. Although he can't see exactly how, the section on selection of the winning proposals must be the key to the strategy he now needs. "Other factors" than the lowest bid will be considered: a company's size and reputation, previous experience in wind farm installations, service and maintenance record for turbines, ability to work effectively with Hydro-Québec and Ministry personnel . . . . The "ability to work effectively"—that's the "out" for the Ministry, the subjective factor to trump all other considerations. He needs to make that the "in" for his company.

❧

It has been a bad day. Dieter is sure that Lynn is rejoicing at her victory. The Provincial Government first, followed immediately by the Federal Government, the one-two punch clearly a coordinated assault on the industry, has put all companies' plans for wind farms in Prince Edward County on hold. He should call Lynn to congratulate her on this stay of execution and remind her that it will only be a matter of time before the industry wipes out her fleeting success. Her citizens' protest coalition has won only the initial skirmish. It's an annoying development, but no more than that. In the big picture, it doesn't matter. The bad news will be reversed, only a question of how much in fees the industry association's lawyers will bleed from their clients before the opposition is ground down; the industry has much deeper pockets than conservation groups. It is willing to spend heavily. There's much to lose, but much more to gain. No, it doesn't matter. Moreover, the scope of the farms in Ontario pales against the possibilities for James Bay.

Dieter makes a cup of coffee, promises himself he won't leave the office until he's solved the puzzle. He still thinks the "Other factors" section of the RFP holds the answer. Everything else is too straightforward to be manipulated to any one company's advantage. What will be critical to the Minister? Something self-serving. Something that enhances her prospects for ultimately becoming Premier. The public never remembers provincial cabinet ministers, only Premiers who accomplish great things. Like Lévesque and Bourassa. The Premier gets all the credit. Like a CEO. The Minister's best shot at becoming a future Premier is to help the current Premier succeed. That's whom his strategy should target. The Premier, first woman to hold that office in Quebec, will be the ultimate decision maker and her paramount goal is to succeed on the next referendum for secession. During her second watch. Which, in a province like Quebec, chronically fickle in its elections, might not happen. It's a matter of moving quickly to position herself to win a majority in the next election. Then she'll stand a good chance of having the referendum pass. *Moving quickly—that's the key.* The Premier can't afford the time it will take to coordinate the activities of several different players in the James Bay project. It has to start soon and show immediate results that the Premier can point to as unambiguously hers and hers alone. Dieter pours himself another cup of coffee in an act of self-congratulation. Next time it will be champagne.

Coffee cup in hand, Dieter puts a call through to Peter Devlin's office in Stamford. It's late, but someone picks up. It's not Peter. When you're CEO of one of the world's largest conglomerates you always have someone around to answer your phone, no matter the time of day or night. Dieter explains who he is and that he has vital information for the CEO regarding a huge contract that Global Energy is in the running for. The person won't give Dieter a number to reach Peter. Dieter leaves his own number for Peter to call back and has to wait only a few minutes before his office phone rings. Caller ID provides no clue who it is—the number has been blocked.

"Hello Dr. Graber, this is Peter Devlin. Why did you call me at this late hour? I'm on my way home in a blinding snowstorm."

"Thank you for responding to my message, Mr. Devlin. Sorry to hear about the weather. You should be in Montreal. It's a gorgeous evening here. But let me get right down to business. I want to discuss James Bay with you."

"Doesn't that pose an antitrust problem for us? I don't think we should proceed without advice of counsel."

"There's no problem if we're discussing a partnership."

"Partnership?"

"A joint proposal."

"Why would I be interested? You must know that Global Energy will succeed on its own."

"Yes, but only for part of the project. Together, we can make a case sufficiently compelling that the government will award us the entire project. Split right down the middle."

"That could happen without a joint venture."

"Possibly, but it would be much less likely— Besides, no single company can match our combined strength. Together, we'll close out everybody else."

"Do you think the government might be willing to award a consortium of our two companies the whole deal?"

"Precisely."

"They never do that on a large project."

"This is different. It's complex. Progress is critical to the government— They won't want to waste time coordinating efforts among different players." There is a long pause. "Peter?— "

"It's an intriguing idea. Let me discuss it with my people. I'll get back to you."

"Time is short. The RFP deadline is mid-February."

"I know. I'll call you tomorrow by noon."

"Please do— If you decide to move ahead with this, we should travel to Germany for you to talk it over with our Managing Director."

"If it comes to that, I can leave the day after tomorrow."

"We could fly together and flesh out our plan on the plane."

"Please don't get ahead of yourself. *If* we go ahead with this and you can get down to Connecticut, you can join me on my company's jet."

Hah! A personal jet at his disposal. Must be a G-5. I'll have one of those when I'm finally Managing Director. My father won't be able to object.

PART TWO

CHAPTER 15

The last day of February. Past the dead of winter. Ralph is thankful he's not one of the dead. He could easily have been . . .

It had snowed heavily in New York City before dawn on the first day of the month. From his West Side condominium overlooking Central Park, he could see that work crews hadn't yet cleared the paths. What few cabs were out would be taken. He put on his winter boots and tied the tops tight.

Though the snow was light and fluffy, trudging knee deep proved tough. Before he reached the park's Center Drive exit to 59th Street, he was out of breath. Sweeping the snow from a bench, he sat down to rest for a few minutes, watch his exhalations condense into clouds that hung in the air in front of his face. No wind, no sound, the city stilled momentarily. The only thing breaking the silence was the steady drumbeat of his heart. He had to get into better shape if he was going to carry his fair share on the canoe trip less than five months away. More visits to the gym. More time on the treadmill with ankle weights. Maybe a little less on the rowing machine. Lower body strength, stamina. The portaging would be more difficult than the paddling.

By the time he arrived at the office, everyone was waiting in the conference room for him to start the monthly staff meeting. Toronto was on the other end of the conference line. He took his seat at the head of the table and asked the partners to describe the assignments taken on since the last meeting. He invited Toronto to talk about the Canadian Government's moratorium on the development of offshore wind farms along the Great Lakes. Would it affect offshore plans in the Gaspé? The Quebec Minister of Natural Resources, what was her view? Would there be any spillover across the border to the Cape Wind project?

"Why are you interested in the Cape Cod project?" asked Mark. "We're not involved."

Mark, ten years younger, always the realist. Not enough of a dreamer. Mark couldn't have built this firm. But he runs it superbly, even as they get stretched thinner and thinner with a burgeoning caseload, environmentalists everywhere flexing their muscles, buoyed by their recent court victories. "Not yet," Ralph said, "but I had drinks with the CEO of Global Energy last night. He's figured out how to get his company involved. He thinks we can help break the logjam."

"Haven't we got our hands full fighting off Block Island's residents?"

"It's never a good idea to turn down our most important client. They're at the forefront— "

And all of a sudden Ralph couldn't breathe. It felt as if a giant hand were crushing his chest . . .

Waking up in the mornings is different now because there's no need for Ralph to get up early, no place to rush to, nowhere at all to go if he doesn't want to. His cardiologist has made it clear there's no need for him to retire. Slow down a little, allocate more work to his partners. He doesn't have to hand over the reins to the firm he's built. But that's what he's chosen to do. He's grown tired of it. Mary Ann sensed that fatigue. Hervé too. And Dieter. And Lynn, in her own way, called him out on it, amazed that he could continue arguing the "wrong side" of cases. Ralph told Mark that he'd be available through May to help with the transition, but not to count on seeing him much. Ralph hasn't gone back to the office yet. He's given serious thought to committing an act of high treason: crossing to the other side and donning the mantle of a conservationist, not necessarily embracing the cause in Lynn's county, but at least fighting the Cape Wind project across the Sound from his Cape Cod home.

While in the hospital, he contacted Lynn, eager to find out how things were going with Jean-Pierre, presumptive traitor to their marriage. He was eager to hear the news but had to exercise restraint to avoid telegraphing his interest. He camouflaged it by asking a favor: would she mind visiting his parents while he was under orders not to travel for a month? She graciously agreed and visited them twice, calling him afterwards with a report each time. Without his asking, Lynn brought up her Christmas holiday and expressed some reservations about reuniting with Jean-Pierre. But when asked, she wouldn't identify anything particular to suggest it wouldn't work out. He decided not to tell her that he has been considering part-time work as a lawyer for a nonprofit organization; he'd play that card later. However, after some serious thought, meticulously evaluating the pros and cons, he'd decided to play the Monique card, rationalizing that the disclosure was less a self-serving act than it was protecting her against further damage. He purchased a disposable cell phone, sent a single text, *Beware Monique*, then discarded the phone after removing and destroying its memory card. He felt like a criminal, but the possibilities that that move opened up were exhilarating.

Close calls focus attention on what matters. One month after his heart episode, one week after he told his partners that his retirement would be effective in a few months, Ralph awoke late one morning and decided to take charge of his love life. Lynn was his first priority, but until he could loosen Jean-Pierre's grip on her, he would create other opportunities. One of those might allow him to move past his obsession with Lynn or, at the very least, make her realize that he wouldn't be available forever. He placed a call to the Ministry of Natural Resources in Quebec City, reached the main receptionist, and was redirected to the Minister's assistant.

"Bonjour, this is Ralph Mackenzie. I would like to speak with Monique Beaumont."

"Do you have business with the Ministry, sir?"

"I do not. This is a personal call."

"The Minister takes personal calls only on her cell phone. Do you have that number?"

"I'm afraid I don't."

"Please let me take a message for her."

"Thank you. Please tell her that Ralph Mackenzie called. We met at McGill's Faculty Club last month. I'm sure she'll remember." He left his cell number.

Instead of waiting for a call that might never come, he puts on a pair of jeans, a turtleneck, and a warm suede jacket and heads for MoMA on a route that will take him through Central Park. Out the window of his condominium it looks like spring. It isn't. It's winter trying hard to become spring. Despite the cold, he stops along the way and sits on an empty bench to consider what he'll say if Monique happens to return his call. Has he lost his mind? Sort of. He's let it out of its cage to fly with the few birds he can see above the bare trees. His thoughts are up there somewhere in *The Song of the Vowels*, that Miró print today extending its reach beyond his office. Whoosh. Sixty-three suddenly wound all the way back to adolescence. On the verge of asking a pretty girl for a date. He removes a glove and takes out his vibrating cell phone. *Private Caller.*

"Hello, this is Ralph."

"Hello, this is Monique. My assistant said your call was personal."

"Yes." Ralph pauses, attempting to rein his thoughts back in from the sky where they've suddenly scattered.

"Ralph, are you there?"

"Yes— Sorry— I'm in Central Park— It's windy."

"Why did you call?"

"I want to invite you to dinner."

"Why is that?"

"I felt a chemistry in our brief meeting."

Monique is silent for a few seconds. "Then why did it take you six weeks to call?"

"I had a minor heart attack."

He knows he's caught her off guard. And why shouldn't she be? What kind of kook makes a call like this? To a cabinet minister no less?

She recovers quickly. "I don't know what to say."

"Say yes."

"Give me a reason to."

"I'm a respectable and interesting person."

"It wouldn't look proper," she says. "You run a law practice contrary to the interests of the environment that my office is charged to protect."

"I did until a week ago. I've retired." It isn't going badly. She hasn't said no. "At worst it'll be a pleasant evening away from the concerns of work."

"That sounds more compelling than it should be."

"Is that a yes?"

Another pause. "Yes— Sure, why not?— When and where did you have in mind?"

"As soon as is convenient for you. Anywhere you like— Montreal, Toronto, Quebec, New York. You choose."

"You're able to travel?"

"The doctor has cleared me to go wherever I want."

"Ordinarily I'd say Montreal, but it happens that I have business in New York next Monday. Would that suit you?"

"I'll pick a restaurant and get back to you— Would you mind giving me your cell number? You appear only as *Private Caller*."

"Appropriate, don't you think?" Monique laughs at her own little joke and gives him her number.

Ralph hadn't been able to summon his birds back into their cage and yet it worked out fine, better than he had any reason to expect. Now those birds are flying free. Soaring. He knows exactly where he'll spend the afternoon. With Brancusi's birds. The collection of those sculptures at MoMA. White marble *Maiastra*. A magical creature. Good in marble, better in bronze, like his favorite in Brancusi's *Bird in Space* series, polished to such high luster it seems as bright as the sun. Reflecting the lights of the overhead spots, it could melt the wings of Icarus—in La Musée des Beaux Arts. He's seen Breughel's masterpiece in Brussels, a museum of the same name as one in Montreal that he'll have to visit with Monique— *Stop— Stop making the mistake you always make when you meet a new woman, stop fantasizing how it could play out—* Do women let themselves run free like this beyond all reason? Or do they hold back until they're sure they aren't about to make another big mistake?

❧

Ralph opens his laptop and drafts another letter to Bill and Jack, this one relating the gist of his most recent conversation with Steve. He's decided not to tell the group about his heart procedure because the doctor has said there has not been permanent damage. There won't be any substantive restrictions on his physical activities. Ralph was a bit surprised to hear that—he'd fully disclosed the nature of the canoe trip to his cardiologist, including the difficulty of portages through woods without the benefit of cleared trails. Yet, apart from the requirement of regular exercise and a healthful diet, the cardiologist's only suggestion was to let others share the burden of carrying the canoe when it would otherwise be his turn. Who would know better than his own physician?

After a light lunch and a few revisions to the letter, he addresses and stamps the envelopes, puts on his winter coat and boots—it has snowed again—and takes the stairway down to the lobby of his building where he deposits the envelopes in the mail slot. He rewards himself for the morning's work with a short walk in the park, returning in time for a nap before his dinner with Monique. He's secured a reservation at Orso on Restaurant Row, Italian food for the French Cabinet Minister. He's warned her to be prepared to witness a host of celebrities; the restaurant is a favorite pre-theater haunt of actors and actresses. Generally hard to get a reservation there, even a week in advance, unless you know someone who knows the owner. Ralph does, a woman he used to date, who is still willing to be a go-between in arranging a table for him from time to time. She asked who the lucky woman is. A government official was all he would say.

❧

Ralph introduces Monique to the maître d' and follows her to a table in a nook at the back of the restaurant. "Two glasses of Feuillatte Brut, please," he says to the maître d'.

"I thought you said this place is Italian."

"It is. The only French item on the menu is champagne. When it comes to food, Italian is my favorite."

"Mine too."

Ralph is never comfortable making the small talk expected when meeting someone new. He found it awkward at Café Boulud when getting together with Lynn, someone he knew well in his deep past. Her attitude had made it difficult. He hopes Monique will be kinder. "Did your day go well?"

"Very well. Thank you for asking, but let's not talk business tonight."

Forget smooth icebreakers. Her pronouncement telegraphs a need to control. The words have a slight edge. But her tone doesn't. "Easy for me to comply now that I've retired."

Monique raises her champagne glass. "To your health."

"And yours. Fortunately nothing's off limits for me except marathons and extreme sports."

"That must be a relief."

"It is. Before my heart attack, I'd started planning a canoe trip with old friends. The doctor says I'm as good to go as if nothing had happened."

She asks where the trip will be. He hopes his French doesn't sound too English. "Between Parc du Mont-Tremblant and Parc la Vérend-rye." She doesn't wince.

"You're an outdoors person?"

"I am indeed. And you?"

She recounts a few tales from her summers at Camp Ouareau as a teenager. "Aren't you and your friends a bit old to be carrying canoes and heavy packs? It's not like you're going to plunk yourselves down at a campsite for ten days to sunbathe and drink beer." She laughs.

"We're going to paddle and portage only five to six hours a day. I think we can handle that." Ralph tells her about the near-tragic canoe trip the group took as campers and his subsequent battle with the Rivière Rouge during the high school reunion.

"I don't have stories like yours, but I've always enjoyed canoeing and camping."

"How about kayaking?"

"Never done it. Seems too dangerous."

"I don't mean whitewater. Not the stuff you see at the Olympics. Only lakes and ponds. Easy for someone who knows her way in a canoe."

The waiter waits for a lull in the conversation before taking their orders. Monique asks for Pappardelle alla Bolognese, Ralph the Brasciole di Maiale, and they agree to share an antipasto of Polpo ai Ferri. He selects a Brunello to accompany the main dishes. "Our champagne should go well with the octopus."

Monique nods. "Let's get another glass— Where do you kayak?"

"Long Pond on Cape Cod."

"Do you have a house there?"

"I built one in Chatham on Nantucket Sound. That's my main house."

"You have another?"

"I had to buy one in the neighboring town to get a parking permit for Long Pond."

"You live in New York City and have two houses on the Cape?"

"I rent out the second house year round. It's a real estate investment— "

Little beads of perspiration have formed on his forehead and neck. He dabs at them with his napkin. He's already managed to find risky territory on the date that is his one chance to hit it off with her. "Do you have children?"

"Two girls—Jeannine, sixteen, and Christine, fourteen."

"Do they like to spend time outdoors?"

He lets her talk about teaching her children to ski and spending weekends and holidays with them at Mont-Tremblant in the winter.

"You have a place up there?"

"My ex-husband and I built a chalet."

"A real estate investment?"

"Not really, but I made it part of my divorce settlement."

Divorce is a place he won't let the conversation travel unless she takes it there. She hasn't. "Are you all good skiers?"

"The girls are comfortable on black diamonds. And off-trail, too."

"I haven't skied in a dozen years. I doubt I could keep up with you."

She describes her daughter's recent accident. "Jeannine has never been this hobbled. Physical therapy until summer."

She paints a picture of Ralph doing his best to keep up with an impaired Jeannine on the slopes. He laughs. "Maybe I ought to stick to kayaking and sailing."

The waiter serves their entrées and opens the wine. Ralph tastes it and nods. "I have cases of different Brunellos in my wine cellar. You'll have to try them."

"We'll see," she says.

"You've talked about your childhood— " he says. "What would you like to know about me?"

CHAPTER 16

How did I get into this? Monique puts her cell phone back into her purse and sits at her desk stunned. It happened too quickly. A date to look forward to. Precisely what she needs after finally finding the resolve to break up with Jean-Pierre. Virtually a blind date though. All she knows about Ralph is what he looks like—a little taller than her, silver hair, blue eyes. Handsome, a lot younger looking than his age. When she first met him, he appeared to be in good shape. A person in control of exercise and diet. He had those small hollows beneath the cheekbones. Not quite a chiseled face. Maybe an outdoors person like her. But she knows almost nothing about him, only the few facts Jean-Pierre revealed during that last disastrous dinner at the Faculty Club. Until a week ago, Ralph was someone she'd never permit herself to go out with, a lawyer for the same big energy companies lambasting her in the press for imposing a moratorium on hydrofracking. Does that matter? She'll soon find out. What does matter, and it confuses her, it's not like her, who from a young age has been careful, deliberate, not given to impulse, who prefers to analyze charts and tables, equations with their variables and constants, who likes to design and build things to last, it confuses her that she fell that easily into agreeing to meet him. Not for a casual coffee or lunch, mind you, but dinner in New York City at a place of his choosing. How could she have succumbed without a second thought? She doesn't like questions she can't answer. Doesn't like not being in control.

But here she is finding herself liking him. He's willing to open up. He can laugh at himself. He might be fun. Jean-Pierre had been fun in the beginning. Unlike Jean-Pierre, Ralph is available. Yet he's not French Canadian and not separatist. A pity. It will be difficult—maybe impossible—to have a long-term relationship with someone who doesn't share her culture and philosophy. Though she doesn't want to turn their date into the grilling typical of a job interview, there's no point wasting time starting something that's destined to fail. With his comments about kayaking and wine, he's already signaled his interest, but this might end up being their only date. *Make no mistake,* she admonishes herself: *This is a date, and it's a chance you shouldn't throw away, but tonight you'll have to break your rule about mixing business with pleasure. You'll have to risk ruining the evening.*

"How did you know?" she asks Ralph.

"Know what?"

"That your parting shot at the Faculty Club would open up everything for you."

"I'm sorry— I don't know what you mean."

"À *la prochaine fois.* You looked straight at me when you said it."

"Yes I did. Purely inadvertent, I suppose. I meant it for Jean-Pierre. It was a dig."

"At his relationship with the former Premier?"

"Partly. But more a challenge. That's all I want to say for now."

"You said you grew up in St-Jean not far from where I was raised in Longueil. Very few English in those cities— "

"You're wondering what it was like to be an English Canadian immersed in a sea of French Canadians?"

"Yes."

"Not as pleasant as this."

"Thank you, but seriously— "

"It seems you'd know— You mentioned Camp Ouareau and I know you graduated from McGill. You must have been one of few French girls in a sea of English."

"And also an English boarding school, but I asked you first."

Ralph describes growing up in a polarized culture in St-Jean, part of a ten percent English minority scattered throughout an otherwise French-Canadian town. He talks about his grandfather's and father's prejudices, especially the attitude of his father's father toward Roman Catholics. Ralph characterizes his own youth as English Protestants versus French Catholics. Going to Sunday School for the sole purpose of developing a plan with his friends for that afternoon's English-French football game in the public park. Not merely who would play what position, but who would take out whom on the other side. Touch football that inevitably turned tackle before the end of the game. Always someone injured.

"Didn't your parents object?"

"Our mothers more than our fathers."

"Did you have any French-Canadian friends?"

"Our next-door neighbor's girl was my age. We played together until we went off to different grade schools."

"In high school?"

"A few French-Canadian boys. Their parents took them out of the local Catholic schools to get a better education and then enroll at McGill."

That statement resonates with her. Her parents had done the same for her, and though the situation is much improved, she's done the same for her girls. "Any French-Canadian girls?"

"One—my partner on the debate team."

"Was McGill more of the same?"

"I had no French-Canadian friends there. We didn't even think much about the French until the FLQ bombings. And the kidnappings."

"And the McGill français demonstration?" she asks. She wasn't yet born at the time of its occurrence, but the event was part of the lore growing up. More than a symbolic goal for the French.

"That stayed peaceful, but nobody was comfortable knowing that right over the mountain Université de Montréal wanted to rise up and consume McGill."

She could have let it rest there, maybe should have, but felt compelled to press on. If there were any possibility with Ralph she had to know where he stood on the politics of the day. "What did you think of the French cause?"

"I lost an English girlfriend to a leader of that movement." Ralph's gaze appears distant, as if he's reliving a bitter experience. "I kept my nose to the grindstone and ignored the unrest. I was an A student, not an activist."

"Must one exclude the other?"

"I suppose not— I knew I'd be heading off to graduate school in the States— It wasn't worth it to get invested in campus politics."

She hates how she's transformed the pleasant evening into a criminal inquiry if not an outright inquisition, but Ralph doesn't seem to mind. With his charming manner, he tolerates her questions even if he doesn't like them. She suspects he'd prefer to talk about the struggles between the French and English than about the girl he lost. "How do you feel about someone who grew up in surroundings different from yours?"

"You mean French Catholic and a member of the Parti Québécois?"

"I guess that's what it amounts to."

"I try to see people for other than their politics."

"Seriously? With your background, that's hard to believe."

"I'm a lawyer."

"So?"

"If you want to succeed as a lawyer, you get used to understanding the other side. Sometimes you can't help but empathize with it."

She takes another sip of wine. "This is good. I guess you know your wines."

"If they're Italian."

She holds her glass up to the light and looks at the distortion of Ralph's face through it. She should ask about his wine cellar. Tonight, she should be acting more like a woman, not a prosecuting attorney. But there's too much history between his people and hers to drop her guard and relax. *Sorry, Ralph, you probably deserve better.* "Don't you think it's easy to say you can accept someone not like you when you don't have to live with her 24/7?"

Ralph appears surprised by the comment. "I thought you'd rather talk about wine and Italian food. Maybe cooking a meal together."

"I would prefer to do that, but— Tell me why someone who likes canoeing and kayaking— "

"Decided to become a lawyer arguing cases against environmentalists like you?"

"Yes."

"My old girlfriend asked me the same thing when we met up again six months ago— Hey, do you mind if I change the topic?"

"Not at all, but let me ask you one more question first." She'd like to pursue his mention of the girlfriend, but decides to save that for later. If there is a later. She knows she's pushing her luck. He's checked the time, probably wants to end the date soon. She better ask now. It would have reared its head at some point anyway. Ralph puts his napkin on the table and looks straight into her eyes. She can't hold his gaze and looks down into her lap instead, rearranges her napkin.

"Doesn't it bother you that I'm an elected representative of the separatist party?"

"No more than I hope it doesn't bother you that I'm not."

"Touché."

"Look Monique— " He sounds exasperated. "I don't view you as extremist. Are you telling me I should?"

"That seems to be a matter of perspective, doesn't it? You know that most English Canadians do view us as extremists."

Ralph takes a deep breath and sees her brace herself. "Since you've been pressing the topic, I presume you'll permit me a tiny speech."

"As you English say, fire away."

"Strap yourself in."

"I'm ready for anything." Okay, she's asked for it and now she's going to hear a closing statement from the polished lawyer.

Ralph finishes off the wine in his glass and leans back in his chair. An arrogant pose. Strike one. The English are about to hold forth.

"I'm sure you believe the English dispossessed the French of their rightful position of prominence in Quebec. As you were growing up, your parents probably spoke of subjugation by the English minority. I haven't heard you talk about your political views, but I'm sure you have a foot in both worlds. You're the champion of the province's natural resources. Whether you like it or not, you see yourself doing good for all citizens of Quebec, even the English. Am I right?"

"Essentially." That's the politically correct answer, the one she'd give in a public interview. It comes naturally.

"I'm sure we disagree about the long-term viability of an independent Quebec— In my opinion, the Parti Québécois is generally too optimistic, at times wildly so, about the future of Quebec as a sovereign nation or in a sovereignty association with the rest of Canada— That said, how I feel about the co-existence of separatists and non-separatists should make you feel comfortable— " Ralph says he respects reasonable people who are thoughtful, no matter their political, cultural, or religious disposition. Says that in his work as a lawyer, he has had to argue positions he didn't fully believe in, and to win at those, even the ones he did believe in strongly, he has had to put himself in his opponents' shoes. "I came to understand that all well-considered positions have value. It's *respect* that makes things work. People with different beliefs can get along if they choose to."

"That's noble, altruistic—and utterly unrealistic—plain naïve," Monique says, no disgust in her tone, merely incredulity that someone as successful in business could make such a disingenuous claim without cracking a smile. Strike two. "I guess you could say *politically correct*."

"I'd call it enlightened— End of speech. Did I answer your question?— Did I pass the test?"

"It wasn't a test. Only a gut check of whether we might be compatible."

"The best way to find out is by kayaking on Long Pond together. Or cycling on the Cape Cod Rail Trail. Not this dissection of our differences."

"You're right."

"And I thought you said you make it a practice to separate your political life from your personal life."

"I do generally, but how can I if we might begin seeing each other?"

"Okay, since you've pestered me with your sensitive questions, let me ask you one. Does it bother you that I'm not fluent in French?"

Now he's asking the questions. He has truly turned the tables on her. And though she does finally want to move on to less potentially inflammatory subjects, it's only fair that she indulge him briefly because he has been willing to tolerate her penetrating questions all evening. "I think you're missing the richness of a different way of expressing yourself— "

"And that's not a politically correct statement?— " says Ralph.

She tries to gauge the expression on his face. It's blank. The lawyer betrays no emotion. Another strike? "How much does language matter? We don't speak each other's professional language—I'm an engineer and you're a lawyer. I'm sure that doesn't bother you."

Ralph shakes his head no. "It doesn't. But you support the continued enforcement of Quebec's Language Bill, don't you?"

She doesn't flinch. Here it is at last. The political correctness evaporates. He's moving in for the kill. She gives what must seem to him as the standard catechism, but it's a catechism she happens to believe. "It rectifies a centuries-old discrimination."

Ralph moves to the edge of his chair and leans toward her. From arrogant to confrontational. "Does it? What discrimination? Did the English force the French to go to school in English? To speak English in places of business? To mark the signage for their businesses in English more prominently than French?"

"Absolutely not," she says. "That's not the point."

"The point is that the Language Bill doesn't only make discrimination legal; it insists on it. I think it betrays a lack of respect."

"And you've already said that respect is paramount," she says, completely unable to suppress a snide tone. She's let him get under her skin. He's proving better at this than she is, though she won't confess that to him.

"Let me say that I certainly understand the passion of the times that led to the passage of Bill 101 three decades ago— "

Monique cuts him off. "Did the political situation in Quebec force you to situate your Canadian office in Toronto instead of Montreal?"

The question seems to take Ralph by surprise. Territory he's likely never talked about openly, the lawyer always careful to say the right thing, especially in front of his Quebec clients. Is she now one of those?

"Toronto offered a more central location for our business. Many of our clients are based in Alberta."

"They're not your clients anymore." She's finally willing to let him off the hook. He'll never admit he's been skewered. She can see that.

"No, they're not."

"It must be difficult to retire from a practice you built yourself."

"I was ready to retire and didn't realize it."

It's an honest and humble admission. A man in touch with himself. Erase one of the strikes. "Enough of this," she says. "I'm sorry. My fault entirely— Tell me, do you still think we can get along?"

"The French and English?"

"No, silly, you and I."

"I find you fascinating," he says. He looks at his watch again. "I wonder if you'd like to have a digestif. Where does a government minister stay in the city?"

"The Pierre this trip. Not usually at such nice places."

"Then let's wind down in the Two E Bar," he says. "Afterwards it'll be an easy cab ride for me to the West Side."

When they arrive at The Pierre, Monique excuses herself to go to her room. She returns in a green satin dress and joins Ralph in the lounge. He's waiting with two cognacs. Handing her one, he says, "I hope I made a good choice."

"It's as if you knew."

"Only a hunch." Ralph looks her up and down as if he's never met her. "Why did you change out of that stunning black dress?"

"Don't you like this one?"

"As much if not more— Hard to say— "

Erase the other strike. "I spilled a little sauce on the other one."

They direct the conversation back to their joint passion for the outdoors. Ralph describes the house he's built on the Cape and suggests she visit.

"Won't it be too cold?"

"Off-season is the best time. No summer hordes to deal with. Why don't you spend a weekend with me at Brave House?"

"Brave House?"

"Cape Codders name their dwellings. Maybe I should have called it Insane Place."

"Why?"

"Its foundation is only twenty feet above sea level and three hundred feet back from the high-tide mark. Even with my breakwall, a monster storm could sweep the house into the ocean."

"Then why did you build it there?"

"There's no more spectacular view of the Sound. From the house, I see both sunrise and sunset. At night there are so many stars visible the sky appears splotched with freckles."

"We can't kayak in this weather," she says.

"We can bike. Or bundle up and walk the beach. Cook up a storm in my kitchen. Visit art galleries. Shop. Plenty to do."

She sniffs her cognac without taking a taste. "My girls usually come home from school on the weekends."

"Doesn't your ex take them sometimes?"

"He does— I guess I could come down in a few weeks."

"That's settled then— Let's toast a wonderful evening together." They touch glasses and finish their cognacs. As she moves to get up and thank him for a wonderful evening, Ralph motions to the waiter for another round. "Tell me about your place at Tremblant. It must be close to where my canoe trip begins."

She tells him that she and her ex built the chalet ten years ago when the girls were learning to ski. Post and beam. A "great room" with a cathedral ceiling, a fieldstone fireplace, and a wall of picture window overlooking the lake and ski trails. Huge kitchen with a quartz-top center island, copper pots and pans hanging from the ceiling. Straight out of an architectural magazine.

"Do you like to cook?" Ralph asks.

"All the time— The time I don't seem to have   ”

The second round of cognacs arrives. They toast again, this time to her upcoming visit to Brave House.

"What are your specialties?"

"Almost everything Italian."

"Not French?"

"Too rich for my taste."

"Wonderful— I keep my wine cellar at Brave House. A proper wine for every Italian dish. Aglianico, Barbaresco, Barolo, Brunello, Chianti Classico, you name it.

"The A, B, C's of Italian wine— Sounds perfect."

"Did your ex like to cook?"

"He preferred to eat what I made for him. He was always too busy with work."

"What does he do?"

"He's a partner at a law firm in Montreal with a largely English clientele. Can you believe it?" They both laugh.

Ralph puts his head back on the armchair and listens to Monique hold forth. She lets him poke his way into the territory of her marriage and its failure. The evening has turned into a superstorm, the type that could sweep away his Brave House. She's overwhelmed by the pace at which they've covered their personal histories, as if there might never be another opportunity to tell them, as if a second date might be too risky if the background checks aren't thorough enough on the first. Without a concrete agenda to guide her, she feels untethered, but the weightlessness feels good. Not like the end of her relationship with Jean-Pierre. Even with this much information shared in this one evening, there are still many unanswered questions. Who is this person whose past is vastly different from hers? How can it be that they click? How much is her loneliness impelling her? Does it matter? Given their profound political differences, is a long-term relationship possible? After talking about Henri and wondering aloud why anybody would get married, she surprises herself by asking, "Why have you never married?"

"Too busy working eighty-hour weeks in a large law firm. Then building my own practice."

His answer comes too quickly. He's been asked this question before. On other first dates no doubt. "No serious relationships?"

"A few. The last woman I was with wanted to marry me, but I couldn't see myself married to her. A silly view, I suppose. We'd been living together for three years."

"Is that what I'm getting into here?— Someone who can't commit?— "

"I can commit— That relationship was more convenient than right."

Again too smooth an answer. "Any girlfriends in college?"

"Yes— " He interrupts himself and looks to her to bail him out, but she says nothing. " —We were childhood friends and dated in high school and college. I thought she was— "

She waits for him to continue, but he doesn't. After watching him struggle to find words, she says, " —Your once-in-a-lifetime soul mate?"

"I guess."

"Why are you still trying? You seem to be doing fine living alone."

"It grows old."

"Maybe at the Cape you can tell me about your disappointments in love."

"There was only one."

It's well past midnight before they run out of topics in their mad rush to discovery. Ralph apologizes for keeping her up late. "I'm sorry. This was selfish of me. I don't have anything I have to do tomorrow. You do."

"Nothing that tonight didn't make better."

They leave the bar and make their way to the coat check. "Thank you," she says. "It's been wonderful. I look forward to seeing you in a few weeks— But please do one thing for me."

"What?"

She reaches up with both hands and musses his neatly parted hair. "You're even more handsome with a windswept look. Like you've been out sailing."

"Goodnight, Monique." He steps outside and into a cab. She watches it drive two blocks south down Fifth Avenue and turn west onto Central Park South.

CHAPTER 17

The weekends with Lynn are good, but here he is now, as usual every weekday evening, sitting alone in his kitchen revising a chapter in the manuscript of the book he's writing with Georges, all the things he's looking forward to—Jules' prom, the summer road trip—seemingly infinitely far away while what he misses most is close by. It's been three months without Monique. He regrets acceding to her request—*Who am I fooling? It was more like her demand*—that he wait until the end of summer when he'll know whether his marriage can be repaired. This separation from Monique is worse than when Lynn and Jules left him. Imagine thinking of it as a separation, as if he and Monique are married. *Maybe we should be.* It's not the allure of what he once enjoyed and then squandered; it's what's now forbidden. Like an excommunication—*yes, that's right. I can't go to mass, can't celebrate her body.* True, he does miss the sex with Monique, but even more he misses the discussions over the future of Quebec that he can no longer share with the woman who will be part of shaping that future. He misses the challenge of a political campaign, the excitement of a rally, the grand speeches that will be coming, the anticipation of victory. Has he made the wrong choice in thinking he can reassemble the puzzle of his marriage? Lynn was right—their years apart have changed her but not him. How did she say it? *The film of your life has jammed in the projector while mine is still playing.* She's left him behind. Their separation should never have happened—he sees now that he was the sole culpable party—but it has, and they simply can't put it back the way it was. Then the fracture with Monique at the Faculty Club. Ralph's sudden appearance jarred him and completely spooked Monique. The rest of the evening spun out of control and crashed. It shouldn't have ended that way.

Jean-Pierre throws back a shot of his favorite cognac. It sears his esophagus all the way down, precisely what he needs but better when two can experience it together. He breaks down, recovers, then can't help himself.

"Jean-Pierre— I hadn't expected to hear from you this soon."

"I hope you're not disappointed."

"Surprised— Why are you calling?"

"I've thought about our last conversation, what you said you wanted from me, and how badly I responded— "

"And?"

"And how I'd like to have dinner with you to start fresh."

"Will it play out any differently?"

"I think it will."

"Jean-Pierre, please— "

"I'm sorry I hurt you."

"What's changed?"

"You'll see— Let's talk— Can we have dinner?"

"Not at the Faculty Club."

"How about my place? We could make Osso Bucco."

"Too risky."

"Why?"

"You know."

"Let's go out then. *Le Petit Italien?*"

"Too many people go there."

"It's one of your favorite places."

"It used to be."

"Please. It will help us remember the good times."

"Okay. But don't think you can persuade me to come to your place afterwards for a cognac."

"We know where that would end up."

❧

Monique is waiting out front, looking in Jean-Pierre's direction. Or maybe looking around her to make sure she doesn't see anyone she recognizes other than him.

"I'm not sure I should do this."

"Hello to you too," he says. He leans in to kiss her on the cheek. She pulls away. Then sitting across from him at the table, she refuses to look into his eyes. Or talk. She wants him to start.

"It's your nickel," she says.

"I have missed you."

"You miss the sex."

"I miss our conversations. I no longer feel plugged into the heart of what's going on in the government."

"You feel that I'm here only as the Minister and you want to talk politics."

"You know that's not what I mean."

"What do you mean?"

"That what we talk about matters. We can help shape history in this province."

It comes across as an answer he's rehearsed to a question he knew she'd ask. There is no personal touch, nothing empathetic. Even he can hear it in his voice.

"That sounds clinical. I'm not one of your graduate students— "

"You know me better than that."

"Do I? Do you know me? Do you know what I want from you?"

"You want me to divorce Lynn and marry you."

"I want you to show you care. Try bringing flowers."

"I do that."

"Not tonight you didn't. It's never the first thing on your mind. You're absorbed in your own agenda." She pauses barely long enough to catch her breath. "And how about this? Ask how Jeannine is coming along with her therapy."

This sounds exactly like his conversation on the beach at Sandbanks with Lynn. *Am I that transparent?* Despite an effort not to, he reacts to her words as if they constitute a personal attack. Why is she being vicious? Maybe she's had a particularly difficult day. How could he know? They no longer talk.

The waiter, who's been standing nearby to catch a lull in their conversation, steps in quickly to take their orders. "Osso Bucco for each of us. Sparkling water. No wine, thank you." The waiter scurries away.

"How many times have I told you this?— I bet Lynn has too."

Jean-Pierre wipes his brow slowly with the back of his hand and tries to compose himself. "Let's start over— Monique, I've missed you. I can't imagine my life without you."

"Too bad you needed prompting— I wish I could believe you."

"You don't believe me?"

"I do believe you. It's what you haven't— "

"What haven't I said?"

"That you feel the same way about Lynn. You can't imagine your life without her. I don't think you understand— It's either her or me— Are you ready to get a divorce?"

"Now is the worst time. Jules' prom and graduation are coming up in June. Then the family holiday in July."

"No divorce then?"

"Not yet— "

"Sounds like *not ever* to me."

"I've been trying to work it out with Lynn."

"A divorce?"

"No."

"Instead of asking me to dinner, you should have said you'd let me know when you're ready to make a life with me. That's what you promised at the Faculty Club."

"I don't know when that will be."

"That's the problem. It will never happen."

"But I miss you terribly. I spend my week thinking about you."

"And I'm sure you love me."

"I do."

"Then you should have the guts to tell Lynn that."

"I'm afraid what it would do to Jules."

"That's weak."

"Don't you care what happens to him?"

"Sure I do— That's not the point— The point is you're not ready to give up either Lynn or me."

She's right. He hasn't thought this through. What on earth has he been thinking about since they broke up? She continues the conversation without him. As if he's not there. It's clearly a monologue she's been waiting to deliver.

"At least I had the guts to divorce my husband."

"Your situation was different."

"I feel sorry for you. You want too much and you'll end up with nothing— I also feel sorry for Lynn."

"I doubt that."

"You haven't been honest with her."

"What? You expect me to tell her about us?"

"She probably suspects. She's a woman after all."

"She has no reason to."

"I'm sure Jules has mentioned something."

"You keep saying that— ”

"Look. *I* can see it. Why can't *you*? You're thinking only of yourself. Not me, not Lynn. You should have brought flowers. You should have asked about Jeannine. What an idiot I am. At the hospital I wanted you there instead of Henri."

The waiter sets down their entrées and a large bottle of sparkling water, then vanishes.

"There's more, Jean-Pierre. You're not the only person in my life. I've met someone else."

He puts the forkful of food about to enter his mouth back on his plate. "Who?"

"None of your business."

"Tell me— Is he one of your colleagues?"

"No. He's not even a separatist. How about that!" Monique takes her first taste. "How's your Osso Bucco?"

"Not as good as usual. How's yours?"

"Better than ever. I've always loved this place."

That's exactly when it struck him. He would lose her if he didn't do something. Here, right here. Now, right now. It was as if time had come to a virtual stop for his benefit. As if a benevolent god had interceded at the moment of his impending loss to let him collect his thoughts and regroup his forces to meet the coming assault. Jean-Pierre looked across the table at Monique and, for the first time in a long while, noticed what she was wearing. Items he had bought for her. Were they a tribute to him or a test to see if he'd notice? It was eerie, this dichotomy of various objects rearing their heads and sticking their tongues out at him. Spitting at him a jumble of words from the book he'd recently finished on philosophy and quantum mechanics, despite Jules' advice to stop reading it because he had no clue. The concepts of quantum mechanics he found enticing. Like how he could be here and in an alternate universe at the same time. Or wished he could be at this very instant. But now, right now, he saw the quantum entanglement disappear before his eyes. Felt the wave function of his love life collapse. No more superposition of Lynn and Monique. Only Monique. It was intoxicating, this way of looking at things. It rendered everything suddenly clear. She was looking at him oddly. He hadn't said a word for a minute and she was about to get up. Walk right out of his life for good.

"I know exactly the right kind."

"What are you talking about?"

"Flowers. Peonies. You love peonies."

"They're my favorite."

"I want to hear all about Christine and Jeannine. I should have been the one with you at the hospital."

"Jean-Pierre, why are you toying with me?"

"I'm not, Monique. I'm deadly serious. I will tell Lynn that we're going to get a divorce. I will find a way to handle it with Jules. I'll tell them tomorrow. Lynn first, then Jules. I will. I'll show Jules that I will still be in his life—science fair, prom, graduation, family holiday, send-off to Germany. All of it. But not married to Lynn."

"How do you expect me to believe you?"

"I don't. But you will see." Monique begins to well up. "Can you do one thing for me?" he says.

"What?"

"Tell the guy you met that it's over between you and him."

CHAPTER 18

The Minister says she's surprised to see two large companies join forces on the James Bay project. To the assembled staff of the Ministry and Hydro-Québec, Peter Devlin explains that Global Energy and International Wind Technologies have other cooperative ventures under discussion, including research and development, not only for wind turbines, but also for voltage transformers and power transmission. He says that joint projects in countries other than Quebec have been planned. Monique smiles at Peter's implication that Quebec is a country. Dieter presents a tentative schedule for ramping up production facilities in the province for both companies. Hervé from Frontière—at Dieter's insistence, the name of the company has been changed to French, an appellation appropriate for a company whose principal installation will be in Quebec's hinterland—and his counterpart Jacques from Énergie Globale speak only in French, summarizing the expansion plans and how those will feed into the project at James Bay. Both Peter and Dieter stress that the implementation timetable for James Bay will in no way depend on how quickly they can grow their operations in Quebec—the combined production capacity of their plants in the United States and Germany is already sufficient to fulfill 100% of the project's needs. The Minister poses several questions relating to the risk to which the Ministry and Hydro-Québec will be exposed if the joint venture falls apart. Peter answers that their proposal has been structured as a joint obligation in the legal sense, meaning that if one party fails to hold up its end of the bargain for whatever reason the other party must complete the project on time within the originally agreed-upon money terms.

"With our proposal you will have in one group the best that each of us can offer," Peter says, looking directly at Monique. "Énergie Globale has more experience in building generators. That is our core strength as you already know from your hydroelectric facilities. Frontière is known to manufacture the best wind towers and turbine blades in the world. Dr. Graber's designs are unsurpassed for durability and reliability."

"I understand, but I'm curious why you didn't each offer a separate proposal, especially if each of you is convinced you could handle the entire project."

"A great question," says Peter. "I'm trying to say, and obviously not well enough, that the combined strengths of our companies will be better for you than either alone. Why have two different sets of five hundred towers for Phase 1 when you could have a thousand identical towers combining the strongest features of each company's design? This is a case where one plus one is more than two. What we offer together is unmatched by any other company in the world. And you'll only have to deal with the management of a single entity, not two or more. That will be much less taxing on your administration."

"What happens to Quebec if you take on too many joint ventures elsewhere and promise the same aggressive delivery schedule? Won't we suffer unacceptable delays?"

"Our independent track records prove that we each run our businesses prudently. We meet deadlines. We don't overcommit. That won't change as we undertake joint proposals. Any failure would damage our reputation. That you find our schedule aggressive is a good thing because *we* feel it's realistic."

"But won't you experience delays that derive solely from the novelty of joining your two enterprises for this endeavor?"

"I understand that one might expect that kind of difficulty from any joint venture, especially a new one, each partner getting used to working with the other. We've anticipated this question and have a two-part answer. First, hoping that we'll be awarded the mandate, we've already made great progress in establishing a project timeline and have identified what might otherwise have been bottlenecks. We believe we've got those worked out and we'll be happy to show you our analysis. Second, we simply can't afford to let you down. This is the single largest wind energy project the world has ever seen. Success is the only acceptable outcome. There is no piece of business in our companies that will receive greater management attention than the installation at James Bay."

"Thank you Mr. Devlin. An illuminating answer." Looking toward Dieter, Monique asks, "I presume you concur with your partner's views."

"Absolutely," Dieter says with as much confidence as he can summon while struggling to suppress his shock at being demoted to a secondary role in the presentation, not only by the Minister but also by Peter. "Madame Minister, it's a 50/50 joint venture—either of us speaks for the other on this project." As he says it, Dieter looks for approval from Peter as much as Monique.

"I must say that your approach is unusual, Dr. Graber. But impressive. Frontière and Énergie Globale both have clean track records working with Hydro-Québec. Thank you, gentlemen. We stand adjourned."

Peter and Dieter confer after the presentation as they drive to Quebec City's airport, Peter for his corporate jet back to Connecticut and Dieter for Frontière's helicopter back to Montreal with Hervé.

"I thought that went well," says Peter.

"Very well," says Dieter. "I think we've given ourselves the best shot to be awarded the entire project."

They shake hands. Peter turns to leave, then turns back to Dieter. "There's something I meant to ask you on the trip back from Germany.

We both drive BMWs. I wonder if you've heard of the performance driving school that BMW offers at its test track in Greenville."

"Yes, but I've never looked into it."

"I've taken the two-day course for the M class. I'm now qualified for their advanced program. I wonder if you'd like to join me for a one-day school in April after we make our final presentation to the Minister."

Dieter is thrilled at the prospect but doesn't want to convey unbridled enthusiasm for Peter's suggestion. In as low-key a tone as he can muster, he says, "I used to drive my car on the track at St-Jovite. It's been a while. Would you consider another two-day course for yourself? Maybe on the first day they'd certify me for the advanced course and then I could join you the second day."

"Let me talk to them. I'll get back to you."

❧

They'd been informed that the Ministry would announce its choices on May 1st. It's now May 10th. Still no word. Friday, the day before Peter is to leave with his wife for two weeks' vacation at one of his favorite spots in Tuscany, a villa nestled among vineyards and olive groves below the town of Cortona. Everything seemed to have gone smoothly at the April presentation for the finalists. Dieter was buoyant afterwards. Even more after his successful weekend with Peter at the BMW school. He can't wait to get back to Munich to trade in his 335i for an M5. No point doing that in Montreal—he'd only get more speeding tickets.

They're all concerned that the call from the Ministry won't come until after Peter leaves for vacation. Jacques Thibault, the CEO of Énergie Globale, has called twice to ask if he should get in touch with his best contact at the Ministry. Peter has said no each time, claiming that when it comes to dealing with the government, patience reaches its pinnacle as a virtue. Not waiting for them to call first would betray anxiety about the outcome. Dieter has also been trying to persuade

Peter to let Hervé contact the Ministry, or if not them, at least Hydro-Québec. Peter won't budge. But he's called Dieter into his office to talk about the situation. Now he's no longer sure what to do. He says he doesn't want to be pestered in Italy, not even for this. He's promised his wife a quiet, restful time with no business. Peter keeps his promises. Dieter asks to be deputized in Peter's absence.

"The Minister regards us as equal partners."

"Dieter, I don't mean any disrespect, but that's not how I read the vibes at either of our meetings with her. Perhaps it's the relative sizes of our companies, or perhaps it's because Global Energy has previously installed equipment at their James Bay site, but I think she'd prefer to deal with me directly."

"Well, I have to tell you that it bothers me not to be considered an equal in this venture. It was my idea. I was the one to approach you."

"All true, but people dynamics can be complicated. They often determine the outcome. Please let me handle this."

Dieter can see that he's not going to change Peter's mind. He approaches it from a different angle. "Then promise me this. If the call comes before you leave today and while I'm still here at your headquarters, you'll include me in the call. You don't have to announce my presence. I promise you I'll say nothing. I need to be part of the final scene for this deal."

Peter hesitates. "You have to understand that I consider that borderline unethical. It's not something I would normally do, but I can see it matters to you. And you're right that you deserve to hear firsthand. But let me make something clear. No matter what you hear, whether you like it or not, whether you disagree with it or not, whether it's about you or not, you will say absolutely nothing. You won't make a sound. You'll kill our prospects if you do and you can be sure I'll call Germany and have you fired."

Dieter has never heard Peter this forceful. He doesn't like the statement that Peter would have no hesitation in talking to his boss to have him removed. But he agrees to Peter's terms because he doesn't want to miss out being there when they learn that they've won. They shake hands. Peter's assistant knocks on the door and says that the call he's been waiting for is holding for him. Peter looks at Dieter and puts a finger to his lips. Then he connects the call through his conference phone.

"Hello?"

"Mr. Devlin?"

"Madame Minister."

"I'm sorry for our delay in getting back to you. We've spent the last ten days deciding how to split the business."

"I'm sure it was a difficult decision."

"There was a difference in view."

"Not surprising," says Peter, "given the scale of the project."

"Your decision to present a joint proposal complicated matters for us."

"I'm sorry to hear that— May I ask in what way?"

"We are comfortable working with Énergie Globale and Frontière, but have only limited experience with International Wind Technologies."

Then Peter surprises both the Minister and Dieter. "I have good news for you."

"I thought I was the deliverer of news today," says the Minister.

"In the interests of full disclosure, I need to let you know that the boards of directors of both Global Energy and International Wind Technologies have approved a merger of the two companies. I will become the CEO of the combined enterprise."

"When are you going to announce it?"

"This weekend, preferably tomorrow when the financial markets are closed worldwide."

Dieter nearly falls off his chair at the conference table. Peter glares at him and puts a finger back to his lips.

"How will the merger affect your joint venture?"

"Only positively. If you select us, you'll be dealing even more cleanly with a single entity. Frontière will be merged into Énergie

Globale and Hervé Boudreau will become its CEO, Jacques Thibault its president."

"What role will Dr. Graber play?"

Peter pauses. Dieter can read his thoughts. *My decision to allow you to overhear the conversation was hasty. But I'm not going to risk signaling that someone else is listening in on our end of the conversation by having you get up and leave. You'll hear the news soon enough anyway.* Dieter is in shock. That alone keeps him silent, although *What the fuck?* is cycling rapidly through his head. He's dying to hear Peter's answer.

"Dieter will relocate to Munich, which has long been his desire, and take charge of R & D for the merged operations." Hearing no response, Peter waits what seems an interminable period before speaking up. "Madame Minister, are you there?"

"Oui, oui— I am here— This piece of news is— Most welcome."

"How so?"

"Off the record, the Premier has authorized me to award anywhere from 50% to 100% of the project to your joint venture— "

"Have you decided?"

"I was leaning toward 70%, but after hearing your news, I am comfortable putting the entire project in your hands, now that I know that you alone will be in charge."

"That's great news— Thank you— I'm glad we have your trust."

"*You* have my trust, Mr. Devlin. And I feel we'll have better control over such an important mission if we can deal not only with a single company but a single person at the top. I assume you have the capacity to handle all of it."

"Without question. As I said in our presentations at your offices, the project will command our full attention."

"Excellent. I will fax you a one-page binder to execute and fax back to us. The complete agreement will be delivered to your office on Monday." She pauses and seems to take a deep breath. "Let me say how happy I am with this result. Congratulations. We look forward to a successful venture."

Dieter can see that Peter is elated, but that he doesn't want to make it obvious. The Minister has maintained a calm tone throughout the conversation. He will too.

"Thank you again. I'm confident you'll be pleased with your selection of us. I'll sign the binder and fax it to you before I leave today. Regarding the other paperwork— "

"Is there a problem?"

"Not at all. Only that I'm leaving tomorrow afternoon for Italy for two weeks' vacation. I'll have my attorneys review the document and overnight it to me for signature."

Dieter grants himself a small pleasure knowing that Peter's vacation won't be as restful as his wife had hoped it would be. He wonders if Peter knows why he's smiling.

"That will be fine. We were the party responsible for the delay— As to announcements, I would like to inform people at the Ministry and Hydro-Québec this evening and prepare a news release for tomorrow. There will be front-page articles in the national newspapers on Monday."

"May I ask you to wait until tomorrow morning to tell anyone except the Premier? We still have to inform our own people about the merger. I'd like them to hear it from me."

You're not fucking kidding, Dieter says under his breath. *We still have to inform our own people? If I hadn't been here in your fucking office, I was going to have been one of those people.*

CHAPTER 19

W hen she sees that it's Jean-Pierre calling, Lynn braces herself for another few days of his hanging around her house . . .

Every Friday afternoon, after her last class, she hurries home to pre-
pare for the weekend, knowing he will arrive ravenous. He expects
a home-cooked meal, eating out not an option because Picton offers
no restaurant equal to any of the good eating establishments in Mon-
treal. Catching up on the week makes Friday evenings pass quickly
and, with or without a bottle of wine, the late-night sex is passionate.
Lying naked afterward touching his body, Lynn wonders how she
survived two and a half years without the feel of it next to hers, only
to be reminded the next day that the blush fades quickly.

Saturday mornings Jean-Pierre reads, prepares lectures, or works
on his book. Lynn used to spend weekends reading and preparing
for the next week's classes, but during the winter she became ab-
sorbed in writing her memoir, documenting the challenges of being
the parent of a transgender child, having to constantly prop up his
self-image while mediating the war between him and his father. Jules
doesn't know that she's writing it; Jean-Pierre keeps asking to take a
peek. She keeps it locked in a drawer of the antique desk in her bed-
room. In the afternoons, Lynn and Jean-Pierre offer to do something
with Jules—a long walk, a movie—but Jules, too, is busy, busier than

ever with the science-fair nationals coming up in April and spending as much time as he can with Amy.

The weekends have settled into a pattern, a routine that brings a degree of comfort, but lacks the spark of excitement Lynn had hoped—naïvely, it now appears—would come with restoring her old life. Her own fault. To find excitement, she should have opened the door to Ralph instead of slamming it shut. During the workweek her thoughts keep drifting to him. A week ago, she couldn't resist calling to see how he was doing. It was an upbeat conversation for the most part—he talked about his upcoming canoe trip and she told him about the family holiday to visit James Bay, the "prize" that Jules won on behalf of the family in their Oscar contest. Then, masking her true question as best she could, she asked, "Are you going to be visiting your parents soon?"

"Not this weekend, but the next."

"Would you like to meet for dinner?"

"I thought you said Jean-Pierre visited every weekend."

"That's a weekend Jules and I are supposed to go to Montreal. I'll make some excuse and stay behind."

Ralph was silent. This was the call she was sure he'd been hoping to receive. She expected him to leap at the opportunity. But she couldn't even hear him breathe. "Ralph?— What's wrong?"

"I was thinking how events often come at us in the wrong order. You know, like a game of Gin Rummy when we draw the card we need after we could have used it."

"Sorry?"

"If you'd made this offer last November or December, even January or February, I'd have jumped at it."

"What's changed?"

"I've met someone."

Her turn to be upstaged. What bad luck. After such a long time with only a few meaningful relationships, Ralph has now met someone?— "Do you think it will go anywhere?"

"You know me— I'm the guy who can't get himself married."

"By your tone, I'm guessing this might be different."

"Who knows? We've had one date. A long evening. But we clicked."

"Damn— Bad timing on my part."

"I don't know. It could be over after she visits me in the Cape."

She hadn't known what to say.

"This is bizarre," said Ralph. "I thought you were working on your marriage."

"I'm supposed to be, but it doesn't feel right."

"You told me you couldn't be involved with two people at the same time. Have you changed your mind?"

"No."

"Are you willing to be with me?"

"I think so."

"That doesn't sound convincing."

"I meant it to be."

"When do you get back from your holiday?"

"Sometime mid-July. We haven't settled on the dates."

"That's after I return from my canoe trip. Give me a call then and we'll compare notes."

"I'll do that— Goodbye, Ralph."

" —For now."

She could hear the disappointment in her voice.

. . . She picks up the phone hesitantly. "Hi Jean-Pierre. What time will you arrive tomorrow?" No answer. "Jean-Pierre?"

"The weekend is off."

"Has something come up?"

"You could say that."

"That's too bad. We need to talk. I've been thinking— "

"Me too."

"I need to talk to you about Monique. I know you're seeing her. I've suspected it all along and now someone's tipped me off."

"Who?"

"So there *is* something between you?"

"Who mentioned her to you? Was it Jules?"

"I got an anonymous text."

"What do you mean anonymous?"

"You know, an outside caller. And when I returned the call, the phone was out of service— Is there something between you?"

"That's why I am calling. I'm sorry for having lied about it."

"You're sorry about *lying*? How about you're sorry that you're having an *affair*!"

"I'm sorry about hurting you, but I want a divorce."

"I do too, you son-of-a-bitch— But have you thought, for even a second, what this will do to Jules or, as usual, are you concerned only about your own welfare?"

"I've thought a lot about how to present it to Jules."

"*Present it?* Like there's some spin that will make it more palatable? Don't you know him at all?"

"Yes, I do."

"Couldn't you have waited until he graduated? Until he entered college? You're such an asshole. This will be the second time you've walked out." She's glad they are doing this by phone. She'd probably have thrown something at him if he were here. A frying pan. A barrage of pots. Sticks and stones. Dishes. Anything and everything.

"You and Jules walked out the first time. Not me. Besides, I don't think it's going to be a surprise to him."

"Maybe not, since he's the one who first told me about her. But that doesn't mean it's not going to upset him. He's been counting on us getting back together."

"He's naïve. He'll get over it."

"That's too cavalier."

"It's not— I just know that he'll adapt. He's good at that."

"How long have you been seeing her?"

"More than a year."

"You should have told me earlier. You could have had the decency to let me get on with my life while you played around."

"I wasn't sure it would work out."

"Typical. Unwilling to take any real risk. Wanting to win either way. Do you realize that you've been unfair to her as well as to me?"

"That's what she claims too. I'm very sorry. I truly hoped we could put our marriage back together. The way it used to be."

"Are you going to get remarried?"

"It's what she wants."

"Is it what you want?"

"Yes— Look, Lynn, you don't love me any more. You've made that clear. We haven't been getting along. Admit it—it's a strain on you, me, and Jules."

"You can't cancel this weekend. You can get away with telling *me* by phone, but not *Jules.* We have to do it together. He'll need both of us."

"Can I stay at your place?"

"Are you kidding? Try Belleville, like you used to do. Tell Monique she'll have to wait another weekend for you."

"Okay."

"Another thing, Jean-Pierre. You owe it to Jules to handle this properly. And you owe it to Suzanne. You haven't forgotten her, have you?"

"Of course not."

"Are you planning to come to his prom? We're supposed to be chaperones."

"Yes I am. And to his science fair finals. And the family road trip."

"There is no family any longer."

"Then maybe Monique and I should take Jules up to James Bay. After all, it's her project he's interested in."

"Not a chance. If Jules still wants to have that holiday, you won't be on it. Not with Monique and not without her."

"That may not be what Jules wants."

"I don't care. I'm tired of this conversation. I'm going to hang up."

After holding it back during the call, Lynn breaks down. Her comatose marriage has finally died. Jean-Pierre has taken it off life support. Even if you can see it coming, even if you want it, pray for it, and ultimately cause it to happen, even if it's what's best for everyone, a death is still a death, an end to everything that was. That alone makes it hard. All those living branches from the past suddenly stop growing; they have no future. She cries for ten minutes, wipes the last tears away when she hears Jules open the front door.

CHAPTER 20

We need to talk. He's heard those words before. Too many girl-friends he couldn't commit to. He's spoken them too. No matter whom they're directed at, no matter the circumstances, they're never well received. A shock even when they're expected. When Monique texted, he expected the worst, and when she called, that's what he got.

"I've been thinking about it, Ralph. We could probably make it work over the short term, even be happy, but we'll never be able to keep our different backgrounds and politics at bay. They're bound to sabotage any relationship we might develop."

The words were sterile, passed along without feeling. Rehearsed. Thoroughly rehearsed. As if she'd been up all morning mouthing it into the mirror, happier each time that the message wasn't going to be delivered face to face. She chose the cowardly route. "Don't you believe that love conquers all?" He tried to mask the cynical tone, but couldn't pull it off.

"Ralph, we've had only one date. There is no love to talk about."

"Not yet, maybe. But didn't you feel the chemistry between us?"

"I did."

"There's something else then, isn't there? No one our age throws away an opportunity like this."

"Our age? You're twenty years older."

"It's not about age. It's about Jean-Pierre, isn't it? He's a better match and you can't let him go even though he's married and cheating on you."

"Not for long. He's going to get divorced."

"Is that what you think? That's not what I've heard."

"From Lynn?— The soul mate who broke your heart?"

That silenced him. Knocked the breath out of him. Froze his brain momentarily. He couldn't have spoken even if the right words were there in front of him on a teleprompter. He'd never mentioned Lynn to Monique. She must have been toying with him over their dinner at Orso and then over cognac at The Pierre. *Tell me about your disappointments in love. There was only one.* She knew all along.

"After you stopped at our table at the Faculty Club, I asked Jean-Pierre how he knew you. He said he was the one who stole your girl at McGill. I'm doing you a favor—you can finally get back at Jean-Pierre and steal his girl."

"You mean doing *yourself* a favor— Are you saying you have no regrets about not visiting me at Brave House?"

"There are always regrets. But there are even greater regrets. Sometimes you have to trade one for the other."

"Do you trust him?"

"I do."

"Sounds like a marriage made in— "

"That's what he promised."

"Monique, you've caught me off guard. A position I seldom find myself in. I don't know what to say."

"Wish us both well."

"You and Jean-Pierre?"

"No, silly. You and me."

She must be suppressing a chuckle, but he was sure she was smiling. She had released the blade of the guillotine. Beheaded him without a second thought. Smooth. The French woman besting the English man. The new Québec.

Ralph is left to wonder whether it was his warning text to Lynn that had precipitated this, Lynn then calling Jean-Pierre out, forcing him to choose, Jean-Pierre realizing that Lynn was his past and Monique his future. He pictures Jean-Pierre and Monique hand in hand leading Quebec into separation from Canada. Although he is having trouble admitting it to himself, he'd concluded after their date that he and Monique would eventually clash over her separatist agenda. She's right. He's the incurable romantic. Far too willing to enter his fantasyland of building a family and being a stepfather to Christine and Jeannine. Better to kill those thoughts before they take root. Better that there be no memories of kayaking together on Lac Tremblant or Long Pond. Yet he can't help but think of himself a loser when it comes to love—always planning his romances down to the most intimate detail, taking them places they never end up.

The asymmetry of information. When you know something that someone else may not know, and even if they do, they don't know that you know. It's been useful to him in court a number of times. It worked for Monique. He wonders if it will work for him now. Ralph finds his cell phone and texts Lynn, *On the off chance that you're—* He hits send but hesitates before continuing. Lynn responds immediately.

Lynn: *That I'm what*
Ralph: *Available*
Lynn: *For what*
Ralph: *Sailing*
Lynn: *Turns out I am*
Ralph: *Great*
Lynn: *Jean Pierre and I are getting divorced*
Ralph: *Were you going to let me know*
Lynn: *I thought you had a new girlfriend*
Ralph: *She disappeared*
Lynn: *Just like that*

Ralph: *Don't want to talk about it now*
Lynn: *When*
Ralph: *This weekend at the Cape*
Lynn: *Tied up this weekend*
Ralph: *Following weekend*
Lynn: *Okay see you then*
Ralph: *Bring your cold weather gear*
Lynn: *I took sailing as a metaphor*
Ralph: *Always the English teacher*
Lynn: *Fires and cooking meals would be great*

CHAPTER 21

Ralph has arranged a special welcome for Lynn at Brave House. He's placed a dozen long stem red roses in a tall crystal vase on the dresser of the master bedroom. It's on the second floor at the front of the house, a room with a sweeping view of Nantucket Sound. Beside the roses, he's left a card welcoming her to the Cape, his home, and his life, signing it "To L from R." While Ralph lies sleeping after their lovemaking the night of her arrival, Lynn sits in the window seat, mesmerized by the choppy scattering of the moon's light off Nantucket Sound. The next morning, she awakes alone but can hear him downstairs clanking around the kitchen. She stays in bed for a while watching the sun's reflection off the water migrate slowly across the wall as the sun rises higher in the sky. Ralph raps lightly on the door and suggests they get going on the day.

As Lynn enters the kitchen, Ralph hands her a gift, the one he'd bought for Monique after they'd dined at Orso.

"Should I unwrap it now?"

"Please. I think we'll want to use it before we head into the village." Lynn tears off the paper to uncover an Italian cookbook. "Why don't you pick out a recipe for tonight?"

While he prepares a frittata for breakfast, she settles on a beet salad for starters, followed by fettucine with shrimp and tomato. "*Gamberetti*—a nicer sounding word than *crevettes*," she says.

"And both more poetic than *shrimp*," he adds.

"Have you made this 'sailor-style' sauce?" she asks.

"Not yet. I bought the book this week."

"Well, you can work on that while I prepare the rest."

After the late breakfast, they drive into downtown Chatham. Ralph takes her to a women's boutique on Main Street. She selects a few summer dresses.

"It'll be a few months before I can wear these," she says.

"They're not much more substantial than negligées," he says. "Try one on tonight and you'll see how easily I can slip it off."

Before she can reach into her purse, he hands his credit card to the salesperson. "Finer shopping than I'm used to in Picton," she says as she waits for the charge to be rung up.

"Sometimes more funky than fine. What can you expect? It's home to an arts community."

"Do you have a favorite gallery?"

"They're all different—it depends on what you're looking for. We'll visit a small one after we pick up the groceries."

As they make their way back along Route 28 after shopping at the Village Market, Ralph says, "I only visit these galleries during the off-season when there's little traffic. In the summer, I get out early for my morning paddle on Long Pond then hunker down at the house for the rest of the day and leave it to the tourists to clog the roads."

"That sounds delightful. But sometimes a little afternoon sail I bet."

"Sometimes. But I prefer not to sail alone." He winks. They arrive at the gallery. He gets out of the car and holds the door open for her. "I saw you examining my paintings this morning. Try to find the artist here whom you think is my favorite."

She walks slowly around the room and pauses at a large oil on canvas.

"Right. I call this series *Big Man with Bigger Fish*. The fisherman's legs and hands are huge, almost grotesque, his head tiny. But the fish dominates the painting."

"I see. Why haven't you bought any of his work?"

"I can't decide among Barney and Morris and Edward and Luther."

"What?"

"The paintings are titled for the fishermen, who all look almost the same to me. Strange. The first time I saw one in this series, I didn't notice the fisherman until I stepped back from the painting. My eyes had been drawn to the fish instead."

She steps back. "How does an artist develop an obsession for a particular image?"

"I'd never thought about it until I visited the Matisse exhibit at the Met—*In Search of Painting*."

"Would you mind seeing it again with me?"

"It's already left."

"I'm sure it's traveling to another museum."

"I'll find out where."

Following Saturday evening's successful venture with the beets and fettucine, the sailor-style sauce turning out particularly tasty, Ralph displays for Lynn some of his campcraft skills. He splits logs into small strips for kindling and uses them together with larger logs to arrange a ceremonial Indian fire. He lights it at the top so that it will burn slowly downward, layer by layer. He pulls the cushions off the sectional couch and props them against the coffee table. Side by side, they lean back and talk for an hour until the fire is nearly spent, Lynn relating the details of her phone call with Jean-Pierre before arriving at the inevitable topic.

"You promised you'd tell me why your new girlfriend vanished from your life. It shocked me—you sounded upbeat about your prospects a month ago."

"I was. We hit it off on our first date and had made plans for a second, but she called it off. Said she was getting back together with her previous boyfriend."

"Do you think she used you to get back at him?"

"No—I believed her when she said their on-again-off-again relationship was over."

"How long had she been with him?"

"Not sure. A few years I think."

"Did you have any doubts whether you and she could make a go of it?"

"A few. We are different in important ways. You know, religion, politics. The core of a person that shines through after the initial glow of infatuation fades. And she had children from a previous marriage."

"Sounds complicated."

"I think it could have worked. I was trying to imagine being a stepfather. The idea was growing on me."

"That's always been your problem, Ralph. You get way ahead of yourself. Back in college you had us married long before we graduated."

"I know. I can't seem to outgrow my fantasies."

"Is our getting back together yet another fantasy?"

"Seems real to me."

"Do you see anything that will get in the way?"

"Nothing at all. Do you?"

"I have some concerns. We've never lived together. That can surface things you never anticipate."

"Then we should live together."

"We'll see."

Ralph adds a few logs to the coals. They ignite quickly. Lulled into a trance by the kaleidoscopic flames, they let the heat envelop them and make love.

❧

The next morning, while Lynn sleeps, Ralph slides into his slippers and cinches a terrycloth bathrobe about his waist. Slowly and quietly he opens the glass door to the deck, closes it behind him, walks to the railing and leans against it. On this crisp late-March day, spring is struggling to announce itself. It's too early in the season to find boats moored beyond the thin strip of his private beach. In the summer there will be a few and some mornings, like today, it will be calm, the water so flat that the boats will seem married to their reflections, the upside-down world as real as the upside-up one.

Lynn has turned his world upside down. Things are not calm. While his life is now filled with a near-breathless excitement, he realizes that she's right—they don't know each other. They haven't lived together. Things won't always go smoothly between them. He used to see matters in black-and-white terms; she always understood that there were complexities frustrating such a simple view. He can only imagine what it's been like for her to raise Jules, encountering not only the usual problems of adolescence but also handling the particular concerns of a transgender person. Nothing black and white there. Still, he's evolved since their college days. Though in court he'd often had to brush white paint over the prosecutor's black or black paint over his opponent's white, he quickly learned how to put himself in the mind of the judge where few issues resolve neatly. That's how it will be with Lynn. And Jules. Ralph expects that he will sometimes find himself squeezed between them, seeing merits and fallacies in each of their arguments, in the end unable to satisfy either one. He will have to take things as they come, adjust to whatever winds prevail.

With the rising of the sun, a light offshore breeze has come up, generating the first ripples on the Sound. He shivers and goes back inside.

❧

A few weeks later, after an afternoon at MoMA strolling through the sculptures and impressionist paintings, they are snuggled against each other in bed at his condominium. She rolls onto her side to face him. He caresses her lower back and soon gets aroused again.

"Wait," she says. "We need to figure out some things."

"Like what?"

"Your heart attack. Your canoe trip. Our summer holidays. Us. Jules. Dieter. Germany. McGill. A lot."

"Have you told Jules about us?"

"It's too early."

"Not if I'm going with you on the road trip in place of Jean-Pierre."

"Telling him about the divorce was bad enough. He's not ready for another father figure in his life."

"I don't understand your reluctance. I've already met him. We had dinner at your place. Why not another father figure when he's already got another mother figure in his life? Jean-Pierre wasn't shy about introducing Monique to Jules or letting her arrange his visit to McGill."

"I suppose you have a point. I'll talk to him next week— I promise."

"With Jules going to college in the fall and living in Montreal, why don't you give up teaching, sell your house in Picton, and come live with me?"

"I think we should give it some time before I relinquish everything I have now. We don't know how it will go between us."

"You're kidding, right?"

"Sort of. But we have a lot of catching up to do. If you're able to take your hands off me long enough, maybe we can talk about the last forty years."

That's what they do for the rest of the weekend in New York. Ralph learns about the parts of the Jean-Pierre years that she hasn't already revealed; Lynn hears about Ralph's career as a trial lawyer defending large energy companies. She continues to pester him about signing on as counsel for an environmental organization.

"I value my free time too much. I didn't retire to start working for someone else. It was my company, my show. I answered only to my clients and to myself."

"Then pro bono. Take on only the cases that interest you. Offer your services—no one will turn you down."

"I'll consider it. After the canoe trip."

"What about your heart? Can it survive all those strenuous portages?"

"I've been exercising regularly."

"You had a close call."

"My cardiologist says I'll be fine."

"Isn't it at least a little insane for a bunch of sixty-somethings to go tromping around the wilderness pretending they're still young? There'll be no way to get help in time if there's an emergency."

"What's insane about it? And by the way, I'm taking a satellite phone."

"You don't know the territory. The last time you guys tried that route you failed."

"We were only campers, all of us fifteen."

"You had adult counselors."

"Who turned out not to be smart."

"You could have drowned in the Rouge River. This time you might not return alive."

"Then I'll die doing what I love. At least I'm not still arguing cases in court."

"Ralph, please don't make light of this. Not now that I'm back in your life."

"C'mon, Lynn— We're older and wiser now. We'll make it through the trip in one piece."

"Doesn't Kiamika care that you have a heart problem?"

He hesitates too long.

"Haven't you told them?"

"I took the required physical a week before my little problem."

"It wasn't merely a little problem. You have to disclose it."

"They'd probably cancel the trip."

"But not informing the camp is irresponsible."

"I've wanted to take this trip for a long time. You don't understand."

"I hope you've told your buddies."

"I haven't and don't intend to— Look— You can count on me to be around."

"I *am* counting on it."

CHAPTER 22

To prepare for their pre-trip excursion, Ralph and Steve spoke by phone every week during April. Each settled into a natural role: Ralph the optimist, certain they can blaze several trails during the course of two weekends, Steve the pragmatist, winnowing the list down to the two longest portages, the ones mostly likely to scuttle the success of the canoe trip unless they are scouted out and marked beforehand. During the most recent call, Steve challenged Ralph to be more realistic in his assessments.

"You should rent a canoe at Cape Cod for a day and practice portaging off-trail. See how far you get through the underbrush before you exhaust yourself."

Steve mentioned that he'd examined Google Maps at a larger scale than the government-issued topographical maps and for the second longest portage found a dirt road they could follow for roughly eight kilometers in lieu of a four-kilometer slog through woods with no known trail. "Which would you rather take?" he asked.

"The dirt road."

"You bet— The math is simple— "

"I get it— Your point?"

"On our two weekends we should focus our entire effort on the one extremely difficult portage."

"Do you trust Google Maps?" Ralph asked.

"Not completely. That's why I like your idea of chartering a sea-plane. We can fly over the area to make sure the road exists."

"Should we fly over the whole route?"

"I don't think that's necessary. Now that we've decided to have the camp director ferry us by truck from the end of the first leg of the trip to the start of the second leg, we'll have few portages after Maison-de-Pierre and they're all short. No swamp, no alder thickets, no bogs, no slog for two or three days to get where the camp truck can deposit us."

"Sounds like a plan— Steve, be honest. Do you think we'll succeed this time around?"

"If we can nail that one long portage."

Ralph returns to the office in mid-May for the first time since his surgery. He's talked with Mark by phone several times about account handoffs and realizes the extent to which he'd already slipped into a mostly ceremonial role as titular head of the practice. Not relegated to figurehead status, more an éminence grise. Mark needs little guidance running the business. Few clients have been concerned with the impending change at the top; only one has left and signed up another firm. Ralph has collected well-wishes from his biggest clients, several commenting that his retirement is well deserved, that he's accomplished a "great deal" for the industry. He wonders whether they intended the double meaning. A few of his former clients have congratulated him on getting out of the business altogether, Hervé for one. He called Ralph at home as soon as he heard the news, but they were able to speak only briefly at the time. But this morning Hervé called again and they had a longer conversation during which he claimed that Ralph would be much happier now that he could finally live "beyond the mountain."

"What does that mean?" Ralph asked.

"You can live strictly according to your own principles. No more having to compromise."

"Where did you dig up that expression?"

"It's my own. I grew up in Outremont, which means 'beyond the mountain,' but many people who live there believe it means they live on the 'wrong side of the mountain,' away from the power base on the other side. I always saw it as being beyond the reach of the problems the other side brings."

"You mean the English?"

"Oui, les anglais."

"I thought you of all people were beyond that."

"Not always."

"Are the Germans any better? How's it going with Dieter?"

"Comme ci, comme ça," Hervé laughed. "Doesn't matter now, does it?"

Ralph didn't know what Hervé was referring to. Likely some change in management structure at the company. Having stepped out of that arena, he didn't want to get drawn back in. Didn't need to know. He didn't respond.

"Anyhow, my favorite English Canadian— You can now get back to your roots."

On the way to his corner office, Ralph pauses at the offices of his partners to say goodbye, shake hands, give a few hugs. They are happy to see him, but eager to get back to work. It's the culture he instilled from the outset. He reserves his biggest embraces for Mark and Mary Ann. To Mark he says, "Mary Ann is going to help me pack up my office today. Tomorrow it's yours." To Mary Ann, "Let's get started before I break down."

"Ralph— Are you okay?" asks Mark. "Is this what you want?"

"It is, but it's hard to see the place I've built and realize this is the last time I'm going to be here— One more time— " One more time standing at the window looking at the people passing on the street below and wondering about the future. One more time staring at the clouds as if they hold the answers.

"No more difficult calls," says Mark. "No more contentious clients. No more government regulations."

"That's the good part. But I'll miss all of you."

As Ralph pivots to enter his office, Mark says, "I have good news. Did you see the paper this morning?"

"No. Since my retirement I've started reading the newspaper at dinner. When the news is well past old. It isn't any easier to digest then, but I like the idea of viewing it from a greater distance, knowing that life has already moved on."

"Quebec announced who's been awarded contracts for James Bay. It's highly unusual— The entire project has gone to the consortium of Global Energy and International Wind Technologies."

"I don't find that surprising."

"But there was a simultaneous announcement that will shock you—a joint communiqué from Munich and Stamford. Global Energy is acquiring International Wind Technologies. Peter Devlin will be the CEO. He ended up getting the whole deal for himself."

Ralph chortles. "What'll happen to Dieter?"

"There will be a shuffling of management. Hervé will run Canada and Dieter will return to Germany to head R & D."

"A better fit for his skills," Ralph says. "I guess you could say he got Peter-principled." Mark groans.

Ralph follows Mary Ann into his office and closes the door. "I have good news too— I'm with someone." During the fifteen years they've worked together, he's often mentioned his newest girlfriends. She's joked with him about whether he thinks he's finally found "the one." She's kidded him about his undue optimism that doesn't ever pan out. But he's never told her that he is "with someone." Ralph can feel his face flush.

"I could tell something was different— You're no longer slicking down your hair. You've got that relaxed look. Who is she?"

"Lynn, my girlfriend in high school and college. We've got back together." He doesn't tell Mary Ann that he had a date with Quebec's Minister of Natural Resources and she's the one who got him to stop using gel in his hair.

"Do you think this is it?"

"It's what I've wanted all my life."

"Is she the woman who called you last fall?"

He hadn't forgotten about that day, the tragic calls with Lynn, Dieter, and Hervé, the resurrection call with Peter, but he had forgotten that he'd taken Mary Ann to dinner and a musical that evening. Forgotten that he told her about his dashed hopes for getting back together with Lynn, wistfully describing her as *the lost love of my youth*, uttering something Lynn had told him in college: *Once the kite gets away, it doesn't come back.*

"I'm happy for you. Maybe these Miró prints had the answer after all. You told me there was a figure you couldn't account for in the etching." She points to *Plate 15* and the figure in the center hidden behind another.

He'd forgotten that he also talked about Miró that night over dinner. "I'm going to send the prints to my place on the Cape." *How little there is to pack up at the end of a career. Only the personal effects.* "Will you please have my Toronto office packed up for me? You can also have that stuff sent to the Cape."

"Anything else?"

"Please make sure my camp friends have completed their physicals and mailed in their forms. The deadline is the end of the week."

Mary Ann begins to tear up. "This is it, isn't it? I'll never see you again."

"We'll be in touch. I'll introduce you to Lynn. We'll all have dinner." He can't imagine that happening and can tell that Mary Ann doubts it as well. She knows him. "Would you mind if I dictate a last letter?" He composes a note to Jack and Bill, copy to Steve, to inform them of the revised plan to blaze only the most difficult portage.

❧

This morning he made the trip from Picton to Montreal in his SUV, the back crammed with gear for the weekend expedition into the wilds, including a cooler carrying a dinner that Lynn prepared from the cookbook he gave her on her first visit to Brave House—lasagna with chicken and mushrooms. He picks up Steve at his office at Mc-Gill. Apart from the dinner at the Faculty Club, he hasn't returned to the campus of his alma mater for more than forty years. Little has changed. Tucked in the middle of Montreal, it wasn't a large campus to begin with. Not much room for expansion. He smiles as he passes the old buildings where he took his classes, remembers the times before Jean-Pierre broke apart his love life. That has changed.

He and Steve exit the city and drive north to Le Second Souffle, the hotel at Mont-Tremblant that Ralph has booked for the night. As they arrive, he wonders how far it is to Monique's chalet, the one he'll never see. He wonders why he's even thinking about that. Tomorrow night's dinner wrapped in foil in the cooler perhaps—that cookbook had been intended for Monique. He's ecstatic to be back together with Lynn, but his brief time with the Minister had a bizarre end. Sudden and surreal. That was the point: she wanted to cut it off before the chemistry had a chance to make something permanent that would be painful to escape.

Lying in bed that night, Ralph thinks back to his date with Monique and imagines that they are kayaking on Lac Tremblant with Jeannine and Christine. How the summer might have turned out had there been more than one date. He sees himself motioning toward the beach across the lake and asking Monique to take the lead. Though he's never met her girls, he knows that they are athletic like their mother, tall for their ages, thin, muscular. He's certain that Jeannine has approached her physical therapy with her mother's tenacity, as if it's a new sport she has to master quickly.

"How does your leg feel?" he asks.

"Stiff. It's a little cramped in here."

"Why don't you pick up the pace and take over from your mother? When we get across the lake, you can stretch." That is all the encouragement Jeannine needs. Stroking furiously, she surges ahead of Monique, who drops back beside Christine.

"Ralph, why don't you chase Jeannine, give her a little competition?"

"She's doing fine by herself. I'd prefer to stay with you and Christine."

The sky is completely clear and the sun is already well above the mountains. Monique inhales the morning, ceases paddling altogether.

"What are you thinking, Maman?" Christine asks.

"How much fun it will be for all four of us to be out here every day."

Then Christine asks Ralph, "Why do you get to be on holiday all the time? Why don't you have a job like Maman?"

Monique answers for him. "He's older than I am and he's already worked a whole career. He's one of the lucky ones who can spend his time doing what he wants."

"Maman, when will *you* retire?"

"When I've finished helping Quebec take its proper place in the world."

Ralph is unsurprised at her answer. He intercedes. "Does that mean you'll never retire?" And then he understands why Monique ended it. One day he'd slip and make a statement like that. Cross into the forbidden territory of her political world, one with values diametrically opposed to his. Sometime, inadvertently perhaps, when they were merely having fun as a family. In this imagined scene, he stops paddling and lets his kayak glide, focuses on the water dripping from his paddle blades onto the lake, making tiny perturbations that barely disturb the surface, ripples that die away quickly, leaving no sign they've ever existed. Inconsequential. Like him. As influential as he was in his sphere, he had little impact on the world at large. He tried to persuade people to go along with his ideas, but often failed.

And for what? A heart attack? This is better—out here on the lake, the only destination the other shore. This is why he's determined to make the canoe trip a success.

At seven the next morning, the seaplane takes off from Lac Duhamel and bears north for the short flight to Carp Lake where they confirm that the dirt road Steve located on Google Maps does indeed exist. The plane turns east to Lac Rouge and then north again, passing over a chain of closely spaced lakes—Elgin, Barrette, Buda, Aldei, and Huot.

"Huot's a small target," Ralph says as they circle the lake before bearing west to Lac Séré. "A big pond more than a lake."

"If we miss," says Steve, "we have to make sure we hit Aldei to the south. I'd hate to pass by Huot on its north side. There's not another lake for a few kilometers and it's not on our route."

They land a few minutes later at the northern tip of Séré, skimming the water and touching down like a great blue heron, a long, slow, splashing glide to a stop. They inflate the raft and load the gear. In halting French, Ralph confirms with the pilot that he'll meet them at the same spot tomorrow afternoon at four. "Vous retournerez demain— Le même endroit à seize heures." The pilot nods, turns the plane toward the other end of the lake and takes off.

They paddle ashore and pitch the tent. Ralph places the cooler in a heavy-duty fish net which he suspends with rope about four meters above the ground between two trees to protect it from inquisitive wildlife. On a different line Steve hangs one of the packs. They take only one pack on the trail—maps and compass, two bars of dark chocolate, six protein bars, eight bottles of water, first aid kit, and matches in a plastic prescription bottle. A single machete.

"Today we'll merely mark the trail," says Steve. "Tomorrow we'll each bring a machete to clear away underbrush."

"We should be sure to get back here by four," Ralph says. "Six hours to find Huot." Six hours might not be enough; what appeared to be a short distance by air would seem a lot longer on the ground, in deep woods. Handing Steve the machete, he takes the map and compass and sets his bearing, walking off in an east-south-easterly direction. He paces off a hundred meters in a straight line and waits for Steve to catch up. The brush at lakeside is thick, not impassable like alder thickets near a marsh, but many young trees growing close together. Ralph works toward higher, drier land. More deciduous trees than he would have liked, none leafed out yet as they will be in a month. He'd hoped for stands of conifers. They'd be spaced farther apart with a soft bed of dead needles—easier for portaging a canoe. After an hour plowing straight ahead, Steve following, marking the trail by cutting away two patches of bark from a tree at the end of each hundred-meter segment, one mark facing the direction they're heading and one the direction they'll return, they stop.

"How are we doing?" asks Steve.

"If my pacing is accurate, we've covered about nine hundred meters. Let's break out some chocolate and rest here for ten minutes."

They continue in this fashion until three in the afternoon, resting every kilometer. "Hey, Mr. Pragmatist," Ralph says. "We need an executive decision. I'm inclined to press on for another hour, then turn around if we don't reach the lake. We'd make it back by five— It stays light until eight."

"We should head back now," says Steve. "You remember what happens when we start to improvise."

Ralph is disappointed. He's sure they are close. "I guess that's why you wanted two weekends to mark this one portage. Can you imagine trying to carry canoes in these woods without a marked trail?"

"For a kilometer or two maybe, but no more," says Steve.

Their fresh blaze marks, exposed white wood against dark bark, are easy to spot. Steve is inclined to continue clearing selectively, but Ralph says no. "We decided to head straight back—let's stick to the plan." They make good time and arrive back at their campsite before four.

"I'm famished," says Steve. "What's for dinner?"

"Better food than we'll have on the actual trip. Lynn sent us off with two large servings of lasagna."

"I'll collect some wood," says Steve.

"No, Mr. Ax-in-the-leg, you've used the machete enough today. Why don't you dig a pit near that flat rock down by the water."

A half hour later they have a fire going. While letting it burn down to hot coals, Ralph cuts several short lengths from a young maple tree and soaks them at the edge of the lake.

"What are you doing?"

"Making a grill. Even double-wrapped in foil, I'm afraid the lasagna will burn if we put it directly on the coals."

"Any beer in the cooler?"

"No alcohol tonight. We'll celebrate tomorrow night back at your place."

Over dinner, sitting around the fire they'd built up again, Ralph asks Steve what had soured his first marriage and how he'd met his second wife. After hearing the story, he asks what it's like to raise a teenager.

"Sounds as if you want a crash course in parenting."

"I've inherited a boy, almost a young man, who's graduating from high school." He thinks about whether to tell Steve that Jules is transgender but decides not to—he's not sure that Jules would approve. He's not sure that Jules approves of him.

They sit silently, listening to the sizzling and popping of the green wood on the fire. Ralph breaks the silence. "Have you done any kayaking?"

"My son and I do serious whitewater. The closest good spot for us is The Seven Sisters— "

"Are you kidding? I almost drowned in those rapids while rafting during a high school reunion."

"My son's an expert. He's become my instructor."

"Nothing that exciting for me anymore," Ralph says. "Only freshwater ponds on the Cape."

"It must be relaxing."

"It's also good exercise. I go at it hard."

"I guess my son and I are in it more for the thrills."

"If you ever want something different, come visit me. My house is right on Nantucket Sound. You could try dealing with waves and currents instead of rapids. Or we could all sail."

"Maybe after my sabbatical."

They chat until the fire burns down again. Ralph sets the alarm on his cell phone for six. "We'll hit the trail by seven. Bacon and eggs for breakfast." He reminds Steve not to get used to this good food.

It takes less than an hour to reach their farthest point of progress from the previous day. The sky clouds over quickly and by eight thirty it has started to drizzle. By nine it's raining heavily, weather not in the forecast. Ralph begins to see what it would be like on the trail in driving rain during next month's trip not knowing precisely where they're headed—every bit as miserable as they were the first day on their last trip as campers at Kiamika. By ten o'clock they are soaked, water streaming down the legs of their jeans, some of it finding its way inside their waterproof boots. After sloshing around for a further fifteen minutes, they are ready to punt on the day and place their bets on the following weekend.

"Let's give it another thirty minutes," says Steve.

The undergrowth begins to thicken as they lose a little elevation. Pushing through the brush is easier now that they're sodden and no longer care about getting wetter. They move faster, pausing only to let Steve mark the trail at regular intervals.

"Do you see that slight depression over there?" Ralph points a little to the left of the direction they've been following.

"That's north of where we want to be, isn't it?" says Steve.

"I don't think so. I've taken us a little south of our intended line. I have a hunch that's a body of water. Let's check it out."

Twenty minutes later they are standing on the shore of a small lake.

"Which one is it?"

"I'm not sure. Anything this small looks about the same from the shoreline."

"What if it's not Huot?"

"Then it would have to be Aldei. It can't be Buda—the map indicates that we'd have crossed a dirt road."

"It doesn't matter," says Steve. "We'll mark this spot clearly and watch for it when we come through in June."

"We should bring spools of yellow ribbon next weekend," Ralph says. "Nothing fancy, only cheap stuff. We can tie it around trees between the ones we've already blazed and double the number of markings."

"I'll ask my wife to buy some. You can figure out how much we need."

Ralph takes off his pack and sits down. The only way his jeans could get wetter would be for him to wade into the lake.

"Not now," says Steve. "I'm drenched."

"It's a trivial calculation. Give me a few seconds— Our trail's about five kilometers long. One ribbon per tree every hundred meters would be fifty ribbons. At an average of two meters in circumference, that would make a hundred meters of ribbon." Ralph stands up and threads his arms through the pack's straps. "At a dollar a meter, one hundred dollars. I'll give you two hundred to be safe."

"You're nuts. Let's get going."

They reach the campsite by one, change into dry clothes and play Gin Rummy for a couple of hours before packing up.

"It looks as if it might stop raining soon, but the ceiling is awfully low," says Steve. "I hope the pilot can get in. We're down to a few protein bars." He looks concerned. This isn't a contingency they've planned for. Google Maps has turned out to be accurate but the Weather Channel has not. Four o'clock comes and goes. Four thirty. Five. A mist begins to settle over the lake. "I think we'd better pitch the tent again. Looks like we're here for the night. No food to cook, but let's light a fire anyway. Do you remember how to do that with wet wood?"

"Sure. All we need is a huge pile of cedar shavings to get it started." But Ralph is not thinking of fire or food. He's thinking of what Lynn will say when they get back, if they get back—they're too old to be taking this trip; they don't know what they're getting into. *Is she wrong?*

"At least we won't have to worry about this next month."

"Worry about what?"

"Whether a seaplane can get in."

Ralph's confidence in being able to start a fire with wet wood in the rain is matched by his skill. Every experienced canoe tripper knows that cedar stays dry inside its bark. He builds a huge pile of thin shavings and cuts the rest of the cedar into kindling-size sticks. They soon have a roaring fire going, hot enough to evaporate the diminishing rain before it reaches the flames.

"You're good," says Steve. "All that time beating down environmentalists hasn't taken the outdoorsman out of you."

"You make it sound as if I club them to death."

"That's probably how they feel after you've finished with them in court."

"Let's hope the fucking plane gets here tomorrow morning. I've seen enough of Lac Séré for one weekend."

They are up at seven without breakfast. Not even a protein bar. Only lake water. The mist is rising. A doe drinking at water's edge on the opposite shore raises her head and sniffs the air. Bends over again to drink, looks in their direction. Steve takes a paddle and slaps the flat of its blade against the surface of the lake, making the same warning sound a beaver does with its tail when there's danger. The deer bolts into the woods.

"I haven't heard that sound in a while," Ralph says. "Reminds me of the time in Bullfrog Bay when we went after the damn frogs keeping us up at night. Remember the bloody massacre?"

"The camp director made us peel potatoes the next day," says Steve. "They almost stripped us of our Leader Awards."

"Yeah, it took some talking to change his mind."

"It doesn't surprise me that you turned into a lawyer."

By seven thirty the sun has started to break through the low-lying clouds. By eight the sky has almost cleared, and forty minutes later they hear the propeller of a plane. It slides to a stop about fifty meters from shore.

"Avez-vous passés une bonne nuit?" asks the pilot with a wry smile as he helps them stow their gear.

"Mais oui," Ralph and Steve answer simultaneously.

CHAPTER 23

Even for Jules, fluent in French and English, with stellar grades and a unique personal essay, there was the usual nail biting around the time colleges sent out their acceptance and rejection letters. Unsurprising to everyone but him, he was accepted, with scholarships, at both Toronto and McGill, the only schools to which he'd applied. Surprising to nobody, he chose McGill, the university where his parents had met, and the one that noted in their acceptance letter that they hoped he would choose the Honours Engineering program after his freshman year. Jules' application to live in a student residence at McGill was also accepted. In his reply, he expressed a preference for Gardner Hall, the one he had visited. Though Jean-Pierre wanted Jules to live with him in Outremont and walk around the mountain through Parc du Mont-Royal to campus every day as he himself had done when he attended McGill, and as Suzanne later did, Jules decided he wanted the experience of living in a dorm.

"At least there's one benefit to you and Dad getting divorced," Jules said to his mother as he read the acceptance letter out loud.

Lynn did not mention that she thinks there's more than one. The announcement of the divorce had not produced the explosion she'd feared. It seemed that Jules had expected it, having already admitted to himself that his efforts to reunite the family had failed. But Lynn knew that it would take him a long time to process his parents' split.

The hurt he hadn't expressed initially would bubble up—she was sure of it. Still, she was glad for the current calm. It has given her a chance to bring up the matter of Ralph's participation in the July road trip to James Bay.

"It's still on, I hope," said Jules.

"If you want it to be. But not with your father. That wouldn't be right."

"Dad's coming to my prom, isn't he?"

"Yes, but the road trip is different. I know you intended it to be a family experience. I'm sorry. That's no longer possible."

"Because you and Dad can't sleep in the same room together? Why not get another room?"

"That won't work. It's more than that. The important point, the thing that hasn't changed, is that you want to take this trip to visit the hydroelectric facilities and to see the site where the wind farms will be installed. You're going to apply for a summer internship up there when the project is underway. That's enough reason not to cancel the holiday."

"Do you think we should still go?"

"Yes. Why I wanted to talk to you about it is that I would like Ralph to join us now that he's a significant part of my life and also in yours."

"I think that's even less appropriate than Dad coming along."

"I understand how you feel, but it's something you'll have to get used to."

"I'm about to go to Germany and then to McGill. Why do I have to get to know him better? Why now?"

"Because it will be good for you. He has a cool apartment in New York City. He has an even cooler house right on Nantucket Sound. You can windsurf there merely by walking out your front door."

"Not *my* front door, Mum. *His* front door."

"*Our* front door. As soon as I can get an appropriate visa, I'm going to leave Picton and move down there with him."

"Don't you see? It's not fair to hurl him at me like this!"

"Hold on, Jules. Do you think for a moment that your father won't bring Monique into your life? He already has. And you'll be living in Montreal when you're attending McGill—you'll be seeing a lot of her."

"That's different. She's an engineer."

"She was. Now she's a politician."

"If you had to ditch Dad, why couldn't you have chosen Dieter instead of Ralph? I like Dieter and I'm going to be spending a month working with him."

The thought of being involved with Dieter makes Lynn wince, but she can't tell Jules why. The only person she's ever confided in about Dieter is Ralph and it took her more than forty years to summon the courage for that. *Raped by the man to whom I'm entrusting Jules' care this summer?* That's not a place she can go. Not now. Not ever. She should probably never have permitted Jules to accept the internship.

"*You* don't get to choose whom I'm attracted to. I feel lucky to have met Ralph again. Don't forget that your father was having an affair behind our backs and lying about it to both of us."

"But I can't imagine you, me, and Ralph making that road trip together."

"I didn't think you could. That's why I'd like you to invite Amy along. Then there will be four of us. For the most part you and Amy can do your thing and Ralph and I can do ours."

"I'll think about it."

❧

On one of his visits to Picton before confessing his affair, Jean-Pierre suggested to Jules, who'd already succeeded in progressing through both stages of a beginner's driver's permit, that he might like to drive to Montreal once a month, sparing his father the round trip. Jules was eager, but Lynn overruled, saying that it didn't matter that he'd qualified for his full license—he still needed more practice driving on major highways to satisfy her that he could do the trip to Montreal alone.

Naturally Jules set about meeting the challenge. After receiving his new passport from Ottawa, he made the three-hour drive to Toronto with his mother as passenger to file an application with the German embassy for a Youth Mobility Visa for his summer internship. On spring break, the two of them shared the drive to Montreal. Satisfied with his performance, Lynn permitted him to drive anywhere alone after that. Before their split, she and Jean-Pierre agreed to share the cost of leasing a used car for him. Jules was thrilled about the freedom he gained by finally having his own wheels. Lynn was thrilled at being liberated from having to transport him everywhere, especially to the Belleville train station now that Jean-Pierre was no longer making the trip to Picton.

Despite his acceptance to McGill, Jules' last semester of high school proved not to be the usual coast toward graduation that seniors heading to college counted on as they wound down their adolescence. Most of his extracurricular time was spent on improving his science fair exhibit for the nationals. Lynn doesn't understand any of the things he's done. She's heard the litany of modifications and improvements often enough that she can play them back verbatim to anyone who wants to listen. She can make his canned presentation, but her knowledge is only superficial—she'd get tripped up at the first question. For the provincials, Jules added a few closely spaced wire nets at one end of the tank to damp out the reflections that had been creating standing waves in the tank. He and Amy built three model turbines, all eggbeater, oriented at different angles on their anchoring pylons for studying the various stresses on the underwater cables. Someone viewing a demonstration could peer through the glass on the side of the tank and see directly how the cables responded to incoming waves. By the time of the nationals, he'd added a powerful fan to the apparatus, securing it to the top end of the tank opposite the wire nets. He encouraged people who stopped by the exhibit to participate by adjusting the fan speed to make larger or smaller waves. The judges were surprised to see the eggbeater design, nothing like what they'd witnessed on any land-based farm. They asked many questions, all of which Jules answered competently without faltering. During the awards ceremony, the judges remarked on the ingenuity of the experiment and said they would have been inclined to rate the project more favorably had he fabricated a real generator and produced an electric current to power a string of miniature lights. In accepting a certificate of achievement, Jules humbly agreed, though he told his parents later that the judges had missed the essential point of the project. Ninth place was a tremendous accomplishment Lynn and Jean-Pierre told him. Jules' teachers agreed. But he had hoped for better. Lynn had to admit that she gained a new appreciation for wind farms, certainly not the aesthetics of turbines, but the technology underpinning them. Nevertheless, Jules' success hasn't changed her view about having a wind farm in her backyard. Thank God they won a restraining order in the county—she almost felt like calling up Dieter and crowing. But talking to Dieter about anything is not something she will ever relish. And she knows her victory will be short-lived; the energy companies will pay their way to having the last laugh.

The science fair had a salutary effect on Jules' social life. After the regional competition at the high school, the other team members left the project, except for Amy. Though Jules was the driving force behind the exhibit's continuing development through the provincials and into the nationals, steering the emphasis from wildlife conservation issues to engineering design, Amy assisted at each stage, particularly in building scale models of the unusual turbines. She and Jules now do homework together and study for tests together and go to first-run films together when the good ones arrive in town. Lynn has repeatedly asked Jules whether he and Amy are officially dating, to which he continually responds that his mother can consider the relationship anything that makes her happy as long as she never asks whether it's *serious*. Amy was also accepted at McGill and, after her financial aid came through, followed Jules' lead by accepting her acceptance. Most weekends Jules drives to Sandbanks. Amy reads a book while he windsurfs. One day in late May he returns from the provincial park and tells Lynn that he and Amy have decided to attend the prom.

"She's your date?"

"We're going to prom, okay? That's all."

Jules rents a traditional black tux. Lynn helps him choose a wrist corsage for Amy. Over his mild complaints, she insists on driving them to the prom. She and Jean-Pierre had agreed months before to serve as chaperones at the event. Jean-Pierre honors his promise despite having filed for divorce. They drive to Amy's house, where all four parents comment that Amy and Jules make a lovely couple, Jules' bright blue cummerbund matching Amy's satin dress. Jules, ever concerned about his height, asks Amy to take off her heels for the photographs. After the mandatory shots for each family's album, Jules, Amy, Jean-Pierre, and Lynn continue on to the prom.

The evening winds the clock back in time for Lynn to her own prom. The gymnasium at her school was festive that night long ago, its centerpiece decoration a large windmill covered with artificial carnations of all colors made from Kleenex tissues. She and Ralph were part of a small group of students who stayed after school every afternoon for a few weeks to make those carnations, until neither of them could stand the idea of flowers any longer. Until the night of the prom when he pinned her with an exquisite purple and white orchid. The windmill's four arms turned slowly throughout the evening, virtually stilling the pace of everything, as if that precious night had been commanded by the graduation gods to last forever. Ralph liked only the slow dances and he and Lynn danced every one of those together. No one cut in on Ralph that night. They were king and queen of the prom. Later they came close to making love. The desire to consummate their relationship had been building all night, the would-be act interrupted only by another couple stumbling into the guest bedroom at the home of the prom-party's host. A tear runs down Lynn's cheek.

"What's wrong?" Jean-Pierre asks.

"I was thinking about my prom night."

"What about it?"

"Nothing— Life will be hard for Jules."

"Don't worry— Things will work out."

"They have for you, haven't they? You got what you wanted."

Lynn wishes there were something to drink with alcohol in it. Thinking about her own fateful night has soured her mood. Being here with Jean-Pierre is difficult. Then, as if those graduation gods decided to speed up time again, the evening draws towards its end.

"It's the final dance," says Jean-Pierre. "How about a last one for old times' sake?" They move to the center of the floor and put on a display of their finest ballroom dancing for the students. Sweeping by Jules and Amy, Lynn overhears a boy say to him, "Your parents are good. How did you turn out so queer?"

"Fuck you," says Jules, not seeing his parents nearby. The boy stops dancing and pushes Jules in the chest. Jules pushes back. The boy takes a pencil from his jacket pocket and stabs Jules. Amy screams as Jules falls to the floor. Jean-Pierre bounds to the spot where Jules is lying and, from behind, puts his arms around the boy as he is about to strike again. Then puts him into a headlock.

"Call the police and an ambulance," Jean-Pierre shouts to Lynn. The teachers and principal clear the gymnasium, ushering students outside and declaring the prom over. Lynn kneels beside Jules and cradles his head in her arms. The principal and a teacher return and take the boy into custody until the police arrive. Jean-Pierre removes Jules' jacket and presses a hand over the patch of blood swelling on Jules' shirt.

"I don't feel good, Dad— Am I going to die?"

"No. You're going to be okay. The ambulance is on its way."

Jean-Pierre opens Jules' shirt and presses his thumb directly over the stab wound from which blood is trickling but not spurting. Amy, also kneeling at Jules' side, sobs in great gasps as if she's the one who has been stabbed.

The police and ambulance arrive simultaneously. Jean-Pierre tells the officers he's going to press charges against the boy. "Please take statements from my wife and my son's girlfriend. I'll give you mine later, after I know he's out of danger."

"I'm going with you," Lynn says. "They can get my statement later too."

"No," says Jean-Pierre. "Stay with Amy and speak to the police. She needs you to calm her down. Please drive her home. Then join me at the hospital." The police are looking at him strangely. He's said all of this in French and seems completely unaware of it.

The paramedics strap Jules onto a stretcher. Amy kisses him on the cheek. "I'm sorry," Jules says. Jean-Pierre climbs into the back of the ambulance. It speeds off, sweeping past a crowd of students still milling in the school parking lot gaping at the spectacle.

Lynn arrives at the hospital an hour after Jean-Pierre and Jules. The doctors have already examined Jules and pronounced him fortunate. Had the pencil penetrated somewhat higher—into the neck—or a little lower—into the heart or lungs—the result could have been tragic. As it is, a puncture wound in the chest is serious, but will only leave a scar as a permanent memento of the prom.

"It'll make me look like an even bigger freak," Jules jokes. "I had to explain the scars on my chest to the doctor. He must have thought that I'm a member of a gang or something."

A tetanus shot, a thorough disinfecting and dressing of the wound, several stitches, some intravenous antibiotic, that's all it took to make him almost good as new, the ER doctor says. He'll be released in the morning with a prescription.

Jean-Pierre pushes a chair to the edge of the hospital bed, sits and takes hold of Jules' hand. He asks about the boy.

"His name is James. He's been bothering me since the start of the year."

"I don't know him," Lynn says. "He's not in any of my English classes."

"His family moved to Picton last summer."

"How does he know about you?" asks Jean-Pierre.

"I was changing for soccer in the locker room one day and he asked how I got the scars. He said I looked like a freak."

"What did you do?"

"Ignored him. He went off to shower."

"Was that it?"

"He sometimes harasses me at lunch. Only when others are around. He thinks he's a big shot."

"You're sure he knows you're transgender?"

"Yeah— But I don't know who would have told him."

Lynn moves from the end of the bed to stand beside Jean-Pierre. He gives her the chair. "Are there any others in the school like him?" she asks.

"Not really."

"What does that mean?"

Jules' eyes close and open. "When James taunts me in public, others sometimes join in, but mostly people tell him to shut up."

"Jules. Jules." Jean-Pierre puts his hand on Jules' forehead. "Please try to stay awake for a minute— Have you reported this to your teacher or the principal?"

"I didn't want to make trouble— It would affect Mum, too."

"I think you should have," Lynn says. "This kind of behavior has no place in a school."

"Or anywhere else," says Jean-Pierre.

Jules turns his head away. "Good luck with that," he mumbles, as if talking only to himself.

"I'm sorry," says Lynn.

Turning back toward his parents, Jules asks, "Dad, what's going to happen to James? Why did you tell the police to press charges?"

"They don't have a choice. Assault is a serious crime. If he's lucky, he'll get away with community service."

"I'm going to insist that James make a public apology at the final assembly," Lynn announces.

"How is that going to happen?" asks Jean-Pierre. "I'm sure he'll be suspended for the rest of the year. Then probably expelled. His family will have to leave town."

"I'll tell the principal that we'll file civil charges unless he makes it happen."

"That might only make matters worse for the school." Jean-Pierre takes Jules' hand again. "You're nodding off— Did they give you a sedative?"

"They gave me an injection."

"Probably the tetanus shot. I'll check on the way out. We'll come back in the morning for your discharge."

"Do you think Amy will visit tomorrow?"

"I'll call her parents," says Lynn. "They'll want to know how you are. I'll ask if Amy can stop by in the afternoon after you're home."

"I love you guys." Jules gestures feebly.

"We love you, too," says Jean-Pierre.

CHAPTER 24

It took Dieter several weeks to process his profound loss. He could sense Ralph's hand in the turn of events. Who could forget his threat in their last call? *Someday one of your deals is going to jump up and bite you. You'll be finished. You won't even see it coming.* Even from retirement, Ralph found a way to win. That's what Dieter continued to think and stew about until Peter Devlin called to say how excited he was that Dieter would be leading the research and development effort for the consolidated company. They talked about how they'd triumphed as a team in the bid for James Bay. Peter was magnanimous in congratulating Dieter for deducing that the Premier would prefer to award the project to a single entity and for having the foresight and courage to propose a joint venture. During that conversation, Dieter learned that Ralph, months before his retirement, had given Peter a heads-up that something huge was brewing at the Ministry. At first it made him even angrier about what Ralph had done. Ralph, the guy he couldn't conquer in the end, the privileged kid now grown up who always seems to come out on top. But, in mulling over Peter's words in the ensuing weeks, Dieter convinces himself that Ralph isn't the one who beat him, not even by the tortuous logic that Ralph brought Peter into the mix before the competition for James Bay was officially announced. Peter's company would have become involved regardless.

And it isn't Peter who undid him. He finally comes to the conclusion that he must have defeated himself and that he can't afford to squander the rest of his life in a petty battle when his lifelong adversary is no longer on the field of play. Dieter himself is not likely to be there much longer either. For most of his life he has been trying to prove himself better than Ralph and good enough in his father's eyes. More than merely good enough—he has striven to be better than his father, to make a greater and longer-lasting contribution to the energy business. Everything traceable to his father for the broken promise when Dieter was only twelve.

After listening to Ralph speak rapturously of his outdoors experiences at summer camp, Dieter had determined to persuade his father to let him go to this magical place called Kiamika the following summer. By Christmas he'd succeeded, and within a few months he'd taken the requisite physical exam. He pestered his mother to purchase the necessary gear—a trunk to store his camp clothes, a sleeping bag and army blanket, waterproof flashlight, trip boots and various other items on the camp's must-have list. He kept bugging her until she finished sewing nametags into the inside of every piece of his camp clothing. As Dieter kept thinking of items to bring, he packed and unpacked the steamer trunk to make sure everything would fit. He talked to Ralph about the daily routine at camp and listened to him describe living in a platform tent in the open air and cooking meals over a fire on a canoe trip.

Dieter began to count off the days until the third week of June when he'd leave on a train from Windsor Station with all the other campers. He imagined his mother crying as she watched him go, his father standing by her side and hardly lifting his hand to wave goodbye. Then, at the end of May, they received news that Dieter's grandmother had been diagnosed with liver cancer and wouldn't survive the summer. His father said they'd have to return to Switzerland for a family get-together immediately after the school year ended. Dieter pleaded to go to camp for a month first and join them overseas afterward for the rest of the summer, but his father insisted that he drop the idea of camp until the following year. He remembers the conversation as if it happened only last week. It has lived with him for fifty years.

"You promised," said Dieter. "I've been counting on this all year."

"Who knew my mother would get sick?" said his father.

"She's *your* mother, not *mine*. I haven't seen her in years."

"All the more reason for you to accompany us."

"She might still be alive when I return from camp."

"We're not going to take that chance."

And that was that. His father had spoken, and broken an important promise. His grandmother survived until the end of August and Dieter never attended summer camp. His father decided that while they were based in Canada an annual family reunion in their home country was more important than anything summer camp in the Laurentian Mountains could offer. "You can camp out in the Alps. They're more impressive than the Laurentians."

"It's not the same," said Dieter. "I won't make a lot of new friends."

"Sure you will. And you can work on your German. That will be more important to you than a few Canadian friends you'll never see again."

There was no arguing with a Swiss father. No arguing with *his* father when Dieter was twelve and no arguing with him much later when Dieter was in his forties and his father wouldn't install him as CEO of the newly formed International Wind Technologies. Dieter realizes that he must let go the grudge against Ralph and the one against his father. Holding onto them has not served him well. And he must finally attend to the other much more important matter that has dogged him for almost as long as he has battled Ralph, the seed of his animosity towards Ralph. He can't explain why he keeps putting it off, why he's waited until now, a week before he's scheduled to leave for Germany, but he can't ignore it any longer. He calls Lynn.

"It's Dieter. I can't imagine you expected to hear from me."

"You must want to be the first to tell me something you have to gloat about."

"Hardly— I've been relieved of my North American command. I'm being sent back to Germany to head up R & D."

"That doesn't sound too bad."

"It's not what I wanted."

"This is why you called?"

"No. I think you know there's something we need to discuss. Can we meet?"

"I don't think that's a good idea."

"Then please do it for me if not yourself."

That's how they end up sitting across from each other at a table at the shabby Montana's restaurant in Belleville. Dieter has taken the train from Montreal and Lynn has made the short drive from Picton. Dieter has reached his quota of speeding tickets before being dealt a license suspension and wants to escape to Germany without further encounters with provincial police. He has no taste for another conversation with the OPP or the fucking Sûreté du Québec.

"For once, I'm all ears," says Lynn as they sit down.

"Thanks for agreeing to come. I know you didn't want to."

"Only coffee for me, please. I don't have a lot of time."

"Okay. I'll be brief. But there are a few things I have to say because they can't remain unsaid and I'm not likely to ever see you again." He tries to gauge Lynn's reaction, but her face is expressionless. "First, I want you to know that I am fully committed to taking Jules under my wing this summer. He's talented and I'm sure he'll learn a lot. I hope it propels him into a successful career."

"That's kind of you."

"It's the least I can do."

"Yes, I suppose it is."

This is not going well. No reason to expect it would, but he had hoped. The wounds run deep. "Second, and by far the most important reason I wanted to meet with you, is that I owe you an apology. I'm not sure an apology will be good enough, especially after such a long time. I'm sure you remember our prom night."

"You mean the *indiscretion*? You planned it all along, didn't you? Your way to get back at Ralph."

"I hadn't even been planning to attend the prom."

"What made you?"

"You're right. I wanted to get back at Ralph. At the party afterwards, when you and he went upstairs, I thought about breaking into the bedroom to interrupt your go at it, but a couple got there before me. It was hilarious to see Ralph stumbling over himself while trying to put his pants back on."

"There was nothing funny about that."

"And then I watched him get shit-faced drunk, two-fisted no less. You weren't far behind."

"I don't need to be reminded."

She probably doesn't. They'd both seen Ralph pass out after vomiting all over the hosts' Oriental rug. After she cleaned up the mess, Dieter had offered them a ride home. He'd slung Ralph over his shoulder and walked right to Ralph's front door. Lynn couldn't have missed the look on his parents' faces. Dieter had talked to them for a long time.

"Do you recall what you said to me when I returned to the car?"

"No."

"You asked if there was anything you could do for me."

"I don't remember."

"You know I've had a crush on you since high school."

"You may not believe it, but I cared for you too at one time."

"Why did you choose Ralph?"

"I don't know. More chemistry I guess. You should have got over it. Do we have to talk about this?"

"We do. Because I've been carrying the guilt all this time and I'm sure you've been carrying the hurt."

Lynn starts to tear up.

"I'm sorry, Lynn. I'm sorry for— For forcing myself on you that night in the back of my car. I wish I had never done it. I wish I'd had the courage to call it what it was and apologize sooner."

"I was so drunk that I imagined you were Ralph. But it was you who raped me, not Ralph."

"I'm sorry. I'd wanted you badly, but I never wanted to hurt you." He hands Lynn his handkerchief. "Are you okay?"

"Do you expect me to forgive you? Is that why you wanted to meet?"

"No, but I needed to apologize."

"Have you ever told Ralph about this?"

"I promised you I wouldn't."

"Well, I finally got up the courage to."

"To tell him about us?"

"Not *us*, Dieter. *You*. I told him that you raped me."

"When did you tell him?"

"Does it matter?"

"To me it does."

"In November last year, on the weekend that Jules visited McGill."

Dieter is stunned. Ralph had a more serious motive to do him in on the James Bay deal than being fired from the Frontière account. That must be what made him set Peter in motion. It was personal, not business. *Ralph played Peter and then Peter played me. All along I thought I was the one in control. Peter with the faster car and grander title. Now I've been sent back to Germany in disgrace. I'll never have the top job, never be able to redeem myself in my father's eyes. I was such a chump to convince myself that it was my own fault I lost the deal and got pushed aside.*

"I need to leave," Lynn says. "Thank you for being willing to keep an eye on Jules this summer. I appreciate it."

Dieter hardly hears her. He's still stuck in the rut of this revelation. But none of it is Lynn's fault. He shouldn't take it out on her. He's apologized for what he did. It's Ralph he needs to get back at. It's always Ralph he needs to get back at. Always Ralph. "There's one more thing."

"What?"

"This is difficult, too, but I think you need to know."

"Know what?"

"Something that I'm guessing Ralph has chosen not to tell you."

"Have you spoken to him?"

"No. But I know he knows."

Lynn's expression hardens. "Is this another of your attempts to get back at Ralph for something he never did to you?"

"No. I'm trying to protect you."

"From Ralph?"

"From Jean-Pierre."

"You mean his affair?"

"He's admitted to it?"

"Yes."

"What is it you think Ralph might have told me?"

"He caught Jean-Pierre and Monique together at McGill's Faculty Club back in January. I happened to be there having dinner with a friend. I know Ralph didn't see me. But I saw Jean-Pierre introduce him to the Minister."

"You've met Jean-Pierre?"

"At the twentieth high school reunion, remember?"

"And Ralph knows the Minister?"

"He does now."

"One more thing, Dieter."

"Yes?"

"It wasn't you who sent me the text?"

"What text?"

"An anonymous text warning me about Monique."

"Not me."

"Are you telling the truth?"

"Yes."

CHAPTER 25

At last, after eight months' gestation, it was like a new life bursting into the world. Sunday, June 23rd its birthday. On the 22nd, Ralph drove from Picton to Steve's place in Montreal for the event. Jack and Bill had flown to Montreal the night before, Jack from Vancouver, Bill from Edmonton. They all stayed at Steve's and left at seven the next morning in Ralph's SUV, arriving at Kiamika a little before ten. The director greeted them in the parking lot near the campcraft area. He said that the first wave of campers would arrive in about a week. Apart from counselors making final preparations, they had the place to themselves.

Seeing the camp again transforms them momentarily into their boyhood selves. They stroll among the white birches taking in the once-familiar sights—waterwheel and slide in the junior swim area, the large raft shaped like a letter C in the senior area. Same lifeguard tower on the dock. Same cement breakwall along the waterfront, though it's now badly cracked and severely askew after years of assault by the lake's winter ice. Rack after rack of canoes by the Counselors' Cabin. The two clay tennis courts near the Dining Hall have gone to seed, a huge climbing wall installed in their place. The Main Lodge has a new exterior but hasn't been altered inside, moose antlers still standing guard over the stone fireplace. The Senior Lodge has been completely rebuilt into a more modern building with fitness equipment in one of the rooms, the old upright piano with cracked ivory keys long gone. Ralph imagines the camp filled with boys. If he listens hard enough, he can almost hear them in their tents flanking the lake. Chasing each other around the Indians & Settlers field playing Capture the Flag. He can hear the founder, clad in ceremonial dress as Kiamika's Big Chief, accepting new braves into the tribe on their first night at Council Ring.

After a short walk through the woods, they pass beneath the wooden archway announcing the outdoor chapel and sit halfway up the tiers of railroad-tie benches built into the hillside that looks out over Bullfrog Bay, the scene of their nighttime massacre almost fifty years ago of the unsuspecting lily pad amphibians.

"It's as if we never left," says Steve. "They said we'd remember these as some of the best times in our lives."

"As a teenager how can you appreciate that?" asks Bill.

"They merely wanted to plant the thought," says Jack, "to help us through the inevitable hard times by having good ones to remember."

Ralph scans the faces of this group of former friends sitting silently staring out at the bay. He wonders whether they, too, are letting themselves be transported back to their days as campers when none of them had any idea what awaited them in life. Or whether now that they're back at the site of some of their fondest memories, they can't help but think of everything that's transpired since they left, afraid to allow themselves an ecstatic moment of nostalgia because they'll soon have to leave it behind. He knows this: they no longer know each other.

They arrive at the southern tip of Lac Rouge at one thirty, take down the canoes and put them in the water with the bows pulled up on shore. They unload the gear from the trailer and place it into the canoes. Ralph reminds the camp director that on day five they'll confirm by satellite phone the pickup the next day at Maison-de-Pierre.

"Good luck guys. Take lots of pictures. We'll use a few in our marketing brochures."

"Okay, only us now," says Steve as the truck drives out of sight. "Easy does it today. We'll make camp in a few hours."

"I wonder if that old cabin still exists," says Jack. "We might have to break another lock."

"You seem in the mood for that," says Ralph. Since he arrived, Jack has been the least enthusiastic of the group. As if he wants to make the point that he's here against his will. "Lighten up, Jack—this is going to be spectacular. Way different from that trip down the Rouge. How about this weather?" Unlike their unfortunate trip as teenagers, the starting day is sunny. There is no wind. They reach Lac Barrette by four thirty. The cabin, or some reincarnation of it, is exactly where it used to be. Unlocked.

"Steve, this time you stay put," says Jack. "Ralph and I will collect firewood. Maybe you and Bill can catch a few trout."

No trout were interested in being eaten that day.

They arise at six, make breakfast, and break camp by seven—the drill that Ralph and Steve established on their two weekends blazing the long portage. By nine the group reaches it, welcomed by a fat band of yellow ribbons wrapped around a maple near the water's edge.

"How sweet!" says Bill. "Couldn't you find an old oak tree?"

"A reminder to come home in one piece," Ralph says, remembering Lynn's words. "It was Steve's idea."

"Actually Ralph's," says Steve. "We thought they'd be easy to spot. You'll find them all along the trail."

"Let me take the canoe on this portage," Ralph says to Steve. Jack has already hoisted a canoe and started up the trail, leaving the rest of them behind. "You can get the next one."

"Are you sure? This is going to be tough."

"Yeah. I'm good. I know this trail well by now."

Yesterday back at camp, he'd prepared the canoe for portaging in the manner he learned long ago, a technique utilizing rope, two paddles, and a tump strap. He used the rope to rig the portage thwart and attach the tump strap at each end to the gunwales a little forward of the thwart. Now, at the start of the trail, he inserts the blades of the paddles into the rigging and ties the shafts to the bow seat right below their grips. With knees bent, he stands at the middle of the canoe, grasps it with both hands at the closer gunwale and lifts it to rest on his thighs. Leaving his right hand on the near gunwale, he reaches over with his left and grasps the far gunwale. He rocks the canoe gently on his thighs, takes a deep breath, and in a single, smooth motion rolls it upside down while raising it clear over his head with both arms extended. Then lowers the canoe slowly and exhales while letting his head pass through the gap between the paddles, allowing their blades to rest on his shoulders. He places the tump strap under the blades and across the top of his head, then adjusts the tumplines a little to lessen the weight pressing against his shoulders. After standing for a minute, arms hanging loosely at his sides, the inverted canoe perfectly balanced on his head, its full weight distributed down his spine and throughout his body, he and the canoe as one, Ralph says to Steve, "Ready to go." The canoe is much heavier than he thought it would be. Maybe he should have persuaded the camp director to supply them with Kevlar canoes. He tires quickly as he climbs through seventy meters in elevation and hurries to catch up to Jack and Bill. After what he judges to be a little more than a kilometer, he calls out to Bill who's a hundred meters ahead of him carrying only a pack. "Let's take a ten-minute break."

Bill shouts ahead to Jack who's striding through the underbrush as if it doesn't exist. "Christ Jack! Slow down. You're a bloody moose. Ralph wants to stop." Jack lifts the canoe from his shoulders without effort and sets it down lightly on its bottom. He removes his pack and places it beside the canoe.

Ralph continues to where Jack is and puts down his canoe with a thump, virtually dropping it the last foot onto the ground. "Easy Ralph," Steve says. "You'll put a hole in the bottom of the canoe. Are you feeling okay? You're sweating like a stuck pig."

"I didn't expect it to be this hot and humid this early in the morning. It's impossible to keep up with Jack."

"Don't even try. Let's switch off after our rest."

"No, I'm getting the hang of it. Let me go to the halfway point. You can take it from there."

Ralph fares much better after the short rest. The land is now essentially level, the trees not as densely packed. He doesn't have to keep tilting the canoe as far back in order to see where he's going. Passing through a small stand of pines, he begins to feel cocky. As Maarten would have done, he shouts back to Steve, "Piece of cake!" The last word comes out as c-a-a-a-k-e as he slips on the bed of needles. His right foot snags a root. "Shit." He struggles to maintain his balance, then stumbles. The bow of the canoe dips and catches the ground, literally stopping him in his tracks. He sinks to his knees. Steve, who's been following closely, removes his pack and rushes to help. He extracts the canoe carefully from Ralph's shoulders to avoid banging his head. Ralph slumps into a sitting position.

"Are you hurt?"

"I banged my right knee and it feels as if the portage thwart cut into my neck."

"Anything else?"

"No— No broken bones— " He examines himself. "No scrapes that I can see. A few bruises and strains. That's all, I think."

"Can you walk?"

He stands and takes a few steps. "Yeah, I'm totally fine— "

"Let's get started again," says Steve. "Jack and Bill will be wondering where we are."

"Please take over," Ralph says.

In twenty minutes they catch up to Jack and Bill who are lying on the ground with their eyes closed, hands clasped behind their heads, big *we're-better-at-this-than-you-are* grins spread across their faces. "What happened to you guys?"

"Ralph decided to stop and pray."

"What?"

"I tripped on a pine root. Went down on both knees. No real damage. Only a few bruises."

"You'll have to do better than that," says Jack.

"Not to worry," says Steve. "We're camping at Lac Seré tonight. Should be there a little after noon. An easy day."

"Plenty of time to fish," says Jack. "You and Bill sucked last night. Ralph and I will show you how."

Ralph appreciates the show of confidence, especially from Jack. More like camp days when the two of them were virtually inseparable. They make good on Jack's boast, each catching a rainbow trout. Ralph cuts off the heads behind the gills and slits the bodies lengthwise right above the spine on each side. He removes the ribs and belly fat, leaving the skin on one side. After washing the four fillets in the lake, he salts and peppers them, and pan-fries them in a little lard. "Hey guys, bring your pannikins. Watch out for bones."

After the meal, Steve discards the fish remains, the cooked and the uncooked, in the woods a couple of hundred meters from the campsite, then scrubs the pannikins and frying pan with sand and rinses them in the lake. A film of oil spreads out on the surface of the water and shimmers a rainbow of colors in the sun.

Next morning, Jack unzips the tent, steps out to take a pee, and comes face to face with a black bear. He freezes. Then starts to talk, softly, soothingly, in as deep a voice as possible, careful not to make any sudden moves. "Get the fuck out of here. Shoo. Scram. Go find your own food."

"What's wrong?" Steve calls out from the tent.

"The fish remains must have invited this bear to breakfast."

"We're going to stay in here," says Bill. "You can offer yourself up for the greater good."

Jack raises his voice. "All of you, get the fuck out here— Now— You'll pay for it if you don't."

They believe him. Jack is by far the strongest. They emerge from the tent, clad only in their Under Armour, and stand beside Jack— four in a row, a cacophony of voices exhorting the bear to leave. Not persuaded by their words, she continues to face them, motionless.

"Let's throw a stick at her."

"No. That'll piss her off."

"She might have cubs nearby."

"Let's sing the old camp song. That should scare her away."

Their middle-age screeching kills whatever curiosity has impelled the bear to hang around. With a toss of her head, she ambles into the woods.

"Okay— No more fishing," says Jack.

Keeping their promise to the camp director, they take hundreds of photos—shots of canoes being paddled and portaged; sunrise filtered through mist rising from a lake; sunset over mountains with a band of clouds at the horizon turning yellow to orange to pink to violet. And one afternoon, the rarest of sights—a moose. Cruising toward their intended campsite on Lac Sunset, gliding past a marshy area, about to put in, they come upon a cow moose. Nearly submerged, she lifts herself from the shallow water and trundles ashore. Ralph and Jack, each in the stern of a canoe, are the first to retrieve their cameras, zoom in, and snap a few photos. Steve and Bill, each in the bow, their packs stowed behind them, can't get to their cameras quickly enough and are able to manage only long-distance shots of a fuzzy object disappearing into the woods.

"Did you hear her crash through the undergrowth?" Ralph says. "Moose don't care what's in their way."

"Like Jack portaging a canoe," says Bill.

Jack laughs the loudest.

Lac Sunset brings another wildlife treasure that night, the fourth night of the trip. One for the ears, not the eyes—the call of the loon, a bird so private it won't let a human get near. But the loon has no problem announcing its presence from afar, cry after cry emanating from the other end of the lake, each with a faint echo off the mountains that sounds like a second loon responding to the calls of the first. Lore has it that you'll sleep soundly after hearing the call of the loon. Lore can be wrong.

Every night after dinner, the four of them sit around the campfire and talk about their years since leaving Kiamika. Everyone gets to be the center of attention for a night. Steve volunteered the first night, Jack the second, and Bill the third. Ralph didn't learn much more about Steve than he already knew from their time together clearing the first portage. Jack, who's already proved himself to be in the best shape, talked about having chosen his father's career. Like his father, he earned a doctorate and became a professor of physical education. By age thirty, he'd secured tenure. He loves his work, but doesn't seem happily married and wasn't willing to offer much about his family life. Said his two children are grown, married, and live in the United States. Has three grandchildren but doesn't visit them often. Ralph asked Jack why he let that happen. "I don't know—it happens" was the evasive response. Ralph didn't press Jack. Now, wrapped in the cocoon of his sleeping bag trying to fall asleep, Ralph wonders what Jack makes of these insistent calls of the loon. Do they awaken something primitive in him or pass right through without stirring anything?

He has the same thought about Bill, who's head of Human Resources at a large Alberta-based oil & gas company, a senior executive, but no one Ralph would have naturally come into contact with in an environmental lawsuit. Like Jack, Bill didn't talk much about his family. He's proud that his son has moved to New York and become a star investment banker, but when asked what it's like to be a father, Bill stared blankly into the fire. When he finally spoke up, all he could manage was, "I missed a lot of my son's birthdays while traveling on business."

"Being a father isn't a highlight of your life?" Ralph asked.

"Why do you ask?"

"I think I'm about to become a stepfather to an adolescent boy who will be a freshman in college in the fall."

"What do you mean by *about to become*?" said Bill.

"It means I haven't proposed yet."

The fourth night the wheel comes around to Ralph. He talks about building the environmental practice at Bourke, Donovan, and Fraser and then breaking away with a handpicked group of young lawyers to establish his own firm. He mentions a few of the high-profile cases he's argued. Jack tosses a few more logs onto the fire, sending sparks high into the air. The wood crackles as tiny pockets of sap boil and explode. Like firecrackers.

"Gee guys, does it get any better than this?" says Ralph.

"No, it doesn't," says Bill. "But if you feel that way about the wilderness, why did you defend companies like mine?"

"Maybe for the same reason you work at one."

"What's that?"

"That's where the money is. It's never been on the side of environmentalists."

"You're right— I make a lot more as head of Human Resources than a top lawyer at a nonprofit."

"I suppose in the back of my mind I thought I could help rein in industry practices whenever I figured they'd compromise the environment."

"At least you were able to retire before the rest of us. Your lifestyle doesn't sound too shabby."

"You have a good life," says Steve.

"Why do we always have to talk about this psychological bullshit?" asks Jack. "For Christ's sake, we're not a bunch of housewives."

"What would you like to talk about instead?" Ralph asks, an edge in his voice.

"If you insist on something depressing, Ralph, tell me why the Montreal Canadiens haven't won a Stanley Cup since '93."

"Why do you care?" says Steve. "Out there in Vancouver don't you now root for the Canucks?"

"Victoria, Steve, Victoria— Too many years in Montreal, that's why— I'll always be a Canadiens fan."

"Think about me," says Bill. "The Oilers haven't made the playoffs since 2006. I haven't had much to cheer about since Gretsky left."

"At least the Canucks made the finals two years ago," says Steve.

"The first time in my life I rooted for the Bruins," says Ralph, only half in jest.

"Christ, you *are* a pussy," says Jack. "They're the Canadiens' long-time rivals. Where's your loyalty? Have you forgotten you were born in Montreal?"

"Who said I'm not still a Canadiens fan?"

"A true Canadiens fan is a Canadiens fan for life. You don't root for rivals, even if they're your new local team."

Steve stands up and stretches. "Easy guys— Our Ralph here was once a star hockey player."

"Floor hockey," says Ralph. "In high school— How do you know that?"

"You told me the first night we camped out a month ago. In the finals you got the crap kicked out of you by a German."

"See," says Bill. "Even out here in the wilderness you have to watch what you say." He and Jack get up and take a pee in the lake. Steve joins them.

"Nice," says Ralph. "Taking care of the environment."

"Okay then," says Steve, after he and the others have sat down again around the fire. "I think there's something you haven't told us."

"Is it your birthday?" asks Bill.

"I have no idea what you mean."

"Sure you do. What about our first portage?"

Ralph gives Steve a look that pleads, *Please don't go there.* "A bit rusty. That's all. I had no trouble today, did I?"

"Today was an easy dirt road. Still, I was watching you carefully."

Jack and Bill move closer.

"It's only a hunch," Steve continues, "but it fits with your letter inviting us to join you on this trip and with the difficulty you had on the first portage."

"Go on," says Bill.

"Yes, please go on," adds Jack.

Ralph meets Steve's stare, then looks away. Gazes into the fire as if expecting an answer to spring from the flames, words to blunt the impact of the coming accusation.

"You're dying, aren't you? This is a bucket list item. I don't buy your having shrugged that off when we were together last month."

"No, I'm not dying. No more than you."

"A heart problem then," says Steve. "That would explain your difficulty with the first portage. It looked as if you were having a heart attack."

Ralph, realizing that he's not likely to escape this discussion without revealing the truth, tries to find words to soften the impact.

"I had a minor heart attack in February. They put in a few stents and sent me home."

A loon calls from the far end of the lake, as if to deny Ralph's claim.

"How did you pass the physical?" Bill asks.

"I took it a week before the episode occurred."

"You should have told the director," says Jack. "This is exactly like— " He doesn't finish the thought.

"I told my cardiologist about the trip and he cleared me to go."

"Well— You could have disclosed that too."

"I was afraid Kiamika would withdraw their support."

"Jesus, Ralph— For good reason," says Steve. "Did you tell your doctor you'd be carrying a canoe? Solo."

"I did."

"And?"

"He suggested that I let the rest of you share that responsibility."

"Why didn't you tell us?"

This time it's Ralph who gets up to stoke the fire, sending a fresh spray of sparks high into the rapidly cooling night, temporarily adding a few stars to the sky. "You'd have called me a pussy if I didn't do my fair share. Right, Jack?"

"Not if you'd been honest and told us why."

"You should have trusted us."

"I'm sorry— I won't carry the canoe— I'm fine."

That conversation, now an hour old, is still raging in Ralph's head. The campfire's coals have long since burned down to nothing, but Steve's words are still burning white hot. It isn't the loon that's been keeping Ralph awake.

The next morning Ralph wakes alone in the tent after a night of fitful sleep, a recurring nightmare growing worse with each cycle. In it he saw how it would end for him, furiously paddling across Long Pond in his kayak, making little headway against the wind, undoubtedly a sign of what it would be like in a few days as they cross the Baskatong Reservoir. Each time through the dream he made it a little farther to the beach on the other side, finally gaining the lee of the shore, sprinting the last stretch to prove to himself that he was still in command, ramming his kayak halfway out of the water as it made land. Then the peculiar image of him making an angel in the sand. He stood to watch himself, admiring the artist and his artistry, then crumpling in pain as a giant fist seized his heart and squeezed the life out of him. Right before he awakened, he rejoined his body in the depression of the angel he'd made. There he was flat on his back staring up at the sky, straight into the sun, as he'd done when Dieter rescued him from drowning in the Lower Rouge and as he'd done years earlier when he rescued himself from drowning in the Upper Rouge. And there were Lynn and Dieter, the sun forming a halo around their heads. As he strained to make out their faces against the blinding brightness, Ralph could see that they were holding hands and smiling down at him.

When he emerges from the tent, dressed and ready for breakfast, the others are sitting around the fire finishing their oatmeal.

"We saved you some," says Steve.

"Hey guys, I lay awake thinking about our conversation last night and I want to apologize. What I did— Didn't do— Was wrong."

They seem surprised at his contriteness. Jack speaks up. "We talked it over before you got up, and feel this should be the last day of the trip. When the van picks us up tomorrow morning, we should drive back to Kiamika— "

"I'm not surprised to hear you say that," says Ralph. "You didn't want to come in the first place."

"Is that true, Jack?" asks Bill.

"I'm here, aren't I? I've been having as good a time as any of you. But we've accomplished what we set out to do. We succeeded where we failed on the original trip."

"What about the Baskatong?" Ralph asks.

"There's nothing left to prove," says Steve.

"What can I do to change your minds?"

Jack hands Ralph some oatmeal as a peace offering. Ralph adds a spoonful of brown sugar and takes a seat beside the others. "Don't you want to see that enormous reservoir again?" There is an unmistakable pleading in his voice.

"We don't want to be responsible for your having another heart attack," says Jack, "and dying out here in the middle of nowhere. That's not the memory we want to take back from this reunion."

Ralph swallows a mouthful of oatmeal. It sticks in his throat. He splutters hoarsely, "My doctor says I'm fine."

"Sure sounds like it," says Steve.

"Could you see any signs of a problem when you and I were marking the trail?"

Steve scoops another few spoonfuls of oatmeal from the pot, sprinkles raisins over it, and adds a little water. "I gave you the benefit of the doubt."

"What do you mean?"

"After the first weekend I suspected. You said you'd been training for six months and you looked lean and fit, but you tired too easily."

Bill, who hasn't said much, speaks up. "How can we be sure your doctor cleared you for this trip? We have only your word for it."

Ralph tosses the rest of his oatmeal onto the coals and empties the pot to smother the dying fire. "We can settle this easily. Let me call my cardiologist on the satellite phone."

Bill, Jack, and Steve look at one another and nod. "Okay," says Jack, "but you'll also have to talk to the director, and you must promise not to carry the canoe again."

"There are hardly any portages left."

"Then it should be easy to make that promise."

"And keep it for a change," Jack mutters, not quite under his breath.

Ralph extracts the phone from his pack and calls the cardiologist's direct line at the hospital. He's surprised that the doctor picks up right away. After telling him what he needs him to do, Ralph hands the phone to Jack, who satisfies himself that Ralph has told the truth. The doctor asks Jack something else. Jack says no. He ends the call.

"What did he ask you?" Ralph asks Jack.

"Whether you've experienced any problems."

"Thank you for saying no."

Ralph calls the camp director, explains the situation, and apologizes. He tells the director that he'll sign a new form releasing the camp from liability. The director is dismayed by the news and initially uncertain what to do. He asks to speak with Jack, who is able to assure him that they'll keep an eye on Ralph and call if they feel he's having trouble.

Lac-de-la-Maison-de-Pierre, day five, the last day of the first leg of the trip, barely rescued from being the last day of the entire trip. The house-of-stone lake that may have once had a house of stone but no longer does. A magnificent long lake with scattered dunes, a few rising as high as thirty meters above the shoreline. The group is subdued. Everyone seems to be in his own head. Partway down the lake, Ralph breaks the silence. "Look guys, I'm sorry for casting a pall over the trip. Let's do something fun. How about skiing these dunes?— We have the time."

"Hear that gentlemen?" says Steve. "The Retired-Lawyer-and-Born-Again-Environmentalist wants us to help him erode the land-scape."

"Not true," says Ralph. "Not the environmentalist, the boy who— "

" —Should know better— " says Jack.

" —Thinks we all need a bit of fun," says Ralph, giving the sign to cut the conversation off there.

They opt for fun, for once again being the teenagers they've long left behind. A group of men who wouldn't have had enough in common to become friends if they'd first met at this point in their lives, but who can indeed allow themselves to be transported back to their shared adolescence, to another universe, nothing around them but sand, air, and water. Grown men needing to act like boys.

"You sure you can handle this, Ralph?"

"Fuck off guys— I'll beat all of you to the top." There is no way he can climb faster than Jack, but he clambers to the top of the tall dune before Bill and Steve, and earns more style points than anyone else as he sends sand flying with punch turns on the way down. As he hits the frigid water, he thinks of what might have been next winter, tackling moguls with Monique and her girls. Would he have been ready for that? Will he be ready to be a presence in Jules' life instead?

Back in the canoes an hour later, the thrill from conquering the dunes still fresh, they paddle vigorously to tomorrow's pickup point at the end of the lake. They set up camp and spend the rest of the afternoon horsing around in the water. Then Ralph announces he's going to prepare a special treat for dinner to celebrate their success on the first leg of the trip—a fresh berry pie.

First he cuts some lard into the remaining flour to make a ball of dough. Then he places the dough on the bottom of an overturned canoe and rolls it out flat using a tin can. He splits the dough into two parts and rolls out each again. He places one part into the bottom of the reflector oven's pan and fills it with wild raspberries, blueberries not yet ripe this early in the summer this far north. He sprinkles the berries with a little sugar. Then places the second sheet of dough over the berries, crimps the edges and pierces the top in several places with a fork to let it breathe. With the bottom of a spoon he paints the top with melted lard and sprinkles it with a little more sugar. As he finishes up, he notices Steve, Jack, and Bill get up from where they've been sitting on the beach and shake out their towels after what appears to have been a brief powwow.

That evening, after their main course, but before Ralph's special dessert, they all sit around the campfire that Jack has built into a bonfire, its flames extending almost to the height of the special bonfire on the final night of the camp season at Kiamika marking the send-off of seniors who will never return as campers. No one ventures to speak. Finally, Jack, despite the fun they've all shared during the day, lobs a grenade in Ralph's direction. He still seems stuck on getting to the bottom of something that's been eating at him since the start of the trip.

"Hey Ralph— You never got married, but you had a huge crush on my sister. Do you ever wonder what happened to her?"

"Hey Jack— You know we were only good friends."

"Seriously? Coming all the way from St-Jean by bus to visit us on weekends, pining away outside the Nature Cabin waiting for her to walk by, writing her letters while she was away at camp, taking her sailing in the evenings when you were head instructor, skiing with us at McGill, hanging around campus hoping to catch her after class— you consider that *only friends*?"

"So?"

"And there was your other flame at college. The person you dated in high school. What's her name?"

"Lynn— Where are you going with this?"

"That you're afraid to seal the deal— You talk a good game, but you can't close— With Lynn you let a lesser guy push you aside, a French Canadian no less. A separatist. I'm surprised you had the balls to succeed as a lawyer."

Bill is wide-eyed. He jabs Jack in the arm. "What are you doing?"

"Yeah, Jack— " Steve interjects. "Haven't we beaten him up enough already?"

Ralph says nothing, glad that Bill and Steve have come to his defense.

"Steve tells me that you have another shot at Lynn. Do you think you can reel her in this time?"

"Why do you care?" Steve asks.

Ralph stares through the fire at Jack's head suspended in flames, his onetime friend turned devil. The center of the bonfire is white hot. Ralph wipes his forehead. This is more like the Steve he spent time with blazing the trail. No longer the inquisitor.

Bill ignores Steve's attempt to silence Jack. " —Jack called you a pussy last night. Show him the balls he claims you don't have."

"It's none of his fucking business!" says Ralph.

"That's right—it isn't," says Steve.

The others wait for Ralph to speak. He's waiting to gather his thoughts. In the dark sky, he can't locate the moon. Maybe it's a new moon. Or not yet risen above the hills. But the three stars of the Summer Triangle and their constellations are clearly identifiable. As bright as Ralph has ever seen them. In a way, Jack hasn't changed—he can still cut through a mass of clutter to see things clearly. But he seemed kinder long ago. His words never stung like this. *And all this only from my rejection of his sister?* Ralph wants to let the matter die. But there's no way to save face without answering.

"Jack is right about Lynn. I was weak back then. I should have fought for her. I wanted to marry her— But his sister Joan?— Yes, I had a crush on her, but that's all. We've all had crushes on girls in our adolescence. With Joan, I never gave it a chance. I embarrassed myself writing those letters to her in French. I thought it was romantic; she thought it was weird. Jack, I'm truly sorry if I hurt her. And you. But I intended no harm. I'm surprised you've carried it all these years—" Apart from the rasping of crickets in the distance, the only sound is the low hiss of the green wood on the fire. Birds apparently down for the night. "I'm not like that now. This time I won't let Lynn get away."

"Do you ever wonder what happened to Joan?" asks Jack. "She's happily married with three children."

"I'm happy for her," says Ralph. "Why can't you be happy for me?"

Jack doesn't answer. No one speaks up. Not even Steve. They look glum.

"What's wrong guys?"

Jack, apparently the self-anointed leader, answers. "Ralph, while you were making the pie, the rest of us had a conference about our decision earlier today to continue the trip into the second leg. We've reconsidered. We think it's wrong to reward you for your failure to trust us. We think it's wrong to take the risk that you'll have a serious heart attack out here. Your satellite phone won't make a difference if that happens. You'll die, and believe it or not, none of us wants that. Not even me. I'm sorry for changing our minds and disappointing you, but it's the right thing. We have already succeeded at what we set out to do."

Ralph stands and walks across the thin strip of beach to the edge of the lake. He's angry with Jack, his onetime best friend. There was no tone of conciliation or forgiveness in his little speech. A loon calls out. Probably the same one as last night. This time to remind Ralph that he was warned by Lynn about the ramifications of not disclosing his medical condition. Amazingly, this feels worse than losing a major court case. But he'll surprise them one last time, make them feel guilty for not supporting him. Strange thought: he wonders if this is what it's like to be Dieter. On the losing end of something important. He wonders how his other one-time best friend is faring across the ocean without the job he wanted even more than he had wanted Lynn.

Ralph finds himself feeling sorry for Dieter, realizes that he's been more fortunate in life than the Swiss boy he used to kill with rubber-tipped arrows in woods not unlike these. Ralph stoops and dips a cupped hand in the lake, splashes water on his face and wipes it off with his T-shirt. Walks slowly back up to the group still seated around the fire watching him intently as he returns. He stands facing them.

"Before we eat our final dessert, I want to propose a toast."

"With what?" Jack asks.

Ralph walks to the tent and comes back with an unopened fifth of Canadian Club.

"Something else you didn't tell us, eh?" says Bill.

"This is it, I swear. I was saving it for our last night together out here in the wilderness. I'd hoped that would be at the Baskatong, but I guess Maison-de-Pierre will have to do."

"Against camp policy," says Jack. "Trust the lawyer to break the rules."

The others look to Jack to see if he's serious. He's smiling.

"I want to thank all of you for agreeing to join me on this trip," says Ralph. "I can't tell you how much it has meant to me. I wish we could finish the second leg, but I understand your concern and appreciate your honesty. I'm sorry that I lost your trust. I showed poor judgment."

"Enough of that," says Steve. "A toast to all of us. It took us nearly fifty years, but we finally made it around this circuit."

There are no glasses to raise. Pannikins seem a poor substitute. Ralph fills them instead with the dessert that's been cooling on a rock by the overturned canoe. They pass around the bottle.

"Nice pie," says Bill. "You haven't lost your touch."

CHAPTER 26

Ralph drove everyone back to Steve's place in Montreal. Jack and Bill stayed the night before flying back west. Steve encouraged Ralph to stay over as well and get some rest before his long drive, but he declined. His farewell: "Goodbye guys, I don't know when I'll see you again. This was our once-in-a-lifetime reunion canoe trip. Maybe you, Steve. When you get back from your sabbatical, you and your son could get in some kayaking and sailing with me at the Cape. Jack and Bill, this is probably it. It was great to see you. I hope you don't feel too let down."

Ralph did not return to the Cape. Instead, he drove to Picton to get ready for the trip to James Bay. He was still feeling like a last-minute stand-in for Jean-Pierre. He knew he shouldn't think of it that way. Jules wouldn't consider him a substitute for his father. Neither would Lynn. He didn't want to assume that parental role. His task was to find the fine balance between becoming too involved and not involved enough, a matter to talk over with Lynn before they were all thrown together on the road trip.

The day after he arrives in Picton, Ralph accompanies Lynn on her early morning walk to the dock at the marina. He begins the conversation he had gone over in his head on the drive back from Kiamika by telling her about the canoe trip and why the second leg was called off. "You were right. I should have told the camp director and my friends about my heart attack. Now I'll always feel that the trip was less than it should have been."

"You've come back none the worse for the wear."

"Physically perhaps, but not in my head."

"It's a matter of trusting people, Ralph, at least those you care about— And speaking of that, I have something to ask you."

"Should I be worried?"

"I don't know. It's about the breakup with your new girlfriend."

"You couldn't call it a breakup—we had only one date. Haven't we already talked about that?"

"I feel there's something you're not telling me. It seems too fortunate that you and I were both suddenly available at the same time."

"Are you against serendipity?"

"Not at all. But it was spooky. You texted me almost as if you knew that my marriage had ended. As if you had orchestrated it."

"Is that what you think? That somehow I managed to convince Jean-Pierre to give up on you? Lynn, you're making too much of this. You're not surprised that your marriage couldn't be put back together, are you?"

"No. But you happened to be available at the precise moment it ended. You have to admit that's a bit weird."

"That's not how I see it. You know that I tend to get ahead of myself. I fantasize. Convince myself that each new girlfriend might finally be the one. All the while hanging on to the memory of you. My former assistant could recite the stories for you, chapter and verse. I made her live every one."

"You were optimistic this time around."

"I guess it may have seemed that way, but I always am." Then, even though he hadn't wanted to go there, he flashed back to the evening with Monique. "We had a wonderful date at a fine restaurant in New York City, went to a bar on Fifth Avenue afterwards. Drank cognac until midnight. I arrived at my condo all excited about my prospects only to have them dashed a week later. I wish I could say it was the first time that ever happened."

This is another of his partial truths. Lynn doesn't even know that his new girlfriend was Monique. Better that she not know. If it ever comes up, he'll deal with it. He hasn't lied, hasn't even twisted the facts. But he hasn't divulged all the facts. This unease of hers will dissipate, he tells himself. It's not like the incident on the canoe trip. Lynn is not as tenacious as Steve. They reach the harbor, step onto the dock and walk to the end where they take off their shoes and socks, sit and dangle their feet in the water. Ralph leans over and kisses Lynn.

"Hey, let's talk about the road trip. Are you sure that Jules is okay with my coming along?"

"He's not."

"Then why are you forcing him to accept it?"

"Because I won't do the trip by myself. It was conceived as a family trip. I'm still thinking of it that way. I'm hoping that you're going to continue to be part of my life—Jules' life and mine."

"I plan to."

"We'll take it as it comes. I'm sure it will work out."

CHAPTER 27

Tired of waiting for his parents to do it, and then with no one in charge after they announced their impending divorce, Jules has taken control of planning the trip to James Bay. He reluctantly accepted his mother's demand that if he still wanted the trip to happen, Ralph would have to come along in place of Jean-Pierre.

"As long as you understand he's no substitute for Dad."

"I never said he was, and you'll see that he won't pretend to be either."

Although he hadn't shown it, the little chat with his parents about their split didn't sit at all well with Jules. "Lame" was the first word out of his mouth when they told him. "You guys didn't try hard enough to make it work. It wasn't that hard." He didn't buy Jean-Pierre's comment that he was too young to understand, couldn't possibly have any appreciation for how a long-term relationship can come unglued and why it is hard to put back together. Much harder than building one of his windmills and making that work, his mother said.

They're right—his parents always think they're right. But even if they didn't get it, Jules does. He understands how important it is to have fun on this holiday. When he's in Germany, he'll be farther from home than he's ever been, by himself in a place where he doesn't know the culture or language, where his English may be understood by some, but his French-Canadian French by no one. Despite his excitement about working at a real engineering research facility, he's a little intimidated at the prospect. Even in Canada, he lives day to day in a situation incomprehensible to most people. He fears venturing into a public restroom, always uses a stall, waits if possible until the restroom empties before he leaves. Now he has a stab wound to prove that his fear is not unfounded. Yet it's Amy he feels sorry for. Because he was responsible for ruining her prom night, he was thrilled when his mother offered to bring her along. Maybe she thinks that will take the pressure off Ralph to be on his best behavior. It won't.

❧

During the first week of July, Jules was watching the late news one night and saw a brief clip about forest fires in northwestern Quebec, blazes threatening the heart of the Cree Nation's homeland. He stayed up past midnight browsing the Internet looking for information about these *feux de forêt*, finding more useful material in French than English, pursuing a long trail of websites until he satisfied himself that the situation had to be taken seriously. While early June was apparently a wet one in Quebec south of the 49th parallel, the northlands were parched, parts without rain for sixty days. Who knew? The forest fire hazard there is now listed as extreme, particularly in the vicinity of the tiny Cree village at Eastmain on James Bay, not far south of the hydroelectric facilities they're scheduled to tour.

The news services report that the wildfires, not yet covering a large area, but already out of control, will likely continue to spread, consuming hundreds of thousands of hectares of forest and sending up plumes of smoke that winds will carry hundreds of kilometers to the east and south. The prevailing winds off James Bay that will someday power two thousand giant turbines that the Quebec Government will soon erect there are now fanning the flames of a potential boreal holocaust worse than any experienced within the past fifty years. Those are the facts impossible to ignore. The holiday trip is in danger of being consumed by natural forces beyond their control.

Jules is not an expert, only a person with an intense self-interest in the outcome. As he sees it, the main risk is not that the forest fire will ultimately reach James Bay Road, scorching the only route to the power generating stations, but that the road will be closed due to poor visibility and air quality. Without heavy sustained rains, that will happen during the next few weeks. Delaying the trip is out of the question—Germany can't be rescheduled. The only smart thing to do is to start the trip a week earlier he tells his mother. She protests, complaining that all their reservations will have to be changed. They'll be lucky if they can reschedule. People make their plans months ahead of time. Jules keeps reminding her that success sometimes comes from being flexible enough to change plans, like getting divorced instead of gluing a marriage back together. Fortunately, as he's come to expect, she ultimately listens to reason. Or perhaps he finally wears her down. He doesn't get why it takes so long. She should simply listen to him in the first place. Then he learns that it was Ralph's arguments as much as his own that convinced her. Ralph offered to change all the reservations. Jules said it would be easier if he did it himself. Now, instead of his father's credit card, he gets to use Ralph's; he likes the thought of making Ralph pay.

❧

Jules planned several activities to break up the long drive to James Bay. The first day they rented canoes and paddled around a lake in Parc la Vérendrye. Jules was impressed at how proficient Ralph is at handling a canoe—he hadn't yet heard the full account of the reunion canoe trip. Ralph showed Jules how to use the J-stroke to keep the canoe on course. How to deal with wind by first heading mostly into it and then tacking mostly downwind, never broadside. Ralph showed Amy how to collect dry kindling to start a fire and then, after it catches, to keep feeding the fire larger and larger pieces of wood. Jules watched Ralph use an ax as easily as his mother uses a kitchen knife. They cooked hotdogs and hamburgers over the fire that Ralph and Amy built, and topped off the picnic with s'mores.

The next day they drove in light rain to Val d'Or and toured a gold mine that had been turned into a museum. The price of admission included the rental of jumpsuits, heavy-duty raincoats, and hardhats with headlamp and battery pack attached for the descent a few hundred meters underground to learn about the hard life of miners. Then they continued their journey northward to the village of Matagami, no more than a hamlet, a place that offers nothing of interest to tourists but a motel that calls itself a hotel, a spot famous for nothing of note except for lying at the start of James Bay Road, the 620-kilometer stretch of highway ending at Radisson, headquarters village for the two hydroelectric generating stations they are scheduled to visit.

Calling James Bay Road a highway is a stretch. It's hard to tell when it was last maintained properly. There are cracks and heaves everywhere. The 100 kph speed limit has to be taken seriously. It's boring, B-O-R-I-N-G as in nothing but boreal forest—low bushes and pink fireweed along the sides of the road, scattered stands of poplar and an occasional white birch, and stretching away to both east and west an endless green ocean of conifers, mostly spruce, more and more stunted in their growth the farther north they travel.

About 260 kilometers beyond Matagami, they arrive at a narrow, single-span, rusted steel, suspension-style bridge across the Rupert River, the longest river in Quebec. Ralph pulls onto the shoulder a little beyond the bridge. They walk back to the middle of the bridge and stand four in a row against the railing to gaze at the famous rapids, an act that would be dangerous if there were any cars passing by. Lynn mentions a great battle the Cree fought and lost here against the White Man. Much as the French lost to the English on the Plains of Abraham more than two hundred and fifty years ago, she says, and for which the English have been paying the price during the last fifty years.

"Mum, what battle with the Cree?"

"The battle over diverting the Rupert's water upstream from here to satisfy our appetite for electric power."

"Who won?"

"The Quebec Government over the protests of the Grand Chief."

"Do you know that Chief Mukash wanted to build wind farms instead of hydroelectric plants?" Ralph interjects. "The Cree may have lost the battle, but not the war."

They all press themselves flat against the bridge's railing as a car whizzes by, the only vehicle they've seen since leaving Matagami.

"I hope the Cree get more money from the government for using their wind than they did for their water," Lynn says.

"You and I will help make sure that happens," says Ralph.

Jules and Amy exchange glances. "And how are you going to do that?" Jules says. "You don't control the government. My father and Monique have more power than you and my mother."

"In a sense, yes, and in a sense, no. Conservationists have more clout than you think. They can slow down civilization's rush to ruin the environment and change people's lives for the worse. They can cause the terms of the deal to be changed. They sometimes even win outright."

"But my mother says you fought on the side of big energy companies against conservationists."

"I did, but I'd like to think I helped keep those companies in check from doing the worst things imaginable. And now I'm going to represent the other side. Your mother and I have been talking about it."

"You haven't told me any of this, Mum."

"You don't like it when I talk about Ralph."

Jules changes the subject. "I can see why these are called the *Oatmeal Rapids*."

"Apparently they were much more impressive before the diversion of the river," says Lynn, unwilling to let the matter drop. Like there's some point she's making that will make a difference. To something and someone, to anything and anyone.

On the road again, Jules notices several vast areas of dead spruce, the trees still standing, their trunks a combination of faded charcoal black and weathered gray white. As they encounter another such area, he says, "Those trees must've been killed in a forest fire years ago. See the low growth that's started up around them? How long do you think it will take for the forest to regenerate here?"

"A good ten to twenty years," says Ralph.

"Probably longer than that," says Lynn.

"Not really," says Ralph. "Most forest fires start from lightning strikes. Nature's way of taking care of things."

"That's what happened near Eastmain," Jules says. "I looked up the latest news last night. The fires are getting closer to this road."

"I'm sure we'll make it up to Radisson and back in time," says Ralph.

"Don't be too sure," counters Lynn.

Ralph gives her a perplexed look. "I thought you were keen on this trip."

"I'm a lot keener now that Jean-Pierre isn't here."

"Mum, give it a rest."

Ralph glares at Jules. "Perhaps we should all give it a rest. This is supposed to be fun."

At Kilometer 381, they arrive at the only filling station before Radisson, a spot that's named and known by its distance from Matagami. A sign that announces there's still a long way to go. The English version of the sign at the old-fashioned pumps instructs them to wait for the "gas boy." He turns out to be a short, stocky man with thinning gray hair who can take directions and make change only in French. *Remplir* is the operative word. Everyone is going to need a full tank for this journey.

Re-entering the highway, they notice a low black band of haze stretching across the western horizon.

"Don't be too sure," Lynn repeats. "I don't think it was such a good idea to travel to Radisson at this time. We might get trapped there."

"We'll be fine." It's not Jules who says that. He's no longer sure. And not Amy—she hasn't spoken a word yet today.

They soon cross the bridge over the Eastmain River. "It's much more depleted than the Rupert," says Amy. Good for her, thinks Jules. She's finally entered the fray. "The banks where water used to be are covered with bushes and grasses— The flow of water is barely a trickle."

"Like the Rupert, it used to be a much more impressive river," Lynn says. "What I didn't point out earlier is that they diverted the Rupert into the Eastmain and the Eastmain into the reservoir we'll visit tomorrow."

"All for good cause," says Ralph. "Quebec now completely satisfies its needs for electric power— "

"At great cost to the ecosystem," says Lynn.

"Only initially— " says Ralph, looking away from the road momentarily to glance at Lynn. He fails to notice a huge heave. The SUV bottoms out. It sounds as if they've left vehicle parts strewn behind them. He checks the rearview mirror and sees nothing on the pavement, but is frazzled enough to slow down for ten kilometers before speeding up again. Going faster makes the boreal forest pass more quickly.

Jules and Amy play a word game. Lynn is in her own world. Ralph seems to want to talk to her, but won't in front of the children. He asks if he can participate in the game.

"You wouldn't be any good at it," says Jules. "You need to speak French."

"Try me. You might be surprised."

It's a further thirty minutes before they arrive at the inn in Radisson, time that couldn't pass quickly enough. Not even the spectacle of Hydro-Québec's massive array of super-high-voltage power lines emanating from a transformer substation covering an area equal to one hundred football fields, a fact they learn the next day, is cause enough for anyone to comment and risk a backlash.

That night after dinner, a surprisingly delicious one for a tiny establishment in the hinterland, when Jules and Amy are lying in separate beds in their own room, Amy asks, "What was that about this afternoon?"

"I'm pissed at my mother."

"You were hard on her. And on Ralph too. Weren't you the one who couldn't wait for this road trip?"

"Yeah, until my parents decided to get divorced. It was supposed to be a family holiday."

"Don't you want to see the generating stations and the site for the wind turbines?"

"I wanted a holiday with my parents— Both of them."

"That's never going to happen again. You'll have to get used to it."

"You sound like my mother. I don't need to take that from you."

"Yes you do. I'm your best friend. Someday you'll thank me."

"I doubt it."

"Please— Let's have a good time on the rest of the trip."

"I don't see how."

"Promise you'll try."

Jules pulls up the covers, buries his head in the pillow, and starts to cry.

CHAPTER 28

The next morning Ralph rouses Lynn at six o'clock, an hour before the dining room opens for breakfast, and suggests they take a walk.

"Where?" she says. "There's nothing to see here."

"Anywhere. We should talk."

Once outside, they realize that there is indeed nothing to see. They walk down the main street, virtually the only street in Radisson, past the only gas station and grocery store, back the way they arrived at the village. Ralph takes Lynn's hand.

"Hey, what was that about yesterday? I didn't expect you to be so sour."

"I don't like Jules' attitude."

"Cut him some slack. On top of everything he regularly deals with, he now has to get used to me hanging around. That's got to be difficult for him. It's asking a lot."

"It's asking for my happiness."

"That's something a child can't understand. It's not how they're wired."

"How would you know? You've never been a parent."

"Ouch— I read, I see, I think, I understand. That's how. You're not seeing it because something else is in the way. What is it?"

"You want to know?"

"I wouldn't have asked otherwise. We were always good at talking."

"Except at the end."

"I couldn't stand the thought of losing you."

"Okay. Two things. They've been bugging me ever since I met with Dieter."

"This has to do with Dieter? I thought he apologized."

"It has to do with us."

Ralph let Lynn talk herself out. She told him about the mystery text message warning her about Monique. That, after a while, she realized it had a double meaning, neither of which was good. The first was obvious: Monique and Jean-Pierre were having an affair. That shouldn't have been a surprise. But the anonymous warning? What was its intention? Friendly or otherwise? The more she thought about it, the more she became convinced it was Ralph who had sent the message. The second meaning was less obvious and didn't occur to her for several weeks. That road also led to Ralph. Monique was the woman he was seeing. And that prevented him from getting together with Lynn for dinner when he was visiting his parents in Kingston. Not only was Jean-Pierre two-timing but also Monique and Ralph.

"Tell me— Am I right?"

Ralph, the trial lawyer who could work his way out of most difficult spots, who often found his way to a partial truth that wasn't incriminating, a way of expressing the facts to make them sound like the complete story, decided to go against his instincts and tell the whole truth and nothing but the truth the third time around, sensing that the stakes were high. If the truth couldn't prevail, then the victory would be hollow, despite having finally won the prize he'd once let slip away. "On both counts, but it's not what you think."

"Convince me."

"Before I try, let me say that you were two-timing too."

"That was different," she said. "It didn't hurt you and, come to think of it, not even Jean-Pierre. For what he did to me, he deserved it."

With that kind of logic, Ralph sees that the task ahead of him will be difficult. He continues anyway: "Remember when I called you in November and you canceled your visit to New York? I told you then that I wouldn't let you go, that it wasn't goodbye, only goodbye for now. I meant it. I have no idea what Dieter could have told you that would have led you to these conclusions— "

"He told me that you were at McGill's Faculty Club and introduced yourself to both Jean-Pierre and Monique."

"How could he have known that?"

"He said he was there too, but that you didn't see him."

"I was shocked to see Jean-Pierre and another woman together. Alone. A younger woman. Extremely attractive. Someone I'd never seen before."

"She's the Minister of Natural Resources. How could you not have seen her before?"

"I'd never met her. The Toronto partners handle our Canadian business for the most part, especially in Quebec, with the government as well as our clients. Also, she hasn't been Minister for very long. I guess I'm more out of touch with the political goings-on in Canada than I thought I was. Anyhow, there was nothing particularly damning about them having dinner together, except that it appeared rather intimate. He sat beside her, not across from her. They leaned toward each other as they talked. It looked as if he wanted to put his hand on her arm at one point. The more I thought about it, the more I assumed it was true. I struggled with whether to let you know. If you knew the warning came from me, you'd have thought it was purely self-serving."

"Wasn't it?"

"Mostly, I suppose. I'm in love with you. I wanted you back. But I also wanted to protect you from further damage at the hands of Jean-Pierre. It was clear from our conversations that you were having trouble recommitting to your marriage."

"What about my second point?"

"After you made it clear that you were going to work on your marriage, as much for the good of Jules as for your own happiness, and that you couldn't be with two men at the same time—or so you said—I realized that I might never get you back. After my heart attack I understood there might not be much time left."

"That's why you jumped at the first woman in sight?"

"I knew that I couldn't be alone for the rest of my life. If Monique was good enough for your husband, why not me?"

"You were trying to get back at Jean-Pierre for stealing me from you?"

"Not consciously. She's an attractive woman and obviously smart and driven. Exactly my type, don't you think?" He hopes she'll see the compliment in that. Yet it seems not to register.

"And younger. Did you sleep with her?"

Ah, Lynn is finally at the crux of it. He knew she was driving towards that. It's not that his potential new girlfriend was Monique, but whether he slept with her. "No. We had only that one date. Then she was supposed to come to Brave House. We might have made love there, but she called off the visit, said that Jean-Pierre was getting a divorce. She wanted to be with him. I had no idea that you and Jean-Pierre had decided to call it quits."

"I didn't know either."

"We learned at the same time?"

"I think you might have known before I did." She laughed. "Ironic in a way."

"But it wasn't an unhappy circumstance for either of us, was it?"

"No, it wasn't— It isn't. Serendipity I think you called it— One more thing. That cookbook you gave me— Did you buy it for Monique?"

"I did. Its author is a celebrity actor who happened to be at the restaurant the night of our one and only date. I thought she'd like it as a memento."

"Why did you give it to me?"

"Because I know you love to cook and I wanted to expand your repertoire to include Italian dishes. They're my favorite."

"It seems out of place for you to give me the present you got for her. There's a story behind the giving of a present. It's a personal thing. You should have sent it to her and got me something else."

"I suppose I should have. Sorry— "

"That's okay. I'm glad you've finally been forthright about all of this. Please don't ever try to mislead me with your lawyerly way of telling the truth. You can do that with others, but not with me. Understand?"

"I do— Is that all?"

"Yes."

"Feel better now?"

"Thank you."

They walk back to the hotel hand in hand, Lynn smiling, Ralph too. When they arrive shortly before seven, Jules and Amy are waiting outside the dining room. As Ralph and Lynn approach, Jules says to Amy, "I promise."

"Promise what?" asks Lynn.

"Nothing," says Jules. "Where were you guys?"

"We went for an early morning walk while you sleepyheads slept," says Lynn.

The dining room is packed, everyone undoubtedly taking the tour of the hydroelectric facility, no other reason to visit Radisson. Partway through breakfast, the manager of the *auberge* enters the room and addresses the guests, says that today's tours might be the last for at least a week. Due to the rapidly encroaching wildfires, James Bay Road will be closed, likely as soon as tomorrow, possibly even later today. But today's tours will take place as planned. Enjoy it while you can, he says.

After breakfast they walk next door to the Hydro-Québec welcome center. Following an introductory video in the amphitheater about the entire James Bay watershed and its hydroelectric complex, they board the bus for the tour of La Grande-1, a "run-of-the-river" generating station using the river's swift current to turn the turbines, no attempt to dam the river and create a reservoir to be used as needed. The plant is entirely above ground. Immaculate. Everything in its place—tools, plumbing, cables, machinery, and storage tanks for oil, all on a larger-than-life scale. Everything labeled clearly in French. No dirt or dust or grease anywhere in sight. It could pass a surprise military inspection. Jules translates the guide's presentation for Amy, reminding her that the afternoon tour of the Robert Bourassa facility will be in English.

The two tours appear to erase all bad feelings from the previous day. The sheer size of the structures they witness and the unfathomable capacity for generating electric power leaves them speechless, all but Jules. Ignoring the attempts of the others to hush him up, he keeps reciting statistics about the generating stations. La Grande-2 is located in a man-made cavern four stories tall, five football fields long, and nearly as far underground as the tour of the gold mine had taken them. Neither Amy nor Lynn need to hear the numbers to marvel at the scale of the enterprise. They say the data means nothing to them. Ralph says he finds the figures compelling and nods in approval. Jules grins. When the group gets back above ground, Jules continues spouting until Amy tells him to shut up.

Jules mentions that his father attended the inauguration of La Grande-2 and has often talked about standing beside Premier Lévesque and past-Premier Bourassa, both of whom expressed awe at the engineering achievement.

"Your father was a political big shot," says Ralph.

"Not an elected official," says Lynn. "But influential. He was René Lévesque's chief of staff."

"I'm sure he'd like to be here now," says Jules.

"Monique and your father can bring you back when you start an internship on the wind farm project," says Lynn.

From the top deck of the observation tower overlooking the island-specked Bourassa reservoir, Ralph remarks how small a large thing can be. The dam, spillway, generating station, transformers, and transmission lines, as impressive as they are, cannot compare with the vastness and power of the river. And the river is a small part of a province in a country in the world. The planet a small part of a solar system within a galaxy within the universe. Sort of like a Matryoshka Doll, he says, except on a much grander scale.

It's been like that for him. He let himself be encased in the world of his job, a small world, but a fulfilling one as long as he allowed himself to keep the blinders on and not question what he was doing. Now he's emerged from the cocoon of that life into a larger one. Now he's with Lynn and with Lynn comes the world of Jules, one completely foreign to him, one for which he has no particular skills to help him cope, other than the will to engage it enthusiastically. Words come to him from long ago, from the pastor's closing benediction on the mornings Ralph was permitted to skip Sunday School and stay in church through the entire service: *May God give to you and to all those you love His comfort and His peace, His light and His joy, in this world and the next— In this world and the next—* The old world has to die to usher in the new. His next world has just begun. Ralph is not a religious person, but he senses a certain spirituality in this place, a connection to others and to himself he hasn't experienced before. He glances over at Lynn standing alone peering out over the reservoir. She seems to be in her own world or galaxy or universe. She looks content.

Back at the inn in late afternoon after the tour of the Bourassa facility, Ralph suggests they retrace the bus's morning route, this time continuing into village of Chisasibi instead of turning off for La Grande-1.

The dirt streets in the largest town in the Cree Nation—four thousand in population, the same as Picton, notes Ralph, a fact only a visitor new to a place seems to know—are lined with small single- and multifamily wooden houses, many with tepees in the front or side yards. They stop to take pictures of the tepees, but with nothing obvious for tourists to do in town, they turn around and return to

La Grande-1, where they traverse the bridge alongside the generating station and continue onto a gravel and dirt road to Longue Pointe.

At the destination, they scramble to the waterfront through low scrub on rocky terrain. Jules chooses several flat stones and skips them out into the windless bay, three hops the best he can do. Ralph, who's been skipping stones his whole life, has one with six. He shows Jules the technique: leaning to his right side to get close to the surface of the water, holding the stone primarily between his right thumb on one side and the index and middle fingers held together on the other, cocking the wrist to be able to put spin on the stone, then releasing it parallel to the water, forcing it to take its first skip not too far from shore. After several botched attempts, Jules catches on. He finds a perfectly smooth stone with a slightly rounded bottom and skips it eight times. He beams.

Echoing Ralph's earlier comment about the scale of things they've seen, Jules states another fact from his pre-trip research. "James Bay is only a small finger of Hudson Bay, but is as large as all of Lake Superior. Imagine two thousand turbines along these shores. If Dad still has any sway with the government, I might be working here as an intern in a few years."

"If you have to build wind farms, I guess this is as good a place as any," says Lynn. "There's not a soul around."

"Don't forget the Cree," says Amy.

"We'd better head back to Matagami," says Ralph, "before they close the road. There's no other way out." Not that he wants a way out of anything at this point. He has come this far and knows he can face whatever might come his way, even a strong wind impeding his progress. But right here, right now, the air is still and the water calm. He takes it as a sign.

CHAPTER 29

It was a sign. They were one of the last cars to pass down James Bay Road before the barriers were erected at Radisson and Matagami. The first order of business after they arrived back in Picton was to see Jules off to Germany. Lynn had agreed to let Jean-Pierre be the one to drive him to Pearson International Airport in Toronto. He picked up Jules at the house in Picton. There was an awkward moment after Jean-Pierre had packed Jules' baggage in the trunk of the car. Lynn gave Jules a hug and Ralph shook his hand while Jean-Pierre looked on.

"Does it feel like home yet, Ralph?" asked Jean-Pierre. Jules punched his father in the arm. "I see that you've already converted Jules."

"Shut up, Jean-Pierre," said Lynn. "Nobody's planning to take your place. You've made your own bed. Now you can sleep in it."

Ralph shook his head gently at Lynn.

"Glad I'm heading out of here," said Jules.

"Me too," said Jean-Pierre.

After Jules and Jean-Pierre leave, Ralph convinces Lynn to walk with him down to the marina.

"What has drawn you to this marina? Yesterday afternoon you insisted on coming here by yourself. It's *my* special spot, you know."

"You and I both like being on the water where we can let our minds run free for a while. Right now, I need to get rid of the thought that it's always going to be like this with Jules and Jean-Pierre."

"Aren't you pleased that Jules saw that his father's behavior was inappropriate?"

"Yes, but there was too much tension in the air."

"It will get better."

They walk the rest of the way without speaking. As they step onto the dock, Ralph says, "Hey, I've got some good news. I've signed on as a pro bono consultant for one of the groups opposing the Cape Wind project at Martha's Vineyard."

"When did that happen?"

"Right before the canoe trip, I let them know I was interested. I found out after I got back."

"And you didn't mention it until now?"

"I wanted to clear it with my former colleagues and clients before agreeing. First call was my former partner Mark. And the second was Peter Devlin at Global Energy. Both had already decided it was best to steer clear of Cape Wind. I think Peter is suffering indigestion from absorbing International Wind Technologies and launching James Bay."

"What about *my* group in Prince Edward County? Are you willing to help us?"

"I've been mulling that over. At first I thought it might be moot because I was planning to convince you to sell your place and move in with me."

"You don't want me to move in with you?"

"I do. But I think you should keep your place here for a while. Even with my contacts, it may take sometime to sort out your visa situation and I bet Jules would like you to keep the Ontario home."

"I was planning on quitting my teaching position to work on my memoir full-time. When I do, I won't be able to afford my mortgage payment."

"I can handle that—I'm going to pay off the mortgage and cover your ongoing costs. I'd like to have a Canadian residence near my parents. They're going to need more of my time."

"You seem to have thought through everything."

"There's one more thing."

"What's that?"

"I'll tell you on the way back."

As Lynn turns to leave, Ralph takes her hand. "Wait." He drops to one knee and takes her other hand. "Lynn, will you marry me?"

She starts to tear up. "I'm not even divorced yet."

"I know. But as soon as you are. I'm not going to let you get away a second time. No more goodbyes."

"You're leaving me no choice?"

"I hope not."

"Yes, of course, I'll marry you."

"I'm glad you accepted. Now I can give you a wedding present."

"Haven't you already given me enough?"

"I missed your birthday, didn't I?"

"I don't celebrate that anymore. I told you why."

"I know. But this time is different."

Ralph leads her to a sailboat in its slip on the other side of the dock. Nothing particularly extravagant, a daysailer with a dark blue hull and white deck like some of the other boats rocking gently in their slips. "I asked around and found out that the owner lives in town. I talked to him yesterday and we agreed on a price. It's now yours. Let's take it out for a sail."

"How did you know?"

"What?"

"That this is the boat I always come to on my walks. I stand on its deck, listen to the halyards slapping against the mast and peer out into the bay, imagine that I am sailing towards the open lake. I never thought that someday I'd be doing it."

"Today is that day."

CHAPTER 30

Jules had been at work a week when he learned that his mother was going to marry Ralph. *Something important to tell you. Please call.* Typical. Sending a text with proper punctuation, the English teacher who can never bring herself to use abbreviations either. He responded with a simple *k*, no period. Dieter offered his office as a private space to make the call.

"What's up, Mum?"

"Jules, there's no easier way to say this than coming straight out with it. Ralph and I are going to get married."

"No way!"

"Yes."

"Are you and Dad even divorced yet?"

"We will be in a month."

"Can't you wait? You know, to see if it's going to work out with Ralph."

"No, the time is right. You sound as if you think I'm doing this to hurt you. I'm not. I'm doing it for me. I didn't think it would upset you this much."

Here she was, trying to be reasonable. It wasn't working. "That's because you didn't think."

"I guess there was no easy way to tell you."

"When is the wedding?"

"In the fall, after you return from Germany. We're going to hold it in Montreal to be convenient for you— When you're settled in at McGill."

"A big wedding?"

"Not big, not small. I was willing to have a civil ceremony this time, but Ralph's never been married. He wants to do it right his first time."

"Will Dad be there?"

"No. He wouldn't want to be."

"Then don't count on me going—Dad and I are the family now. Besides, I'll be too busy with my courses. College is harder than high school, you know."

"Aren't you happy for me?"

The conversation almost ended there. He was still reeling, but wouldn't let himself tell her that he'd been rocked by the news. He said they could talk again in a few days after he'd processed all of it.

"What do you mean *all of it*? What is there to *process*?"

"What life will be like without you and Dad together. Having Ralph around when I visit you."

"You and I lived without your father for nearly three years. We got used to being without him."

"That's the point. It was only you and me. Now Ralph will be there."

"You're making way too much of this. You saw firsthand on our trip to James Bay how nice he is."

"Your news makes me glad I'll be living in Gardner Hall for most of the year. Alone, but right around the mountain from Dad if I need him."

"You know you can count on me too."

"I used to think that. Now you seem to care more about Ralph than me."

"That's not true, Jules. And not fair. You'll get used to it. You might even grow to like it—windsurfing at Cape Cod, trips to New York City."

"What about Picton? You have to keep our home there. Otherwise they won't let me stay in residence at college— And Picton is where Amy lives."

"I've decided that I'll keep our house a while longer. At least until you adjust to the changes."

"I can't talk about this now. I'm at work. Dieter was kind enough to let me use his office— I'll call you back in a few days."

Dieter returned as Jules finished the call. He asked Jules if everything was okay at home.

"Only if you think that my mother getting married is good news."

The pronouncement appeared to rattle Dieter. He looked as if he'd been told his best friend had died. Jules had expected compassion from Dieter. Having shared his feelings about the divorce, he thought Dieter would understand how hard it was for him to accept that his mother would remarry this soon. As if she'd been having an affair behind his back and could hardly wait to jettison his father. "Is there something you haven't told me?" said Jules.

"There is," said Dieter. "It's complicated. Since we were kids, I've had a soft spot for your mother."

"You and Ralph don't like each other, do you?"

"Not at all— But better that your mother tell you the story than me. After all, I'm only your boss for the summer."

"You're more than that. You're my mentor."

Dieter smiled.

To distract himself from thinking about his mother's upcoming wedding, Jules engages his work project with a passion, arriving every day early in the morning and leaving a little before midnight. Dieter has paired him with a second-year engineering student, Renate, the only female in the summer program. At Dieter's urging, the two interns continue Jules' research into optimal configurations for anchoring pylons for offshore turbines. Dieter promises to take them via the corporate helicopter for an aerial view of the massive wind farm off the coast of Denmark.

"You have a great future in wind engineering," he tells Jules privately one morning. "I can see you running this R&D operation someday."

"I'd have to learn the language and move to Germany."

"Worse things could happen."

Worse things already have. There is virtually no one he can talk to about life as a transgender person. His mother and father, but they now seem a world away. As is Amy. Maybe Dieter someday. He wonders whether his mother has told Ralph. Probably. He seemed too eager to please on the James Bay trip, as if he already knew and was being careful not to step into dangerous territory. Jules doesn't know whether he can accept Ralph as a stepfather. Stepgrandfather maybe? Or perhaps a general-purpose uncle—everybody has lots of those. He had only one true father, one who never knew his only child was a son, not a daughter. Then a grandfather who became his surrogate father, but who actively resisted accepting him as a son. No, he won't go through any of that with Ralph—Ralph will *not* be his stepfather. He won't let Ralph try to impose that on him. Much easier to look to Dieter as a role model.

Jules doesn't call his mother back for a week. He's surprised that she hasn't tried to reach him again after not hearing from him for more than a few days. He was right—she has Ralph on her mind now, not him. At least she's upbeat when she answers the phone.

"How's it going? Learning any German?"

"A little. I'm working with this cool girl, Renate. She's teaching me some. Yesterday Dieter flew us both in the company's helicopter to inspect the offshore wind farms in Denmark."

"Then Dieter's keeping his promise to take good care of you?"

"I'm taking care of myself."

His mother falls into one of her long silences, as she does whenever he snaps at her and she anticipates some kind of bombshell from him . . .

"Have you thought any more about my wedding?"

"Yes, and I've talked it over with Dieter. I'll agree to come if you invite him."

"No point in that. There's no way he will come."

"You're wrong. He said it would bring *closure* to everything since your childhood together. Said that if he could attend the high school prom alone knowing that you were going with Ralph, he could certainly come to your wedding. I asked him what that meant. He told me to ask you."

"Now is not the time— Hey Jules, this is absolutely nuts. Dieter should never have said anything to you. I think that inviting him to my wedding is even less appropriate than inviting your father."

"Mum, he didn't say anything to me. It was as if he were talking to himself and I just happened to be there. I like Dieter more than Ralph. If he wants to come, you should invite him. Anyhow, it's not a discussion. Those are my conditions—*Dieter and Dad*. Both. And Monique, too, if Dad wants her to accompany him."

"That's an awful lot to swallow, Jules. It's *my* wedding, you know, not *yours*. I don't think Ralph will agree."

"No more than I've had to swallow. You know that— And oh, I almost forgot—I've already talked it over with Amy. Since we'll both be living in Montreal, I've asked her to come."

"Anybody else?"

His mother hasn't even tried to disguise her disgust with how the conversation is proceeding. Oddly pleased at her frustration with him, Jules keeps on. "Maybe Renate."

"Why are you doing this?"

"If I'm going to be forced to have a bad time, I want a lot of people there who can cheer me up."

"Ralph won't think any of this is a good idea. It's not what the day is supposed to be about. It's about us, not you."

"If he wants to marry you, he'll figure out a way to get used to it. He and I got along better on our road trip than you and I did. Don't you remember?"

"I'm glad you won't mind having Ralph around after all."

"You keep reminding me it's not my choice."

"Jules, you're not being reasonable."

"Under the circumstances how can you expect me to be?"

"I was hoping for something different."

"Mum, everything will be different from now on."

He means it as an assertion of his independence, that he is striking out on his own, no other route available after his mother's decision to cast off his father and welcome Ralph aboard. But his tone sounds harsh, even to him. By her gasp, he can tell she is taken aback.

"Jules, Jules— I can't leave this hanging— We need to talk some more— The two of us."

"Not when I'm at work."

"No. When you're back home. It'll be better face to face."

"There won't be much time. I have a lot to do before McGill."

"We'll make time. The day after you return, let's take the ferry to Wolfe Island. You can tell me all about Germany. After lunch we'll drive by the wind farm and get a close-up view. How about it?— You owe me that."

He can hear it in her voice. Earnest, but not demanding, not pleading, not angry or scolding. She's trying. Harder than she had at any time during the trip to James Bay. He hesitates.

"Yes, Mum, I do."